MW00777272

PRAISE FOR
MOUNTAIN MYSTERIES

"GREAT !! BOOK This is one fine read. A good mystery that reads like a literary piece." —Wooley, Amazon Vine Voice Reviewer

"*A LIFE FOR A LIFE* is one of the most satisfying books I've read this year. Everything about the book delighted me. *A Life for a Life* has also been compared to *To Kill a Mockingbird*. Both are character-driven and back a strong message of forgiveness, redemption and acceptance." —Ana Manwaring, writer, blogger, creative writing instructor

"FIVE STARS! Lynda McDaniel has that wonderfully appealing way of weaving a story, much in the manner of Fannie Flagg. The tale immediately drew me in." —Deb, Amazon Hall of Fame Top 100 Reviewer

"GREAT PACING—I COULDN' T PUT IT DOWN. I highly recommend this book, but read *A Life for a Life* first, so you can truly appreciate all that Abit accomplishes in *The Roads to Damascus*." —Malena E., author and playwright

"THE MOST SATISFYING MYSTERY I've read in ages." — Joan Nienhuis, book blogger

MORE REVIEWS FROM READERS

"I JUST FINISHED *THE ROAD TO DAMASCUS*, having previously read *A Life for a Life*. Like delicious hors d'oeuvres, they left me panting for the next installment. I hope to God the delightful Fiona becomes Abit's second half. Ireland is a very important part of Appalachia's soul; it seems fitting that Abit finds fulfillment in an Irish rose. I find Lynda's fiction revealing of the human condition."

"A GENTLE SOUL. I found it difficult to put the book down. It flowed so easily. ... Read this one. I think you'll fall for Abit."

"RIVETING SUSPENSE AND PLOT TWISTS. In contrast to the often inauthentic characters in so many novels I have read, Abit, Della and Alex (and now Fiona!) come across as utterly real – people I would like to meet."

"SWEET, EXCITING COMING-OF-AGE STORY of Abit Bradshaw. We met and fell in love with Abit in *A Life for a Life*. Now Abit is challenged to explore a world he didn't know existed. Come along on Abit's adventure; it won't disappoint!"

"I COULDN'T PUT IT DOWN. Once again, it left me wanting more ... The characters are well drawn and totally engaging, but what is most captivating is the metaphysical thread that gently supports each character's journey of growth."

"**AFTER** *A LIFE FOR A LIFE*, **I WAS EAGERLY ANTICIPATING THIS SEQUEL**, and I was not disappointed. The suspense and plot twists were as riveting as before. … I also appreciated the author's insights into the complicated relationship between the local people and the increasing numbers of former city-dwellers moving into their communities."

Also by Lynda McDaniel

FICTION
A Life for a Life
The Roads to Damascus
NONFICTION
Words at Work
How Not to Sound Stupid When You Write
Highroad Guide to the N.C. Mountains
Insider's Guide to North Carolina's Mountains
Asheville: A View from the Top

Welcome
the Little Children
A Mystery Novel

Lynda McDaniel

Published in 2018 by Lynda McDaniel Books.

ISBN: 978-0-9977808-6-4

Printed in the United States of America

Dedicated to loving families of all stripes.

1994

1

Della

"I don't know what to do with this."

I was working in the back of the store, and I could've sworn I heard someone calling me. But when I looked out front, no one was there.

It wasn't the first time I'd heard phantom customers. Probably wishful thinking, though over the past ten years, I had built up the trade at Coburn's General Store, a small grocery I'd bought in Laurel Falls, N.C. (Not even the locals knew who Coburn was, but the name came with the deed. And no one would've called it anything else, no matter what I renamed it.)

I'd gone back to cutting a large round of cheddar into wedges when I heard: "I *said*, I don't know what to do with this."

That time I walked to the cheese counter and looked around. "Down here," someone barked. "I want to know how to use *this*."

I glanced down at a little girl dressed in standard-issue jeans and T-shirt who couldn't have been more than seven years old. Her round, full face framed by blond curly hair frowned at me as she held up a bulging can of chickpeas. "Some old woman gave this to us from the Rolling Store."

"Oh, I see," was all I could think to say. I'd learned that catch-all expression from my neighbor Mildred Bradshaw, perfect for times when I found myself at a loss for words. And the sight of a remarkably composed little girl holding a can of beans that could've blown any minute had that effect on me.

I stepped around the counter and bent down. "May I?" I asked, taking away the bean bomb and setting it on the floor behind the counter where it couldn't do much harm. "The Rolling Store took its last run out of Laurel Falls in 1990, so you've had that can at least four years."

"I don't know about that," she said, crossing her arms in front of her chest. "It was in the back of the cupboard when I was scrabbling for something to make dinner with. And like I've been trying to tell you, I don't know what to do with it."

"You'd better not do anything with it. It's about to explode, well past its expiration date."

"What a rip-off. You give away something that's no good." She punctuated her feelings with a stomp of her little sneaker-clad foot.

"I stand by my merchandise," I said, motioning for her to follow me. "Why don't you pick out something to replace it?"

Her frown eased as she wandered the aisles, picking up different items and studying them. Eventually, she grabbed a can and said, "I'll swap for this." A tin of Petrossian Caviar, something I stocked for a rich customer who ordered it more to impress her guests than a love of the delicacy. (Normally, no one else would be buying caviar at $90 a can, but this new customer was shaping up to be anything but normal.) I must have made a face at the costly swap, because the little imp started chuckling. "I was just kidding with you. I figured it was the most expensive thing in the store, whatever it is. How 'bout this?" She held up a $4 can of salmon.

"Let's make it two of those." I reached for another can and set them both on the counter. "How many are you cooking for?

"Four, though Mama doesn't eat much. But Daddy and my brother, Dee, eat plenty. I have to serve myself first to make sure I get enough nourishment."

Why is this child shopping for her family and making and serving them dinner? I thought. *And why isn't she in school?* Then I remembered it was Saturday. But still, something about the scene unnerved me.

She interrupted my thoughts. "I'm fussing over dinner because Mama's sick," she said, her hands on her hips, standing her ground.

I was trying hard to keep a promise to mind my own business. At least most days. A few years ago when I helped my next-door neighbor and best friend, Abit Bradshaw, track down a trio of con artists, I told everyone afterwards that I planned to stay clear of other people's problems. They laughed, but I'd managed to confine my enduring reporter's nosiness (from a former life) to friends and family.

Until now.

Something about a little girl cooking for her father and brother irked me enough to ask more questions. She beat me to it.

"I know what you're thinking. Why doesn't my father do the cooking? He's just awful at it, and I don't think he's fakin' it. And my brother is only a little feller. Dee's just six years old."

I looked closer to make sure she wasn't really a miniature adult. She was bossy and self-assured in a way I never was at her age. But I liked her spunk. "So, what's your name?" I asked.

"Astrid." She thrust out her chin in a defiant way.

"Oh, that's a nice name. You don't hear it much anymore."

"Yeah, there's a good reason for that. The kids at school make terrible fun of it."

When I asked what they said about it, her face crump led, and I could tell she was struggling not to cry. "I'll tell you what," I added quickly. "Let's not sully this space with anything from the schoolyard, okay?" She looked puzzled. "What I mean is, it's a lovely name in my store. You can consider this a safe zone." She nodded and relaxed her stance. "Why don't we have a Coke or cookies or something?" I asked. "I'm starving."

"Do you have anything that's not sugary? I haven't had any lunch, and I get a little dizzy if I eat sweets when I'm this hungry."

"How old did you say you were?"

"I didn't. But I'm eight years old. What's it to you?"

Wow. That little bruiser didn't hold back. If I were still a reporter writing profiles as I did back in D.C., I'd have started taking notes. I wondered again about her size and age—and worried she may not be getting the "nourishment" she needed.

I grabbed some of the cheddar cheese I'd been cutting and a few rounds of dry-cured salami, then sliced whole wheat bread and an apple. I set them on the table in the back and added a couple of fizzy waters. I wasn't sure if a kid her age would like the sharp cheese and peppery meat, but she gobbled it all down, as if she thought she'd better stock up while she could. But I also got the impression she'd be a force to reckon with at her own dining table— she positioned her elbows in a way that told me she was well-practiced at protecting her food. I had to scramble to get some, though I didn't care about that.

We finished our snack with coffee. I fixed hers like I used to for Abit—mostly milk with a slug of coffee. She drank that right down. When I opened a tin of chocolate chip cookies I'd made the night before, her eyes opened wide; she took two of the biggest ones.

While she ate them, systematically nibbling around the edges, I tried to think who she reminded me of. I chuckled when it hit me—Nancy Drew. I'd read all those books when I was a girl, and I still remembered how composed and worldly she seemed for someone her age. I asked Astrid if she'd read those books, too, but she wrinkled her nose.

"Actually," she said between bites, "I prefer the Hardy Boys." She wiped her mouth on a paper towel and asked, "Do you have any recipes for what to do with that salmon (pronounced *SAL-man*)? I don't believe I've ever had it before."

After I set her up in the back with a couple of easy cookbooks and paper and pen, she got busy copying. I had to explain what some words meant, but otherwise, she sailed along. As I cleared our plates and cups, I asked, "Say, Astrid, would you like this tin of cookies to take home?"

Her face lit up, but just as quickly a shadow fell over it. "I'd better not," was all she said before returning to her recipes.

She was working away when I left to check on my dog, Jake. He was getting older, and I liked to bring him down to the store in the afternoon, once the nosy health inspector was safely on his way back to Newland after spot checks around the county.

As we came in the back door, I called out, "Hey, Astrid, I'd like you to meet my dog." Jake was already sniffing around, eager to see who or what was new in the store. But she'd left. Just a slip of paper on the counter with the words: THANK YOU.

A sadness crept over me as I read her eight-year-old's scrawl. The same feeling I had when I first saw her. I laid the note back on the counter and told myself I was being silly. She was just fine.

2

Abit

"Whoa! Stop! You almost backed into the band saw I'm running over here. Dangerously close to being like the butcher who backed into his meat grinder and got a little behind in his work."

That was Shiloh. I'd hired him because, well, I was a little behind in my work. And he made some of the prettiest dovetail joints I'd ever seen. We'd met at The Hicks, or the Hickson School of American Studies in Boone, N.C. After my jaunt through the Virginia mountains to find con artists who'd messed with me and the school, I went back there to learn more about woodworking and wood carving. Two year ago, I moved home to Laurel Falls and set up my woodshop in a corner of the family barn. Next door to Della Kincaid, right where I wanted to be.

Della had seen somethin' in me no one else ever had, and I didn't want to venture too far from that. And she'd brainstorm with me sometimes when I was designing new furniture. So would Alex, her ex-husband and now boyfriend, when he wasn't in D.C. or somewhere covering a news story.

Even though my woodshop stood in the shadow of my parents' house, I liked working there. I'd taken out the dividing wall between two stalls so I had a good-sized space for making large pieces of furniture. The walls were mostly logs and chinking, but I covered one in rough-cut pine that gave me space to organize tools and such. I added a strong floor so I had a sturdy place to set all them power tools.

At first, when I started building furniture, I didn't know what to make. But then I recalled the things that stirred me the first time I saw them—like that sideboard at Ila Pittman's while I was traipsing through Virginia. Or the dining table at Alex's. And hoosiers had always been a favorite. Ever since I was a kid, I'd watched Mama crank the sifter handle under the built-in flour bin to make it snow into her bowl. Hoosiers also have a pull-out countertop for more room to pat out biscuits and a large cabinet below for storage. All them nooks and crannies gave me places to add special touches. Mostly carvings on the legs or at the top, but sometimes I'd chisel out a place for ceramic or enameled inlays from local artists. As more tourists and second home people came to live nearby, my business was on the rise.

Shiloh, aka Bob Greene, had a religious conversion of sorts while at The Hicks. He hooked up with some of the Buddhists who came there every summer, but unlike their serious devotion, he seemed to cherry-pick whatever suited him. He changed his appearance by dressing only in loose clothing, mostly black hippie pants and black T-shirts, and growing a long wispy mustache that gave him the air of a magician. That impression grew stronger when, after a meditation break, he'd slip into the woodshop without me knowing it.

Shiloh seemed to have specially taken to the notion of the laughing Buddha; he liked nothin' better than telling jokes. His repertoire was growing, though he repeated his jokes a lot, or at least I heard them over and over when different folks came into the shop. Even so, some of them made me laugh every time. Some of them.

I needed a break, so I headed over to Della's. I dusted off my overalls (I used to worry they made me look like a hillbilly, but they were the best thing for the kind of work I did); whistled for my dog, Millie, a black-and-white fiest who took up with me in Virginia; and walked down the mossy steps to the store. It was a blustery day for May; I figured a rain storm was on the way. When I opened the front door, a gust of wind snuck in behind me and blew some papers onto the floor. I picked them up and couldn't help but read the top one.

"Hey, Della. Who're you mad at?" I shouted toward the back, since I couldn't see her anywheres out front. I looked down to see Millie and Della's dog, Jake, some kind of yellow hound, already tussling—their way of saying howdy.

"I'm not mad at anyone," Della said, carrying a case of homemade jams to the front.

I'd swear in the ten year I'd known her, Della hadn't changed a lick, but somehow that day, she looked different. It took a minute before it dawned on me she'd cut her hair to an inch or so below her ears, like she wore it when I first met her. Her hair was still that pretty reddish gold, though there were more gray streaks. But that was it. Me? I'd grown to almost six feet three inches and filled out a lot. Of course, I'd started as a kid and come June I'd be twenty-five.

"So why did you have this note by your phone saying ASS TURD?"

"Where?" she asked, a frown crossing her face. "That's not exactly my style of swearing, you know; I'm a little more traditional. Let me see that." She took the paper from me and turned it over. "Oh, for heaven's sake."

"What?"

"A little girl named Astrid was in here earlier, and she didn't want to tell me what the bullies at school called her. She skipped out while I was upstairs and left me a THANK YOU on this side of the paper, but I hadn't realized she'd written something on the back. Those bullies must have skewed her name to ASS TURD."

Oh, man, I knew what Laurel Falls bullies were like. Probably the same everywhere. And a name like Astrid was just different enough to whet their appetites. A dozen year back, they were mean about my names. As if sharing

13

Daddy's name of Vester (with Junior tacked on to make matters worse) weren't bad enough, the nickname of Abit made them downright giddy. A bit slow. A bit stupid. Or a bit retarded when they really wanted to pile on. But who could blame them when my own daddy called me that? Not long after I was born, he told everyone, "He's a bit slow" to make *him* feel better, letting folks know *he* knew his kid wasn't as smart as most. Turned out, I learned a lot at The Hicks, and while I wasn't much good at math and such, I'd found my groove, you might say, in wood. That was about the same time I started telling people my name was V.J. (a nickname Della came up with).

"Laurel Falls Elementary is missing a bet," I said after thinking about ASS TURD. "You know how schools are always doing bake sales for new books or uniforms? Well, our school should set up a panel of 10-year-olds to judge the names parents wanted to give their newborn babies." I started laughing, imagining all them kids in striped T-shirts sitting at a table, discussing the merits of any given name, all serious-like.

I could tell Della didn't get what I was saying, so I went on. "Take the name Astrid. Her parents could've come to the school, paid $5 and asked the panel what would happen to the name Astrid on the playground. Those kids wouldn't even have to think about it—ASS and TURD would've come to them in the blink of an eye. Or remember that guy—head of the Forest Service—Richard Everhardt? I mean, what were his parents thinking? No wonder he was so grumpy, given what he likely put up with on the playground. No question they called him Dick Neverhard. And poor Mr. Peterson, the science teacher. The kids all said ..."

"Yeah, yeah, I get it," Della interrupted, but she was laughing. "I think you're onto something, Mister."

"So who is she? Surely not a customer?"

"Well, in a way she is. She came in by herself holding an old can of beans, long expired after Cleva gave it to her years ago from the Rolling Store."

I'd ridden shotgun on the Rollin' Store for Duane Dockery back in 1985, taking food and supplies into the backwoods for folks who couldn't make the trek into town, a long tradition that went back a good fifty year to when the Rollin' Store started as an open-bed truck. But that big ol' bus got to be a drag on Della's business after a while, and by 1990, Duane parked it for the last time behind the store. Della used it for storage after that. Too good to take to the scrap yard, she said, especially with Duane's fine paintings of flowers and vines on the side of the bus, which still looked good after all these year.

"Okay, but why was she in here all alone?" I asked.

Della filled me in on what she knew about Astrid and her ailing mama—news she'd gotten when she called her best friend, Cleva Hall, after the little girl left. Cleva'd retired from being a teacher and principal in the county, but she still knew everything going on. "She said Astrid's mother and father moved here some fifteen years ago to homestead, but neither one of them knew much about the land or living in the country."

"Sounds like you," I added, taking a big sip of the coffee she'd poured me.

"Thanks for the vote of confidence, pal." She smacked my hand as I reached for one of her chocolate chip cookies, but I knew she was just kiddin' around. Besides, I hadn't meant to sound mean. Della'd struggled a lot when she first bought Daddy's store, but she'd made her way better than most—outsiders or locals.

"Anyway, Cleva said her mother wasn't well; she got the impression it was not so much physical as mental. She's sad all the time, won't eat, and spends much of her time in her bedroom. The father is smart enough, according to Cleva, but there aren't that many places to work around here; he takes what odd jobs he can find. Cleva didn't know how they made enough money to live on, though the father may have some kind of trust fund."

"Next time ASS TURD comes in, let me know. I'd like to meet her," I said. "Maybe tell her how I used to be bullied—and that it gets better."

Within a couple of days, Della called. Astrid was back for more cooking ideas. As I walked down to the store, Millie in tow, I thought about how hard Mama had worked making our meals; that was a lot to put on a little girl.

Della introduced us, and oncet we'd said our howdy-dos, we started in like a house a fire. She petted Millie while I gave her some ideas about outsmarting them bullies and getting on with her life, though given she was only eight year old, I wasn't sure how much "getting on" she could manage. It felt good to share my woeful tales in the hopes of helping someone else, though at some point, I started worrying all this might be too much for a little girl to carry. But she was drinking in every word, looking up at me like Millie did when I'd tell her she was a good dog.

When I was leaving, I heard Astrid tell Della to be sure to let "that boy" know next time she stopped by and added, "He has some valuable information to share." I looked back and saw Della smiling. You couldn't help but.

A week later, I checked with Della to see when Astrid might be coming over because I wanted to talk with her again. She had a funny look on her face when she asked, "Aren't you a little behind in your work?"

At first I couldn't imagine why she was talking to me that way. Then it hit. "Has Shiloh been over here telling you jokes?"

She kinda snorted. "Just left. Funny guy, that Shiloh. But he's sure fond of patchouli, isn't he?"

"Yeah, he loves the stuff. It took me a year to get the old cow smell out of the barn—now I've got that to deal with."

"Well, I believe I'd take eau de cow to this," she said, fanning the air with her hand. "Which reminds me—I haven't seen your work lately, and there's something I want to order. When's a good time to stop by?"

"Shiloh's off tomorrow, so anytime. I'll air out the place."

I went over to Coburn's a few more times when Astrid was there, just to see how things were going for her. I was trying to live up to that revelation I'd had while on my trip through Virginia: be kind. Something I figured came to me from Jesus, from the way he lived his life. It wasn't that easy to do, though it *was* easy round Astrid. And Jake and Millie liked her, too. She was as crazy about dogs as me and Della.

It was a nice time in all our lives. I wished it could've stayed like that.

3

Della

Astrid came by the store several more times. She'd wave and toss out a quick hi before walking the aisles or looking through cookbooks. When I'd ask what she'd cooked the night before, she'd stop to think for a moment before judiciously recapping every step in her meal-making. I bet she was doing a good job because if a cook was pleased with her creations, her family or guests often enjoyed them even more.

Early on, we established that she could help herself to any drink or snack in the store (or "refreshments" as she called them). I wanted her to feel welcome. She wouldn't take anything when she first got there—she'd dig right in and get to work. In a while, though, she'd wipe her brow after so much exhausting work, like only a kid can pull off, and take a much-needed pull from a can of soda.

I got a kick out of her precociousness, and yet I'd've been happier watching her play softball or jump rope or whatever kids did for fun. But I consoled myself that she seemed to be enjoying herself, and I liked having her around.

One afternoon I needed to go to the SuperMart out on the highway. I didn't like to patronize that place—the father of our former sheriff owned it, and he'd always disliked me because I'd beaten him on the bid for Coburn's. (I guessed he'd had his heart set on a grocery monopoly in the metropolis of Laurel Falls.) Anyway, I asked Astrid if she'd like to go along so I could show her different cuts of meat (something I didn't carry), especially the cheaper ones that needed to be braised or slow cooked to make them tender. We had fun together—Astrid checked out every aisle, marveling at institutional-sized cans of tomatoes and all the glass jars of penny candy that rivaled anything from my youth. When I bought her an ice cream cone, you'd have thought I'd knit her a sweater.

When we got back to Coburn's, Astrid took off on her old bike, which I could just make out had once been pink and festooned with colorful tassels (faded and brittle now). She'd told me she knew it looked "bedraggled," but it got her where she wanted to go. Which that day, I presumed, was home. She'd never mentioned where she lived, but I didn't think it could be too far from the store. I doubted she was strong enough to ride a long way over steep dirt roads.

A few days later, following one of our afternoon sessions (school had let out for summer), a thunderstorm rolled through just as Astrid was ready to cycle home. I offered to give her a ride. She seemed nervous about accepting, but the rain looked steady and flashes of lightening concerned me. We loaded her small bike into the back of the Jeep, and I said, "Where to?"

"Not far. Do you know where Hanging Dog is?"

I nodded and turned right out of the parking lot. We rode along in comfortable silence until I asked, "What did you say your father and mother's names were?"

"I didn't." She crossed her arms over her chest.

I'd've chuckled if she hadn't looked so serious. "Okay, what are your father and mother's names?"

"Daddy and Mama." When I laughed, she did, too. A beat later, she said, "Enoch and Lilah. Enoch and Lilah Holt."

"Those are good names around these parts."

She stayed quiet after that. When I turned onto her road, she said in a low voice, "I'm not supposed to bring anyone home."

"Why not?" I asked, lapsing into my nosy self.

"It's tawdry." I loved that kid's vocabulary, particularly when she misused bigger words in a way that had its own logic. "But maybe Daddy won't be home."

No such luck.

Enoch Holt stood on the front porch as we made our way up their rutted driveway. As he loomed over us, Astrid became agitated. "I usually walk my bike from here. You can let me out now." I was determined to meet her parents, so I ignored her. "Really. Just let me out now," she said, her little sneaker stomping the footwell.

I parked close to the house and told her to run on to the porch; I'd bring her bike. It was pouring rain now, and I had on a raincoat. But she headed to the back of the Jeep and took her bike as soon as I got it close to the ground. She was already drenched as she pushed it under the overhang and hit the kickstand with her foot.

"Get inside and change, Astrid," her father said as she stepped up on the porch. He put his hand on her back and practically pushed her toward the front door. She turned and looked at me over her shoulder, then disappeared behind a closed door.

"Who are you?" her father asked. He gave the impression of being scrawny, not so much by stature as posture and attitude. His light brown hair curled down around the collar of a wrinkled linen shirt hanging over loose black pants. "Oh, wait," he added, "you must be that person who took my daughter to the SuperMart without ever asking me or her mother if that was okay."

For once, I was speechless. I could well imagine that any number of people could have told Enoch they'd seen Astrid with that woman from Coburn's—maybe when he was out on one of his odd jobs. And I got it that parents had the right to know who was driving their kid around, but they also had an obligation to feed her well and care for her. As I saw it, we weren't even close in the wrongdoing department.

"I'm sorry," I said. "You're right. I should have checked first to see if I could take her to that store. She came to me looking for cooking ideas, and I just thought of it as a fun trip to see different ingredients for dinner. But as long as you brought that up, maybe you can explain why a little girl is saddled with so much responsibility for her family's meals."

He pulled on his beard. "I don't see how that's any of your concern," he said before turning and going inside. I heard the lock click into place.

The rain had let up, so I stood there a moment, hoping the door would fly open and Astrid would run out to play. I was surprised by how nice the house looked—a good-sized, hand-built cabin from one of those kits popular a decade or two ago. It had aged well, though it needed work around the deck and windows. When she didn't come out, I worried I'd gotten her in serious trouble with her father. Sure, I'd been reaching out to someone who'd come asking for help, but I knew I hadn't handled things well.

As I put the Jeep in reverse, I saw the curtain on one of the windows twitch. I looked closer as a hand opened the curtain wider and a woman's face pressed against the glass. We locked eyes and stared at each other for a few seconds. Then she let the curtain fall back into place.

That was the last time I laid eyes on Lilah Holt.

4

Abit

Evening was coming on, but I decided to do a little more work. I was still building my business, and I wanted to get some orders out as soon as possible. Shiloh came wandering in from the back. "Working late?" he asked, scratching his back against a rough-hewn post. "I could stay and help for a bit, seeing as how you're a little behind in your work."

"Okay, thanks," I said, "though it's time you came up with some fresh material."

He laughed and went back to work. Shiloh was easy enough to be round, and I'd given him his own key so he could come and go as needed, what with his meditations and who knew what else. I didn't know much about his life outside the shop—he never shared anything—but then again, I didn't really want to. He just did his work and told his jokes, especially when people talked about something serious. At The Hicks, one of my counselors told me people could use humor to hide from others. But the way I saw it, that was his business.

Shiloh started putting the finishing touches on my latest hoosier. On the front of the flour bin, I'd set an enameled inlay with a scene that reminded me of the grassy slopes at The Hicks, dotted with wildflowers and a couple of them gorgeous Jersey cows. I thought the cabinet was one of my best so far, and I wanted to get a photograph for my sample book.

I'd bought a good camera offa Cleva Hall. She'd taken up photography when she quit working, but after a while, she found she didn't get out to shoot much. She gave me a few lessons, and I taught myself a good bit on my own, especially about lighting.

As I was pulling lights outta the back room, I heard, "Hey, Rabbit." That would be Fiona. Standing in the doorway, her red hair backlit by the late sun and glowing like a halo.

"Hey, yourself," I said. She walked over and gave me a big hug. We were both still shy about showing affection with other people round, but Fiona must not've seen Shiloh working on the backside of the hoosier. She laid a big kiss on me, and shy or not, I wasn't gonna pass that up.

Fiona O'Donnell had a way about her—confidant but not stuck up—that won my heart the first time I saw her. I'd met her at a storytelling festival in Virginia. (That's where she got the mistaken notion my name was Rabbit. When she'd asked my name, I was so dumbstruck by how pretty she was with her red hair and freckles and big green eyes that I answered, "er, Abit." It stuck, but just between us. No one else would dare call me Rabbit, but then again I didn't reckon anyone else wanted to.)

She'd come over from Ireland, visiting her Auntie Chloe, who was one of the finest storytellers I'd ever heard (and I'd heard plenty, over time). Fiona went home that summer to finish her nursing school, but she came back for a visit a time or two between semesters. When she moved to America two year ago, she settled first near Galax, Virginia, where her aunt lived. Even so, we managed to see a good bit of one another. Just about a year ago, she got herself a job at the hospital in Newland and a garage apartment nearby behind an old lady's house. We'd been seeing each other regular-like ever since. And playing in a bluegrass band. I think me and Bessie (my bass fiddle) were invited to join the band because of Fiona. Man, she played the best fiddle this side of Ireland and told stories almost as good as her aunt. And sang!

"I thought you had to work tonight," I said when we came up for air.

"I caught a break—Sharyn wanted to swap shifts with me. So I was hoping we could go to dinner ..." She kinda flinched and the color started rising up her neck. She'd noticed Shiloh. "Hello, Shiloh. I didn't see you," she said, straightening her uniform, as though it had been messed with. (We hadn't had time for that.)

"Apparently not," he said unhelpfully, that smirk of his cutting across his face. "Say, while I've got a medical professional here, I wonder if you could answer a question for me." Fiona looked cautious but nodded for him to go ahead. "What is the difference between an oral thermometer and a rectal thermometer?"

Fiona seemed to know he weren't serious and played along. "I don't know, Shiloh, what *is* the difference?"

"The taste."

She threw her head back and gave a big belly laugh. I didn't find his joke all that funny, but I'd always found laughter contagious, so I joined in. I wasn't much good at telling jokes myself, but I thought it was a skill to keep after. I'd've loved to make Fiona laugh like that. I hoped maybe if I paid close attention, found some kinda rhythm, I could come up with witty, funny things to say to make her happy.

After we got calmed down, Fiona said she could help out if afterwards I'd take her to McGregor's up toward Crossnore. I'd showed Fiona a thing or two about woodworking, and her old man back in Ireland taught her how to sand something smooth as silk. He may not have known much about raising two kids on his own (her mother had died on the young side), but best I could tell, he knew his way round a woodshop.

We all worked hard (well, Shiloh worked as hard as he ever did) for a coupla hours, so Fiona and I were starving by the time we got to the restaurant. I'd been there oncet before with Della, and I knew it cost a good bit. But so did being late with orders and having customers mad at me. Besides, I wanted to pay Fiona back in a way she wanted. I couldn't say no to that lass. At least that's what I thought at the time.

5

Della

Tuesday afternoon, I heard the familiar rattle that never failed to make my heart quicken—a Mercedes heading toward the store after a long drive down from D.C. Alex Covington, Pulitzer Prize-winning journalist, accidental plagiarist, intentional philanderer, and finally someone who got his act together. Fortunately, that dieselly sound didn't seem to bother anyone much anymore, what with Abit still driving Alex's old model—the Merc—and folks in the community owning their own brands of noisy cars and trucks. It only sounded louder that day because of the relative quiet of Astrid riding off on her bike.

She'd called earlier and said she had a surprise for me. Could she come over for tea? I said of course.

When Astrid arrived, she carried a foil-wrapped package with great seriousness. Without even saying hello, she marched straight to the table in the back and placed her surprise in the center. While I made tea, she teased me with what it was. Finally, she unwrapped it and proudly announced she'd taught herself to bake scones. I found a china plate worthy of her efforts; as I put them on it, I couldn't help but notice their odd shape and weight. I made a mental note to slather them with plenty of lemon curd. The way I saw it, you could put lemon curd on cardboard, and it would be worth the chew.

In spite of their odd appearance, though, the scones were moist and flaky. While I munched, a bittersweet feeling took hold of me as I imagined a little girl baking in a hot kitchen, working hard at a counter she'd have trouble reaching.

I had to get up and wait on a couple of customers, and by the time I got back, Astrid was in a state. She told me she had to go because she was "crestfallen" that her scones weren't good enough. She'd left some for her mother and had to get home before she tried them. She seemed shaken, and I worried about her riding home on those bumpy dirt roads. I offered a ride, but she waved me off as she just about ran out the front door.

Alex joined me as I watched Astrid ride away, a sad little silhouette on the horizon. We headed into the store, where I started cleaning up the tea fixings while Alex lavished Jake with rubs behind the ears and silly talk. Next, he grabbed a scone and then me, giving me a pretty nice glad-to-be-back kiss.

He still lived much of the time in D.C. in the house we shared before the divorce, before I moved to Laurel Falls. Life had a way of twisting back on itself, and I was grateful fate had brought us together again. In a different way, but one that suited us both. He wrote freelance for some of the heavy hitters in D.C., and I enjoyed living closer to nature, though I wouldn't trade anything for the occasional visit back to D.C. and my old stomping grounds.

"These aren't up to your usual," he said after a big bite of scone, "but they're just fine for a weary traveler." Jake was hanging around Alex, hoping for crumbs.

"I didn't bake those. Astrid did." He looked puzzled, so I filled him in on my young protégé and her family. "Her father—Enoch, if you can believe that biblical name—is the only adult in that cabin, though Astrid comes in a close second. Her mother, Lilah, is apparently bummed out on life and …," I paused, trying to get at a niggling feeling. "Oh, I don't know. Something isn't right in that household, and not just because the mother is sick. I haven't met Astrid's little brother yet. His name is Dusk, but already at age six, he's figured out he hates his name and goes by Dee. Which reminds, me. Abit thinks expecting parents should pay to have a focus group—led by school bullies—counsel them on names they want to give their kids to see how they'll stand up on the playground."

Alex laughed. "That's a good idea. I'll have to talk to him about that tomorrow." He helped himself to another scone and started scrounging around in the fridge I kept in the back. "He wants to run some designs by me. I tried telling him I'm a wordsmith, not a woodsmith, but for some reason, the kid appreciates my opinion."

We spent the better part of a week together before Alex had to leave suddenly after a call from one of his editors. The tragic deaths of Nicole Brown Simpson and Ron Goldman had just made the news, and his editor wanted him to go to L.A. to cover the story. He wasn't happy about working on what seemed like a tabloid story, though we both knew something like that could turn mainstream overnight.

Alex was throwing things into his suitcase when he stopped and asked me to come with him. I felt a frisson of excitement at the idea of getting out of Laurel Falls and heading to California. It seemed like ages since I went anywhere farther than Asheville or D.C. But I didn't have anyone to help in the store. Billie Davis, my longtime assistant, had moved part time to Charlotte to be close to her elderly mother. Mary Lou Dockery, Duane's ex-wife, was learning the ropes, but she'd told me she wasn't ready to work on her own; she felt comfortable only when I was in the back or upstairs in my apartment.

Jake and I walked Alex to his car, and while we stood there, making stupid conversation to delay his leaving, we saw Abit and Fiona come out of Abit's woodshop. We waved at them, and Fiona returned our wave while Abit shouted a hello and goodbye to Alex. I loved seeing them like that. They belonged together, and not just because of their red hair and freckles and comely statures. Like two puzzle pieces that had been searching for each other, their countenances shouted *found* as they walked toward Fiona's car.

Alex and I looked at each other and smiled. He'd accidentally called Abit *our boy* any number of times; now we didn't even pretend it was an accident. We'd known him for almost a decade, and in all the important ways, he *was* our boy.

Alex finished loading the car, and I kissed him goodbye with all kinds of regrets.

Not long after that, the sheriff pulled up.

6

Abit

I cursed when I saw the sheriff walking up to Della's store just as Millie and me were heading down there for some afternoon coffee and company. That reminded me of the summer nine year ago when Della and I worked together to find a killer. I stood in the driveway back then and watched Sheriff Brower—long gone now after being voted out of office last year—and a half dozen other lawmen call on Della in her upstairs apartment.

This time it was only the new sheriff stepping inside Della's store. He was a big guy—maybe six foot three inches like me but with two hundred fifty pounds hanging on his bones. He was nice enough looking, though that stupid sheriff's hat didn't do him any favors.

I saw him turn the OPEN sign around to CLOSED and heard the door lock click into place. I watched them through the plate glass window talking serious-like. Pretty soon, the sheriff looked up and motioned for me to move on. I felt fifteen year old again. The sheriff may have changed, but the way they treated me never seemed to.

Sheriff Aaron Horne had a nicer personality than Brower, I had to give him that. But he had the most irritating voice. Booming and grating. No wonder it took only a month of campaigning before he'd gotten the nickname Airhorn.

And he was a lot cooler. He played guitar in a lawman's rock 'n' roll band called the Rolling Stops. I'd heard them a time or two, and they weren't bad. But still, it was good he only played guitar. If he sang with that voice of his, "Stop!" woulda taken on more meaning than just the second half of the band's name.

I didn't have any plans that evening since Fiona was working, so I decided to wait and visit with Della before heading home. When I came back from The Hicks and reworked the barn behind the house for my woodshop, I swore I'd never live in my parents' house again, and I got lucky. I found a fine little cabin I could afford a few mile out next to Chatauga Lake, where I could take a swim after work on warm evenings. After busy days shared with Shiloh, I needed a peaceful place to go.

While I waited on Airhorn to leave—I really wanted to find out what was going on—I settled down on the walnut bench I'd made for the front of the store. I felt the finish for any rough spots that might need repair and recalled how Della'd gotten kinda choked up when I'd delivered it. I felt proud, too; it took all my wood skills to make.

At first glance, it looked like any bench with a high back, but when you got up closer, you could see it had some rounded spots at the top. I carved them to look like people we knew, a tribute to all the folks who used to sit out there—me in my chair, them on an old bench or two. Like Wilkie Cartwright and Jasper O'Farrell and Pudge Buchanan. Wilkie moved to Linville when he finally, after a couple of breakups, got married, and Pudge had passed. Jasper still lived close by, but I didn't see him much anymore. I missed them all; they'd been there with me when I'd had nowhere else to go.

After a long wait, I gave up and went back up to the shop. Shiloh was still there, not exactly working, but I guessed he didn't have nowhere to go, either. So we started in on some finishing work. We were working and talking, and I asked him a question. He must not've heard me over the sander because he said, "How's that?" I repeated what I'd asked, and next thing I knew he was doubled over laughing.

"What? What are you laughing about?"

"I said, 'cows ass,' but you answered as though I'd said, 'How's that?'" He was still chuckling when he added, "I just love that joke. It works *every* time."

It took me a minute to get it. I *had* answered like he'd said *how's that*? The whole thing was just stupid enough to make me laugh, too.

"Now there's a joke even *you* could pull off with Fiona," he said. I thought he might be right.

We worked a while longer, and then I heard Airhorn's voice. I told Shiloh to close up when he was ready, and Millie and I walked back down to the store. Airhorn gave me a look like *I thought I told you to git*, but, hey, it's a free country. Della waved goodbye as he drove off and then motioned me inside. It was right at closing time, so she locked the door again and made sure the CLOSED sign was still facing out.

"Astrid's mother is missing."

"What does that mean?"

"All I know is she's been gone for almost a week now. Enoch didn't report it to Horne for a few days because she's taken off before, but usually for only a day or two. Horne started looking into it, and he wanted to know if I could contribute anything. The word's out that I've spent time with Astrid, so I told him all I knew."

"Which was?"

"Not much. Just about her father being what felt like overly protective, and her mother acting severely depressed. But I stressed that I was just guessing. As you know, I'm trying to keep my nose out of other people's business."

"Yeah, but somebody needs to find that little girl's mother."

"That's Horne's job, honey."

"Well, if you do go out investigating again, I'd like to come along," I said. "I'll never forget that summer we worked together to find out what had happened to Lucy

Sanchez." She gave me one of her looks, and I quickly added, "I didn't mean it like that. I know this ain't a game. But you've got to admit, that was a helluva summer."

Della frowned. "Let's hope this one doesn't shape up like that one."

7

Della

A couple of days later, I was planting zinnias in beds along the front of the store when Horne pulled up and rolled down his window. "Can you come with me? I need to talk to that father and little girl again."

"Why me? I've got a store to run." Of course I wanted to go, but I was busy, and it seemed to me he was breaking all kinds of police procedures by dragging me along.

"For one thing, I'm short staffed. And you know that little girl. Maybe she'll talk to you. I've already been out to the Holt's twice—I didn't get much information from the father and not a peep from his daughter. The second time I brought along her second-grade teacher, her favorite according to her father, but even she couldn't get her to talk."

His keen attention to a missing person surprised me. In D.C. they never had the personnel or budget to investigate every adult who went missing, especially if it didn't seem suspicious. After all, people voluntarily upped and left, never to be heard from again. Though just walking off and leaving two children behind did seem extreme. I was lost in thought when he added, "I need someone local I can trust, and my gut says I can trust you."

I didn't know where Horne had lived before Laurel Falls, but it wasn't nearby. It would take years before he knew the community, or rather before they'd let him. And I did know Astrid better than he did. Besides, who was I kidding? I *wanted* to get involved. A troubling sense of sameness had seeped into my life. Open the store, close the store, open the store again. I longed to be outside those four walls and doing something different.

Horne piqued my curiosity when he added a couple of details that contradicted the idea Lilah had left on her own volition. Like the way she'd posted two doctor's appointments (without any doctors' names) on a calendar later in July with exclamation points in red—as though she were looking forward to them. And all of her clothes appeared to be hanging in her closet.

"That doesn't sound like a woman running away," Horne said, trying his best to convince me.

But I had a store to run. I'd never hear the end of it if I closed early. Customers expected I'd be open certain hours, and I owed them that. I couldn't just go off on a chase.

Or could I?

I told Horne I needed to make a call. He drove off to run an errand and said he'd check back shortly. I got ahold of Mary Lou, and we talked about her concerns. I assured her I thought she was ready to run the store solo—and not just because I wanted the afternoon off. When I asked what could go wrong that she couldn't handle on her own, she gave in.

By the time Mary Lou arrived, Sheriff Horne was out front again. On the drive over to the Holt's, he repeated his notion that Astrid might talk with me since I was the only person who'd broken through the family's self-imposed isolation.

But Astrid wouldn't budge. All I could figure was that in her eight-year-old logic, I was the only new thing in their lives, so I'd somehow scared off her mother. Astrid put her hands on her hips and told us was she wasn't "talking to the authorities." Then she turned and ran to her room.

After that, Horne grilled Enoch on the back deck. That left me alone to look around the house and grounds. I was fascinated by how far off the grid they lived: a large garden area, their own well, solar panels on the roof, plus the ubiquitous propane tank behind the house. Real hermits, other than Enoch trying his hand at odd jobs around the county.

Inside, the cabin looked well-kept and bright. The living area and kitchen combined into one big room. The kitchen sported all the latest appliances, and I could easily imagine Astrid working away in there. When I spotted the little stool she needed to reach the counters, my heart cramped. The home she was trying so hard to hold together had just come apart.

Persian rugs and artwork reminded me that Cleva had mentioned something about a trust fund. But Astrid hadn't spoken of any relatives. I got the impression the kids had had the sanctity of family secrets drummed into them, which was probably why Enoch reacted so harshly when I drove up with Astrid a couple of weeks ago. He wasn't only angry with me, but also with Astrid for seeking me out and breaking the family code.

In the hallway next to the kitchen, I noticed a crowded bulletin board with papers and articles and some school pictures of the kids pinned to it. A couple of photographs of Astrid with her mother caught my eye. Though I didn't understand why at the time, I snatched one and put it in my pocket.

I walked toward the back deck where the sheriff and Enoch were still talking. I knew Horne thought Enoch was guilty of harming his wife; statistics backed up his kneejerk assumption. I wedged myself behind a cluster of potted plants, out of their sightlines but close enough to hear what they were saying.

"Like I've said a dozen times already, I was here. All night. I didn't know she'd gone. She'd [inaudible], and I didn't know until the next morning when Astrid said she couldn't find her mother."

"You had no idea your wife was missing? I find that hard to believe."

The tension was palpable until Enoch broke the stalemate. "We sleep in separate rooms, okay?"

"So you didn't get along? Did you have a fight?"

"In fact, sheriff, we got along better with separate rooms. My wife was in no shape to handle the kids by herself, so we stayed together the best we could. In this case, that was a good thing. For the kids."

Suddenly, a little boy I hadn't seen before ran out of the back door and over to his father. I presumed it was Dee—an adorable little guy with blond curls and a chubby waistline. Where had he been all that time? Quietly waiting in his room? God, what kind of life did these kids have? I remembered staying out of sight, trying to avoid my parents' ire, but this seemed in a different league. They were all like zombies, moving around, not really seeing or caring for each other, just bumping into one another at meal times. Meals an eight year old prepared!

Dee started wailing, and I peeked out enough to see Enoch comfort him. I heard Enoch mention lunch and the little boy nodded his head vigorously. Lunch? It was past two o'clock. I guessed Astrid was on strike, or to be fair, too upset to make their lunches. *Oh, man,* I thought, *this family is so screwed up, I might report them to family services myself.*

Something about Dee reminded me of Abit, back when I first met him. Abit was older, of course, but everyone had called him retarded for so long, he believed them and acted younger. He'd broken through that yoke with the help of the school and people who believed in him. I hoped someday Astrid and Dee would get the same chance to live fully, without fear.

When the three of them headed to the kitchen, I extricated myself from the foliage and joined them. Enoch began chopping carrots, the thwack of his knife on the cutting board louder with each strike. He kept shaking his head, telling Horne over and over that he didn't know what had happened to Lilah. Finally he put the knife down, picked up Dee, who'd started to cry, and gently rocked him. "Listen Sheriff, I don't want to talk about this in front of the children."

"It's hot in here," Dee whined. "Let's go out to the *screamed-in* porch." Enoch and I shared a smile. Precious incarnate. He gently lowered him onto the couch on the porch and gave him a few carrot sticks to eat—or play with, as it turned out. Enoch seemed deeply troubled for his son, and I'd watched him be kind with Astrid. I was beginning to see another side to the guy.

8

Della

Horne left in a huff after Enoch refused a house search without a warrant. I had to hurry after him to make sure I got a ride home. We didn't say much as we raced down the road. More than likely, Horne was mentally collecting facts to make his case for the warrant, and I was busy trying to get those kids off my mind. Horne dropped me at my store with barely a goodbye before speeding toward the county seat.

He got the warrant with no trouble; he had a harder time convincing me to be there that evening when the officers conducted the search. I didn't see what I had to contribute, but Horne said it would be a big help to him. At least Coburn's would be closed then, so I didn't have to worry about daycare.

The evening sky radiated a rosy light that belied the task ahead. Horne's men were already busy when we arrived, and Horne rushed to join them. Without anything specific to do, I just poked around and paid attention.

Enoch spoke quietly to Astrid, who was still not talking to me, though she did offer a weak little hi from behind his leg. It was obvious she was willing to cook all those meals because she loved her father and wanted to please him. Awful stereotypes at play for a little girl and her eight-year-old naiveté, but at that point, she didn't need a feminist manifesto. She needed love.

Enoch asked them to search the kids' rooms first. When they'd finished with Astrid's, he carefully tidied up before easing her back in there and closing the door. He held Dee while they searched his room.

I made my way back to Astrid's room and knocked on the door. She opened it without speaking and then flopped back on her bed. I'd assumed she'd be torn up about her mother, but she surprised me. She actually seemed more at ease than I'd seen before. Even as crazy as my drunken mother had been, I knew she loved me, best she could, and I would have missed her when I was as young as Astrid. But at the Holt's, I got a dark feeling that Astrid didn't have much to miss.

I really wanted to talk with her. She was whip-smart and, no doubt, would have picked up on anything untoward going on between her folks. But I couldn't budge her. I gave up. When I stood to leave, she finally spoke.

"I'll talk to that boy who drove the Rolling Store," she said.

"He didn't drive the bus," I told her, ever the stickler for detail.

"You know what I mean. The one who knows about bullies." I wondered why she didn't use Abit's name; I remembered introducing them at the store. She did that mind-reading thing again. "I know what you call him, but I won't use that name. I know why he's called that."

What a kid. I did feel a pang of guilt that we still called him Abit, but to those of us who'd known him so long, it was just a nickname—and a habit. I tried to explain that I often called him Mister to dodge the issue, but I could tell that didn't satisfy her. Finally, I mentioned I was the one who'd given him the nickname V.J.

"Really?" she said, looking up at me for the first time. She looked puzzled, furrowing her little brow in her best impersonation of an adult. I explained those were initials.

"What do they stand for?"

"Vester Junior."

"What kind of name is that?"

"That's why he goes by his initials." She nodded her approval, not quite smiling but showing a hint of her natural spunk.

"I figured that Rolling Store was where he got away from his ... his ... crappy life, and I want to see what that might feel like. I'll talk to him there."

"The bus is out of gas and can't go anywhere," I told her.

"We don't have to go anywhere, I just want a tour. I want to imagine being in there and driving around giving people food and other things they need. And maybe driving away and never coming back." That took my breath away. When I didn't say anything, she stared at me and said, "Well?"

"It's mostly filled with storage for the store."

"Are the front seats full?"

"No."

"Okay, we'll sit in the seats, and you can watch through the windows." As though she knew the sheriff would require that. Eight going on twenty-eight.

I convinced her to follow me when I went into the living room and brought Horne up to date. He looked at me as though I'd lost my mind, but when he saw Astrid standing there, arms akimbo, feet firmly planted on the floor, he knew better than to object. He looked over at Enoch, who nodded his approval.

"Okay, but it's late now. Do it tomorrow. Keep me informed—and keep an eye on them."

9

Abit

"What the hell are you suggesting?"

I wasn't mad at Della—just that damned sheriff for thinking she had to be my chaperone while I talked to Astrid. Della tried explaining it to me, but I interrupted her. "Oh, I get it all right. He thinks I'm a pervert."

"No, honey, I don't think Sheriff Horne does. He's just anticipating what others might say."

"Oh, great. So it's not just one guy, it's the whole fuckin' community."

She hugged me before getting in the Jeep to go get little Astrid.

I was working in the woodshop when the Jeep returned and parked in front of the store. Della waved at me as I started down the steps, and Astrid ran to the back where we parked the bus. I noticed Della had to lift Astrid so she could reach the high steps of the bus. I didn't dare touch her. My own mother was surely looking out the window, thinking the darkest thoughts.

I settled behind the wheel while Astrid stroked the back of the fake leather seat like it was something special. Cinderella's carriage fixin' to take her away.

Della brought us a couple of sodas and closed Astrid's door. She motioned that she'd be across the way on an old chair out back. Not too close, but close enough she could keep an eye on me, for god's sake. I didn't know who was watching the store, but I'd seen people leaving with bags of groceries, so I figured Mary Lou was inside.

After looking round and getting settled into a seat about three times her size, Astrid asked, "What was it like, driving around in this bus, bringing things to people in need?"

"Well, I didn't drive. I was in the seat you're in."

"And what about seeing all those people? That musta been exciting."

At first, just the contrary folks popped into my mind, the ones who never liked what we brought—too big a can, not the right brand, too small a can. But then I saw the faces of mothers who'd run out of milk for their young'uns or the folks who were happy to get them giveaway items Della always sent, things that didn't sell so well in the store but meant the world to others.

"I loved it. Most of the time," I answered. "People really liked seeing us come lumbering down their roads." I flashed on the kids, all trusting and happy, dressed in saggy underwears or sometimes nothin' at all. "Especially them kids."

"Oh, I can still feel how thrilling it was to see that bus coming down our road. Something from the outside world showing up at our door. I was only four, but I remember. I guess that was after you'd gone off to school. You wouldn't know about how Mama got upset with that old woman who rode along. One day, I don't know what happened, but Mama came running out of the house, her face all twisted, and she told 'em to never come back. That seemed unfair to me and Daddy. We didn't get a say in something that was part of our lives, too."

Della had told me how growed up Astrid acted. Before now, we'd mostly talked about bullies and such, so I hadn't seen that side of her. I couldn't believe she was only eight year old. I looked over some questions Della gave me, just in case we ran outta things to say, and asked her how her mother acted the last time she saw her.

"Same as always," Astrid said. "Sad. Quiet. Locked in her room most of the time."

"*Her* room?" I asked.

"Yeah, we all have our own rooms," Astrid answered with an innocence that tugged at me. She was quiet for a while, so I started trying to find another question to ask. Then she piped up again. "Did you ever think about driving out to the highway and never coming back?"

"I did sometimes, but like I said, I wasn't driving, so I couldn't exactly take a run for it. But I'll tell you, I sure had them thoughts while I was traveling through Virginia a few year back."

"But you came back home. Settled right back where you'd growed up at your parent's home."

"Well, not exactly. That's just my shop, and I pay them rent for that space. And first I went back to school in Boone for a coupla year."

"Big deal. That's just up the road, and school is like being in a prison your parents send you to."

I didn't bother to explain that those were the best times of my life. I'd've wished the same for her, but she was too smart to go to a school for special people. Funny, I'd never thought about it like that before, but I kinda felt sorry for her, missing out on somewhere like The Hicks. "I came back to live next door to Della," I said. "And now I've got my own place out on Chatauga Lake."

She just nodded at that. "But you know what I'm talking about, don't you? That feeling of getting away."

I did. Sometimes I still did. My thoughts drifted off to just how much, especially at her age, I wanted to escape. Get away from all the bullies and people who looked down on me. But things had improved oncet I went to The Hicks and then had my own cabin to go to. When I went swimming of an evening, I'd get down under the water and block out the rest of the world. I could hear sounds and see the light changing, everything getting slow and kinda muffled. Soft. Peaceful. Like you wished life were.

Her voice cut like a razor through my thoughts when she said, "I think that's what my mama did. First, she left us in her head. When that wasn't enough, she just got to moving and decided never to come back." She started crying, silent tears running down her face onto her little striped T-shirt. "I guess me and Dee drove her crazy. Though, you know, Mama could be fun, baking cookies and even singing some old love songs she told us were by the Beatles, whoever they were. But not much lately. She had these Dark Days, I called them. Or Tiptoe Days—that's what Dee called them. And then she and Daddy would get into it. Arguing, fighting, cursing. Did your daddy hit your mama?"

"Not that I ever saw. To tell you the truth, they didn't seem to care enough to fight. They just ignored each other."

"Well, I wished that were true at our house. They don't seem to care much for each other, either, but sometimes they're ready to kill one another. It scared me and Dee, especially when the chopping knife came out."

"Your daddy drew a knife on your mama?" I asked, my voice crackin'.

"No, the other way around." Astrid paused and added, "But you know, those fights happened less than the silence. I swear, that was worse."

We sat quite-like for a while, and I was just about ready to signal Della that we were done when Astrid said, "My daddy has a friend who might be able to help. She comes to visit sometimes when Mama goes away. She's a lot happier than Mama. And I'm pretty sure he went off to see her from time to time because he'd come home smelling different—some kind of sweet perfume. Though that hasn't happened lately."

"Do you know where she lives?"

"She said she was from over near Spruce Pine. Maybe she knows why Mama went away."

"Hey, listen, Astrid, there are any number of things that could've happened to your mama," I said, scrambling to make her feel better. "Maybe she was going for a visit somewhere, to get her wits about her, and then something waylaid her. It wasn't your fault."

That started her crying again, and I felt like an idiot. Man, what was I thinking? I was just trying to ease the pain of her mama leaving, blaming someone else for keeping her from coming home. I guessed what she said had triggered somethin' for me. I'd always felt I weren't good enough for my parents, and I wanted to let her know that she—and Dee—*were* enough. More than enough.

After a while, she turned off the waterworks, wiped her face, and started telling me about finding a new suitcase, hidden in the back of her mother's closet one day when she was playing hide-and-seek with Dee. She said it was just a little suitcase and thought it would be good for her doll clothes. That's why she went back looking for it, but it was gone.

After that, she told me all kinds of things, as if a stopper had popped, and everything came pouring out. Like how the night her mama left, she'd heard her parents fighting. Really loud. Banging things, maybe a glass breaking against the wall. She and Dee just huddled in their rooms, afraid to even look out. When I asked if anyone had cried out for help, she shook her head. "No, nothing like that," she said as she tried to brush tears off her T-shirt.

And then, just like that, the stopper was back. She folded her arms over her chest, letting me know our conversation was over. She patted the dashboard and said, "Someday, I'm gonna get out of here."

10

Della

For a while, I watched Abit and Astrid from that old chair, but it dug into my back, so I moved to the front of the store. Besides, I knew I didn't have to keep an eye on Abit.

I sat on the bench he'd made for the store, running my hand along Wilkie Cartwright's head, noticing how smooth the gleaming wood felt. We'd placed the bench under the overhang to keep it from warping in the rain or drying out in the summer sun. It was so lovely, I suggested we store it somewhere protected from the weather during the cold and rainy winter. Abit surprised me with a stern no! He made me promise to always leave it out front; he'd repair any damages or replace it, if necessary.

As I waited, I realized how odd it was that I never sat in front of my own store. Up until that day, I'd only admired the bench when I opened each morning and closed in the evening. Of course, I stayed busy inside, but I vowed to sit there more often.

I heard Abit call me, so I walked toward the back. When I reached the passenger door, he cranked it open from the driver's side. Astrid jumped off, not like someone escaping, just ready to go home. She called over her shoulder, thanking Abit for the bus tour.

Abit stepped down, that crooked smile of his telling me he'd gotten some good information. I whispered to him to try calling the sheriff's office; I wanted Horne to know as soon as possible what she'd told him. When we pulled away from the store, Abit stood in the driveway, waving goodbye. Astrid rolled down her window and leaned out to wave back.

As the Jeep made its way up the Holt's drive, I was surprised to see Horne standing outside talking with Enoch. Astrid jumped out the second I stopped and ran to her father. He gave her a hug and told her to run inside, just like the first time I met him, only without the push. I nodded at Enoch but stayed by the Jeep. Horne said something to him and came over my way.

"We finished up last night," Horne said, "but I needed to come out this morning to ask Enoch a few more questions. We didn't find anything untoward. No missing knives or hidden guns. We confirmed that Mrs. Holt hadn't taken many clothes, just what she was wearing; maybe a couple of other things, best Holt could tell. Though I don't know what man would notice that kind of thing. I never had any idea about my wife's favorites."

Figures, I thought to myself. I asked if they'd found anything interesting. "A journal," he said. "Bizarro, I'll tell you. I'd like you to take a looksee. The entries range from weepy and loving to ready to kill Enoch and kids."

I was about to tell him that more than likely every mother had experienced that range of emotions, but from the look on his face, I thought better of it. Maybe Lilah's diary was more graphic. I said I'd look it over in the next couple of days and get back to him. Horne went on about exploring every possibility, including suicide. I was glad the kids were off in their rooms.

"In fact, it was more what we *didn't* find. Mrs. Holt's suitcase was missing, but Holt swore she'd given that to the Goodwill months ago. Did you learn anything from the girl?"

"Well, Abit did. I think we should head back to the store so you two can talk."

"Astrid said her mama had bought a new suitcase, which she hid in her closet," Abit told us. We were sitting in the back, and no one else was in the store. "Astrid found it when her and Dee were playin' and ..."

"Maybe Holt found the new suitcase, and they fought," Horne said. "He could've accidentally killed her, covering it all up by burying the body and suitcase. Maybe *in* the suitcase."

"As I was trying to tell you," Abit said, his voice sharp with irritation for being interrupted (or more like dismissed). "Astrid said the new suitcase was really small. She thought it was for her, maybe, or for her doll clothes." I smiled thinking about that little bruiser playing with dolls, but hey, why not? "If it was that small," he went on, "I can't see her daddy stuffing a body in it."

Abit shared the rest of his talk with Astrid. Again, Horne took the darkest view of everything. Like Tiptoe Days. That was something I was familiar with, and I knew they didn't lead to murder. But when Abit mentioned that Lilah wielded a knife at Enoch on several occasions, Enoch had had a girlfriend, and Astrid's parents argued violently the night Lilah went missing, I began to worry Horne might be right.

"We need to go back out there again," Horne said. "No telling what took place that night—or might be going on right now."

11

Abit

The next day, I saw Della go off with Airhorn, and for oncet I didn't feel even a twinge of envy. I was too busy with my own troubles.

I was glad I'd been able to help out, talking with Astrid and all. And I'd been true to her words when I recounted our conversation. I did leave out the part about how she was ready to leave it all behind. That seemed too personal, of a moment. As I saw it, who wouldn't want to leave after what she'd been living through? Besides, it didn't have anything to do with her missing mama.

My troubles started when Fiona and I were on our way to a concert the night before. Our band was just the warmup act, but the main act, Josh Hill and the Highlanders, was one of the best bluegrass bands in the state. We were getting noticed.

I'd had to take out the backseat so I could fit Bessie in the Merc—the neck safely resting on the console between the two front seats. Then Millie hopped in and made a nest of the old blankets I'd put back there. So far so good. Then while I was driving, I told Fiona about Astrid and little

Dee. "Oh, those poor wee'uns," she said, looking like something had happened to one of her own. I just nodded, not understanding where things would end up.

That evening, we sounded real good, and folks came up after and told me and Fiona that we played and sang like a perfect couple. We both smiled. I flashed on the good times we were enjoying together, and I reckoned Fiona was doing the same.

Later, I drove her back to the woodshop, where she'd left her car. As we rode along, I felt so happy, reliving our music and fun evening. When we pulled up, we sat in the Merc, under the security light shining over the family house and Della's store; it felt like we were on a stage, everything bigger than life.

I wished we were going on to my cabin, but Fiona said she couldn't. She had to be at work at six o'clock the next morning; she was assisting some doctor with a new procedure and wanted to be fresh. I could tell how excited she was to get to work with that doctor—her face kinda lit up—and I wanted to support her, so I didn't do any of my usual begging and teasing about staying over.

We were both reluctant to call it an evening, so we just sat there, quiet-like, holding hands. After a while, Fiona asked, "When should we get married?"

"Cows ass?"

"Why are you saying 'cows ass'?"

Well, so much for Shiloh's joke. I kept talking, acting like I hadn't just said something that stupid. "If it were up to me, we'd run off to Gatlinburg right now and say 'I do.'" And I was only kinda kidding. I'd've given anything if I'd left it at that. But like a damn fool, I went on. "What's your hurry?"

"Honestly? I can't wait to have kids. Talking about those wee'uns, the ones who lost their mam, I want to bring up ours with all the love you and I wished we'd both had."

A stabbing pain cut through my chest. I couldn't speak.

"Rabbit? Say something."

I still couldn't say anything, even though I knew every second I didn't answer was gonna hurt both of us. "We never talked about kids before," was all I could muster.

"I guess we haven't, but I assumed …"

"I don't want any kids," I blurted out, kinda loud. Fiona's face went all white; she looked like I'd struck her. "I can't bring someone into this world with my, my, uh, traits." I was flashing on all the bullying and shaming and contempt I'd faced. You had to be a madman to want to inflict that on a little kid.

"Are you mad, Rabbit? You're wonderful. There's nothing wrong with you. I'd bring one hundred children like you into the world."

That image was so sad, I started talking faster, as if my words could outrun my sorrows. "I love you for saying that, Fiona, but you don't know what it's been like."

"We could help our kids, and if they turned out half as good as you, I'd be happy."

I figured that was a good note to quit on. I kissed her goodnight and hugged her a little harder than usual.

12

Abit

Damnedest thing. Otis Cale, who didn't live that far from the Holt's as the crow flies, called the sheriff to say his dog came home dragging a woman's sweater and took it to his bed. Otis didn't think much of it till later that day when the dog came home with a brassiere in his mouth.

Airhorn put out a call to law enforcement within a circle round Laurel Falls, and his deputy organized a sweep for Tuesday, using the extra cops and volunteers. All the whitewater and rock-climbing rescue groups showed up, too, along with the curious and the kind.

They formed five groups, with each taking one of the four directions out from Otis's house and the othern round Enoch's house. Even Shiloh joined us. The only thing his group found was stuff like soda cans and the usual garbage. They did bring back a wallet, but it looked like it'd been out there a long time; an old receipt in it from 1969 bore that out. That was long before Astrid's parents even lived there.

One of the groups found some rusted barrel hoops, broken bottles, and a moonshine still. It was melting into the ground after so many years, but they said you could still see where the revenuers took an ax to it. And Jonny Porter stepped in a hornets' nest in the ground; he was saved from a world of hurt by his baggy overalls.

Ida Carithers nearly tripped over a purse. Everyone got real excited when they discovered Lilah Holt's old library card inside, along with a hanky and red lipstick. Come to find out, that place was an old hiding spot of Astrid's. Just a bunch of whatnot her mama had given her to play with. Later, Astrid told us she'd forgotten all about it since that was back when she was a "child."

The group heading north from Otis Cale's had the roughest time. They faced a steep cliff overlooking a good-sized creek (especially after our rainy spring) that nobody much wanted to deal with. It needed someone really fit, and Bill Davis, Billie Davis's husband, volunteered. He managed to scale down to where he found an old suitcase (the same one Otis's dog had discovered) in a tangled, forgotten spot, like someone stuck it there to hide it. Up on top of the cliff, just off to the left, the rest of his group found a place where some tree branches were broke and the ground looked scraped, all the way down to the water's edge. Since the rains had eased and we hadn't had any in more than a week, the damage still looked fresh, something that could have happened the night Mrs. Holt was out all alone.

Stories went wild, especially after Horne confirmed the suitcase had belonged to Astrid's mama. People round here had imaginations darker than Hollywood, and oncet you got them all together, they cooked up some downright scary notions: *She was killed and pushed down the cliff, then floated away... She was running scared and slipped and hit her head as she fell... Some pervert killed and buried her.*

But no one really knew.

And, of course, people were calling Sheriff Horne, sure they'd spotted her. But Della said Airhorn was familiar with the power of suggestion—or the itch to be in the news—and discounted most of them. He told Della he was beginning to believe Astrid's mama had been hurt by someone who likely pushed her down into the creek. He talked on about it having a good current, and how her body could have washed up anywhere as the creek made its way to the river, then on to the ocean. The misery of all that gave me the shivers.

I could see from my woodshop that the store got real busy over the next week, like the summer of '85. Lots of people showed up, mostly to congregate and swap stories about what was going on. Better than dwelling on their own lives.

13

Della

Horne's still calling Enoch a person of interest, but I think he's just stumped."

I was filling in Cleva and Alex on the news from the past week. Alex had flown into Asheville from L.A., picked up his car at the airport, and driven to Laurel Falls. Together we made chicken korma with a vegetable biryani for the three of us. He brought Kingfisher beer from Asheville, and I contributed mango sorbet from the freezer at the store.

We talked about how, after the first flurry of the investigation, things had come to a standstill. Horne wanted to pin it on Enoch, but the facts didn't line up. "Horne keeps saying that Astrid's mother was depressed, and Enoch snapped," I said. "But that doesn't cut it for me. If being depressed leads to getting murdered, I'd be six feet under now. I don't need to tell either of you that I'd had some trouble getting oriented to this place."

"Honey, just because you're born here don't mean it comes easy," Cleva said. "Sometimes I get the blues, too. Or I get so mad, I just want to pinch someone's head off. I reckon it's like that the world over. Get two people in a room, anywhere, and the likelihood of a head-pinching doubles."

After dinner, Alex poured three glasses of iced coffee he'd brewed earlier and added his two cents. "That sheriff needs to cut the father some slack. Enoch sounds as though he's better with the kids than that mother ever was, not exactly a hothead ready to snap. He's the one who tried to find work and serve as both parents to his kids." Alex's voice grew louder as he stuck up for not just Enoch, but every man who worked at being kind to his family. He was a convert to that group, and as the saying goes, there's nothing like a convert's zeal. He sipped his coffee before going on. "Over the years, I've known lots of people like them—idealistic, aka stupid transplants from big cities. They quickly found it's not easy living here, though Della has managed rather nicely." He clinked my glass and then looked at Cleva. "Not that I don't enjoy your homeland, Cleva. It's wonderful to come for a visit." They clinked glasses.

"And why is Horne horning in on your time, Della?" Alex added, trying to make it sound like a casual quip, but I knew him too well. "You're not law enforcement or even a reporter anymore. I think he's got his eye on you."

I waved off his comment. "Oh, he just needs some help, and he *is* a galoot—not too smooth with kids or women. I suppose I help that way." My turn to sip coffee and pull my thoughts together. "I've spent a good amount of time with that family, and I can't shake the feeling they aren't particularly upset Lilah's gone. Their lives *are* chaotic because of everything going on, but there doesn't seem to be much sadness beyond that. Kids are wired to love or at least count on their parents—their survival rests on that. We've all heard disturbing studies about abused kids going back to hug their oppressors. But the last time I saw the three of them, they seemed more like a family *without* Lilah. Oh, and that reminds me. Horne drove out to question Maddie Kramer, the woman Enoch was seeing on the side. She told him they only got together occasionally and had broken it off recently. He said she seemed credible."

I'd spent time over the past week reading Lilah's diary, and Horne's description—bizarro—was spot on. I shared with Alex and Cleva how she seemed to write whatever came to mind, things that sounded more like Stephen King than a troubled mother. Watching critters come up the bathroom drains. Imagining she was stabbing everyone she knew. Chattering over and over about the stupidest things.

Meanwhile, Horne had also discovered a few things from public records. They'd paid cash for the land and the cabin kit from Rocky Top Cabins, something that supported the assumption that one of them had money.

"Whoo!" Cleva interrupted. "Land prices sure have skyrocketed. It's to the point now where families are building small villages on the farms their great-grandparents carved out of the wilderness. Grown children are just flat out unable to afford land of their own these days."

I knew that was true for Abit. I was glad he'd moved away from his folks and found that rental cabin on the lake, but if he ever wanted to own his own place, I didn't know what he'd do. I did know he'd never live on his parents' land. The woodshop was one thing. Living there? No way.

"When Horne tried to trace deeper into their story, he hit a dead end," I went on. "Their Social Security records didn't go back that far, just twenty years or so. Of course, not everyone gets a Social Security number at a young age. Again, that speaks of money—no jobs after school or during the summers. Enoch told Horne he hadn't gone to college and claimed he couldn't remember his high school. Given his age, I bet he went through an extended doper phase. Same with Lilah. Horne reluctantly admitted he didn't have anything to charge Enoch with except some marijuana they found during the search. I couldn't believe it when he said he wouldn't bother—Enoch and the kids had enough to worry about without that. Brower would have threatened the electric chair."

"Ain't that the truth," Cleva said, polishing off her mango sorbet. I'd noticed Cleva's speech returning to her roots more since she'd retired from the school system.

Alex got up and started to clear the table. The kitchen and living room were one big room, up above the store and overlooking the mountains, where streaks of pink and gold danced behind their majestic peaks, closing out the longest day of the year. "Della told me they ran you off, Cleva, while you were giving away extra food from the Rolling Store," Alex said. "So much for gratitude."

"It was that wife, the mother of them two kids," Cleva said, using her spoon for emphasis. "She came running out one day with a big wooden spoon in her hand, held up high above her head. 'You get off our land and quit pumping these kids for information about us.' I didn't know what to make of that. I'd only said howdy to that little girl; I handed her a can of beans and hightailed it back to the bus. That woman scared the shit outta me, even if it was just a wooden spoon."

The phone rang. Everything was close in the small apartment, and I caught it on the third ring. When I hung up, I told them, "The sheriff has a new lead. He wants to run it by me tomorrow afternoon."

Alex smirked, but I just laughed at him.

14

Della

Alex left the next morning, heading home to finish his pretrial stories on the Simpson/Goldman murders. After Mary Lou showed up, I drove to the sheriff's office, where Horne filled me in on the latest developments while he packed a briefcase.

"When I picked up the phone, a woman blurted out, 'I saw someone who might be your gal.' The caller, who wouldn't give her name, went on to say she saw 'the gal' climb into a Potash 3K truck out at the big truck stop on Highway 221. She said she didn't know what the hell potash was, so it'd caught her eye. Doesn't sound all that reliable to me, but I need to check it out."

"Well, I don't know about you, but I don't know what potash is either," I confessed.

"Well, er, I've heard of it. It's …"

"Fertilize." That was Lonnie Parker. He'd been deputy ever since I'd moved to Laurel Falls—and for years before that. When Sheriff Cunningham had a heart attack in 1984, Lonnie expected to be promoted, since candidates for sheriff didn't have to run for office when a vacancy opened due to illness or death. He thought he'd slip right into the sheriff position after serving as deputy for so long. But the powers that be chose Brower, whose father wielded considerable influence in the county. Brower served almost a decade before getting voted out in favor of Horne. "Or technically, nutrient forms of the element potassium—K, hence the initial in the company name," Lonnie added.

Horne scowled. "Oh yeah, it's the stuff that makes up fertilizer."

"There's an echo in here."

That was likely the boldest thing I'd ever heard Lonnie say. I worried the chip on his shoulder was getting so big it was about to fall off and explode. If he kept it up, he wasn't long for that job, with dim prospects for what else he could do in the county.

"Okay, but what does the 3 have to do with it?" I asked. "Some kind of chemical significance?"

"I doubt it ma'am. Work it out for yourself," Lonnie said.

It took me a minute. "Oh, come on. KKK? In 1994? Surely not."

Lonnie and Horne looked at me as though I'd just fallen off a potash truck. Horne went on. "I called the company—it's based in Charlotte—so I need to run down there and talk with the owner. He said he'd make sure the driver—David Dibble—would be around. He also promised to keep quiet about this until we had a chance to get there."

"We?" Lonnie asked.

"Yeah, I was hoping Ms. Kincaid would come along, this being a woman's issue and all."

Horne's explanation was so flimsy, I had to work at not laughing. I felt bad for Lonnie and made an apologetic face at him. He'd helped me out on several occasions, and I wanted to stay friends. Not to mention his mother was the best baker in the county. Lonnie liberally shared her goods—with people he liked (which meant Horne would never get to sample the pillowy texture and silky icing of her legendary cinnamon rolls.)

Lonnie went back to typing a report, about what I couldn't imagine. Rolling stops and DUI were the county's usual crimes. No wonder his interest was piqued by this case.

"Hey, Horne, slow down. You missed the turn."

"Yeah, but we're making great time." Big smile. *Oh, great,* I thought, *another comedian like Shiloh.* "Don't worry. I know where I'm going. You might want to pay attention. It's a shortcut worth remembering."

That plus light traffic meant we made it to Charlotte in under two hours. Just as well. We didn't have much to say to one another once we'd exhausted the "what ifs" surrounding the case. I was grateful for the quiet.

When we pulled into the Potash 3K Inc. parking lot, the Charlotte police were already there. Out of professional courtesy, Horne had called ahead to a buddy on the force he'd met when they were going through law-enforcement training.

The company owner, Bud Maguire, greeted Horne friendly enough. He was a typical looking guy in those parts: just shy of six feet tall, thinning hair, sizeable gut hanging over his belt. I tried not to think in stereotypes, but there was a reason something was stereotypical—it happened a lot. Horne introduced me, and Maguire looked at me as if to say, "What are *you* doing here?" but that happened a lot, too. I held his stare, and he finally looked away.

After Horne explained more about the situation, Maguire picked up the phone and mumbled into it. Soon there was a knock on the door.

"You wanted to see me, Mr. Maguire?" A tall, skinny kid who couldn't have been more than twenty years old stuck his head in. He looked around the room and saw the sheriff standing near the door. The color drained from his face. "What's this about?"

"I'm the one asking questions, son," Horne said. After we all got seated and settled, Horne formally confirmed that he was talking with David Dibble, the truck driver. Then he bore down hard. Dibble twitched and squirmed, running his fingers through black hair too short to ruffle. At one point, I thought I saw tears well up in his eyes, and

I couldn't blame him. The interview wasn't going well, and Horne's voice in that small office was about to make *me* cry.

Maguire had already confirmed that Dibble had been in our area on the day Lilah left home, but Horne asked Dibble anyway.

"Yes sir, that's my route."

"Did you pick this woman up?" Horne held up the photo that had been printed in the *Mountain Weekly*, and likely other papers as well. I'd seen her only that one time in her bedroom window, but that image was burned into my brain. Lank blond hair surrounding a round face (like Astrid's) with dead eyes.

"I was at the truck stop along 221, just getting ready to pull out when I saw the woman you're asking about. She waved at me, like she was in trouble, and I rolled down my window a little. It was raining hard, and she asked me if I was going anywhere near Chester—she'd missed her bus and had an important doctor's appointment downtown. I felt sorry for her, so I told her to hop in."

"Where did you drop her in Chester?"

"Well, it's kinda hard to describe." He paused for a moment and seemed to struggle to find the right words. "We were on 221, and you know how the highway bypasses the town? She told me to pull over—she'd make her way from there. I was just as glad. Cities like that don't want trucks barreling through town, so I did what she asked."

"Can you narrow the place down for us? Where exactly did you stop to let her out?"

"I honestly don't know. I was having to pay close attention to the road—it was still raining hard." He paused again and closed his eyes; after a few moments, he added, "I recall pulling up at this place that had a shelter—I don't know, maybe a city bus shelter or something like that. That's where I let her out."

"What time would this have been?" When the kid hesitated, Horne spat, "Approximately."

"I guess it was around noon. I'd pulled over at the truck stop for coffee about ten o'clock, took a fifteen, twenty minute break, and was back on the road with her by half past ten."

"Man, there are so many things wrong with that story," Horne barked. "I used to live in Chester, and they don't have city buses. You couldn't have stopped at a bus shelter."

"Hey, I didn't say that was definite. Just something like that." He paused, then nervously looked over at his boss. "Listen, Mr. Maguire. I'm sorry about breaking the company rules and all, but if you'd seen this woman, getting wet in the rain and begging for help …" Maguire waved him off. He had bigger worries.

"What did you two talk about?"

"I just told you she was the quiet type. She did say it felt good to be out of that 'godforsaken holler.' And I'm beginning to see why."

"Just leave out the editorializing. Not doing you a lick of good," Horne said. "Why didn't you come forward? You could have saved us valuable time. If someone hadn't reported your vehicle and company name, we'd never have known."

"I didn't know anything had happened to her. I live down here, and I haven't got the time to read newspapers or watch TV, if the story even made it on our news."

"We need to search his truck," Horne said to the owner. Maguire and the kid exchanged glances. "I can get a warrant, but that will take time," Horne went on. "Time you don't want to lose, either." Maguire nodded.

Horne must have arranged for his buddy to guard the truck, because the same Charlotte police officer was standing next to a Potash 3K truck in an area where several others were parked.

They both gloved up and went over the truck. I watched them work, and after a while, Horne stuck his head out and held up a striped scarf before putting it in an evidence bag. He later told me it was wedged between the passenger seat and the door. Even from a distance I could see a brownish red stain smeared across it. He bagged it and kept looking. Later, his sidekick found a button—one of those barrel-shaped buttons popular on barn coats.

When we got back to Maguire's office, I swear that kid had sweated off a pound or two. Horne held up the bag with the bloody scarf in it. "Son, can you explain this?"

Maguire answered for him. "That scarf don't mean shit. It looks like more rust than blood. If what you told me stands, that woman was running away, likely through a bunch of fields. She'd probably cut herself on barbed wire and staunched the flow with the only thing she had handy."

"We could sit here and make up what-ifs till the sun goes down, but your driver here is the last one to see her alive. And now this," he said, holding up the scarf bag again. "I don't have any choice but to hold you in our county jail." He cleared his throat and gave the Miranda Warning.

"Are you arresting me?" Dibble asked, his voice cracking.

"No, son, just holding you as a suspect. I've got 72 hours before I either press charges or let you go. In the meantime, I plan to get at the truth."

I wasn't sure where that "son" business started, but Horne was piling it on. It reminded me of a mean old father, before belting his kid, saying, "Now, son, this is going to hurt me more than you." Yeah, right.

As we left, Dibble's hands cuffed behind his back, Maguire assured him he'd get the company attorney on this and explain to his mother that he was just giving evidence. "We'll see you back here in no time."

That depended on how you defined "no time."

Horne spent close to an hour in Charlotte traffic trying to find the crime lab. En route, I got a good look at the barrel-shaped button through the evidence bag. I'd had a similar coat when I was a kid, and it brought back memories of how some creepy man tried to get me in his car, telling me he wanted to take a closer look at those "pretty buttons." I ran home, but images of those buttons stuck in my mind—and I'd never bought anything sporting them.

When Horne finally found the lab, he parked and ran in, leaving me in charge of Dibble in the backseat behind the metal grid. Horne didn't think the kid was dangerous, and I *knew* he wasn't. The only thing he was guilty of was being kind enough to offer a ride to someone in need. Neither one of us said a word while we waited.

On our way home, we got bogged down in heavy rush hour traffic, reminding me how glad I was I rarely had to deal with that anymore. Dibble kept making nervous little mewlings and mumblings. It was a long ride back.

Once we pulled into the sheriff's parking area, I rushed to my car and drove home in record time. I couldn't recall when I'd been so glad to see my little apartment above the store. I let Jake out for a run, picked at a few leftovers, and crashed.

The next morning, Horne called to let me know Dibble was still locked up—as though that made the world a safer place. I could tell by the way he talked that even he knew he hadn't found a vicious killer. But there was no one else to blame, and he wanted to show some fast results. Trouble was, that scrawny kid and the whole scene just didn't add up to homicide—yet, anyway.

"The real reason I'm calling," Horne went on, "is I drove over to the Holt's and sat on the porch while Mr. Milquetoast (his nickname for Enoch—just because he didn't swagger and act tough) searched the house for his wife's medical records. He found some information stashed in a file in her bedside table, tucked under a bunch of things no one would look under—nail clippers, nail file, book marks, stuff like that."

Horne said Enoch seemed surprised by all the brochures and articles Lilah had collected about bipolar disorder. She'd also made a list of the best medications and circled a couple in red. Enoch recalled a spell when she'd acted more like her old self, but that disappeared about three months ago. He also found a small personal calendar with the doctor's appointment scheduled for the day she went missing (still no doctor's name). I thought it was odd that calendar didn't include the July doctor's appointments like the one she kept in the kitchen.

"Maybe she stopped taking her pills," I told Horne. I mentioned that I'd had a friend in D.C. who was bipolar. He was one of the most charming, entertaining guys I knew. Until he'd stopped taking his medicine. One day I was driving up Connecticut Avenue, and I saw him ambling up the middle of the road, disheveled and lost in a dirty trench coat. I gave him a ride home, but I don't believe he ever realized who I was. It took him months to get back to the person I knew—and that I knew he wanted to be. I hoped Lilah, if she were still alive, had a good supply of her meds with her.

15

Abit

We played a gig Friday night in Burnsville, and Fiona sang so sweet, I figured she had to be okay with what we'd talked about a few nights ago. (I hadn't seen her since then. She'd been busy at work—at least that's what she said.) Her fan club was growing, her singing and fiddling warming people's hearts. Not to mention how pretty she was, her red hair pulled back with combs and a red checkered shirt I hadn't seen before. I was so busy admiring her I almost missed my cue when we were playing "Are You Missing Me."

I joined her on vocals and kept up my part on the bass. Truth be known, I had a bit of a fan club myself. And Millie had turned into a regular mascot for the band. Everyone loved that dog; she was real quiet and never howled or messed around while we played.

We finished up the program with "Little Cabin Home on the Hill," and the crowd let us know they'd enjoyed the evening by clapping and demanding an encore. "Midnight Flyer" was always good for that. Months later, I pondered our music choices that night. I couldn't help but wonder if them songs had been a sign.

We packed up, and the rest of the band rode home with Ed Neblett, our guitar player, while I gave Fiona a ride to her car parked at my woodshop. As we headed back, I tried chatting about the gig, but Fiona wasn't having it. We rode in silence long enough to make me squirm. Finally, she said, "Rabbit, not having kids would be like cutting off a limb. A part of me would be missing."

I let that sit out there a while, trying to think of the right way to shape my answer. A few minutes later, I said, "I just can't do it, Fiona. I don't want any kid to go through what I've been through. Not a chance."

"But you've shown them. You're handsome and smart and good at what you do. And you wouldn't have gone to the Hicks. Or met me."

I pulled the car into a wide spot next to the road; I didn't want to be driving and discussing my future at the same time. I could tell she'd been working on this problem, and she was right—my life was in a good place, especially with Fiona in it. But I wouldn't—couldn't— budge on the kid thing. "That's like saying someone couldn't be in the Special Olympics if he hadn't gone to the Gulf War and had his leg blown off."

Something changed real bad inside the Merc, and I knew I'd gone too far. "Okay, wait. I know that was a lousy comparison," I said, pleading-like. "I wouldn't take anything for meeting you—but I'd like to think we'd've met anyway. Somehow. *Not* because I'd been tormented and shamed for most of my life and screwed by a bunch of con artists."

"I thought you said you were over all that shite," she said.

"I am. The same way you're over your mother's death. It no longer ruins every day, but it's still with me."

"You could be part of our wee'uns' lives. You're working for yourself, so you could be there as they grow up. Shape their lives. And maybe your parents could help out, from time to time."

"NO!" I shouted, scaring both Millie and Fiona. "I'm not having them involved in any child rearing, even if I did ever plan to have any. Not that I do."

I pulled back on the road, and I thought we'd never get back to the shop. The silence hung so heavy I had trouble breathing; I pushed down harder on the accelerator. After what felt like a thousand mile, I said, "We could adopt."

"Not part of my plan, *V.J.*," was all she said. I pressed her on it, but she didn't say another word. When we pulled up at her car outside the woodshop, she jumped out, leaned back in to say she'd think about it, then slammed the Merc's door. Hard.

I decided to sleep on the cot in my woodshop with Millie in her bed by my side. I didn't trust myself to drive home to the cabin. It felt like every bone in my body was broke. And while I was lying there, unable to sleep, I realized she hadn't called me Rabbit.

A few nights later, I started awake and threw the covers off. I'd been dreaming about being buried alive. I felt better after some deep breaths of fresh air, realizing it was just a bad dream—until real life came to mind. Fiona. Gone. No wonder I dreamed that, because that was how my life felt. Covered in shit.

We'd had a date Saturday evening, but she'd stood me up. Years ago, Fiona'd told me I'd knocked the talk out of her, but I guessed she'd found her voice again. She didn't show at our last gig, either. I could tell the fans missed her—and not just her voice and fiddle playing. Like me, they missed *her*.

I lay there forever, trying to get back to sleep. Finally I gave up. The sun hadn't even come up yet, but I got dressed and gave Millie a walk round the lake. Then we drove to the shop, but I couldn't face another hoosier or sideboard or table. I sat in the Merc 'til I saw Della's light go on in the store; I knew she was brewing some good coffee. It was well before opening time, so I had to knock on the front door. She came out from the back, scowling at whatever fool was trying to get in early. When she saw it was me, she smiled real big, which boosted my spirits. A little.

"Howdy, Mister. What brings you out so early? Need to get out an order?"

"Yes and no. I do have orders to get out, but mostly I couldn't sleep. Fiona's gone."

"Oh, where'd she go? To Galax to see her aunt?"

"No, gone. As in left me." I hadn't been able to talk to even Della about it.

Della looked so sad my heart ached all the more. She poured us both some coffee, and I started to explain about the kids. "I could love it, especially the parts that reminded me of Fiona. But not Daddy. What if that young'un looked like him and made me think of him every day? And what if our kid took after *me*? All them hateful things at school—the taunts and teases piling up 'til they squash the hope right out of you."

"I didn't know you'd ever lost hope, Abit."

"I had 'til you moved here."

"Oh, I see."

"You sound like Mama."

"She taught me."

"Oh, I see." I said, smiling a little for the first time in days.

We got down to some serious talk for a while, and like always, I felt better afterwards. At least enough to go to work. But I sulked through most of the day until even Shiloh got annoyed. I told him the news, and he said he was sorry. Then he tried to cheer me up with one of his stupid jokes.

"What's the difference between a porcupine and a Porsche?" he asked. I shrugged. "The porcupine has the pricks on the outside."

I just turned the sander up a notch. (I'd later come to see that so-called joke as another weird coincidence.)

"Okay, be that way," he shouted over the noise. "You know, you're not doing either of us a favor moping about." He went on for a while and gave up. Like I'd already done.

16

Della

Monday morning, Horne called early to let me know the crime lab results. The reddish streaks on the scarf were rust mixed with Lilah's blood type (O negative, something he'd learned from the files Enoch found). Bud Maguire's idea that she'd cut her hand on a barbed wire fence while traipsing across fields became the most likely scenario. There was more of that wicked stuff stretched across the county than at Sing Sing and San Quentin combined. That plus a lack of motive, and Horne surely knew he needed to let that poor mope out of jail.

Instead, he worked overtime to turn common sense into a conspiracy theory. The attorney for the potash company called later on Monday, complaining in rather unlawyerly language that Horne had "piss poor" evidence. But Horne still clung to the fact that Dibble was the last person to see her alive.

Until he wasn't.

Horne stopped by the store around nine o'clock Tuesday morning to tell me he'd gotten a call from someone in Chester who'd seen Lilah. "Do you want to ride along?" he asked. "I need to talk to this woman, and you've got a better way with them than I do. It needs a woman's touch. I'll fill you in on the ride down there." He didn't even wait for my answer before driving off.

I didn't know what decade he'd dredged up "woman's touch" from but that put me off the idea of riding in the car with him for a couple of hours. Not to mention his assumption that I'd say yes. But I think we both knew I'd end up going along.

I tried Mary Lou, but she wasn't at home. Just as I put the phone down, I saw Abit and Millie heading toward the store. I'd never ask him, and not just because he had too many bad memories from when his father owned the store. He had better things to do.

As soon as he and Millie walked through the door, he picked up on my mood. "Hey, Della. Everything all right? You look worried."

"Oh, I don't have anyone to keep the store, and I really need—well, *want*—to go with Horne." I bent down to scratch Millie behind her ears, and she rolled over on her back, sizeable white paws flopping over her white teddy-bear chest.

"Don't look at me," Abit said, unnecessarily.

"Honey, I never would. But Billie's still out of town and Mary Lou isn't home."

"Well, we're waiting on a delivery of maple wood, and Shiloh can't finish that sideboard 'til it comes in. He could hold down the store. I'm not saying he'd do a great sales job, but he won't clean out the till."

I liked Shiloh, even if he was a bit of a poseur. I got a kick out of him whenever we chatted in back over a coffee. But hold down the store? Abit must have read my mind, because he added, "He may not be perfect, but you'd get outta here."

Shiloh came down, and I gave him a quick overview. The register wasn't anything fancy; all he had to do was ring things up. We agreed on an hourly rate, but before he'd let me go, he gave me a Buddhist lecture about being kind to criminals and not exacting revenge. I was already planning on doing the first and not the second. It was Horne he should've been lecturing.

On the drive to Chester, Horne was both excited about the new lead and disappointed Dibble didn't appear to be guilty. "I didn't find anything—not a scratch on him. No sign of struggle. And that company attorney called again because the seventy-two hours were up. I had to release Dibble."

Oh, that pesky U.S. Constitution, I thought to myself. Besides, the more he explained the new lead, the more it seemed Dibble *had* dropped Lilah off in Chester like he'd said.

"You know how the *Mountain Weekly* and a few other local papers published Mrs. Holt's photo with a brief story about her disappearance?" Horne asked. "Well, this woman we're going to see"—he looked down at a note lying on the front seat—"Ralphine Dawson told me she recognized the woman from the newspaper story, but what really made her stick in her mind was she was pulling one of those 'newfangled suitcases on wheels.' I wanted to tell her they'd been around for a while, but what would be the point? Anyway, she went on to describe Mrs. Holt at the Chester Trailways station and swears it was the day *after* Dibble allegedly dropped her off outside of town. That was a couple of weeks ago now, so I want to talk with her to make sure she's not a drunk."

"What was Dawson doing at the bus station?"

"She's a janitor there."

I could only guess he had something against janitors, assuming they were all drunks. I didn't bother to ask why because we'd just pulled up at the station.

"It caught my eye 'cause I'd never seen one like that," Ralphine told us. "Suitcase, I mean. I'd like to get me one of them—but a bit bigger. Not that I go anywheres—at least not yet. I just clean up after people who do." Ralphine had a lined face that made her look older than she likely was, maybe forty-five or fifty. But she had a spark about her that hadn't been extinguished by the daily detritus at the station. She'd held on to expectations of a life filled with travel and adventure. I liked her and believed her.

Horne still seemed to have doubts. He pulled out a small mug-shot book he'd prepared back at the office—five pictures from his records plus Lilah's. Ralphine was shaking her head as she went through the first three, but on the fourth, her finger stabbed Lilah in the middle of her face. "That's her!"

"And you're sure it wasn't Thursday when you saw her."

Ralphine nodded her head vigorously. "That's my day off."

We thanked her, and I slipped her a twenty dollar bill, just because. She stuffed it in her apron and nodded her thanks.

Horne talked with the station manager, who explained he had no way to know where Lilah was headed. He was cooperative, though, and gave Horne a list of drivers. "It won't be easy to reach them; they're out on the road so much. I can let you talk to the ones here now, and I'll put up that woman's photograph and story in the drivers' breakroom."

They went over schedules while I sat in the waiting area and people-watched. The station bustled on a Friday, hosting an amazing mix of humanity, from college students to migrant workers to ne'er-do-wells and mothers with more children than they could handle. The racket was deafening.

Horne came over to get me, a big smile on his face. He'd caught a break. Only two buses went out that day during the most likely timeframe, and one of those drivers was due back in an hour. He apologized to me for the delay, but I didn't mind. I'd spotted a bookstore a block or two over.

I didn't get to a real bookstore often enough. I browsed through row after row of books, not even caring what the subject was. They were all beautiful, new, and fascinating. I bought one on bluegrass music I thought Abit would enjoy and the latest Michael Connelly mystery for me. At the coffee shop inside the bookstore—a pairing as natural as Shakespeare in the Globe Theater—I ordered a latte and chicken sandwich; I was starving.

But a couple of hours—and too many coffees and muffins—later, even I was getting tired of hanging out there (and good-natured bookstore employees were starting to give me funny looks). Horne was supposed to come get me when he finished, but I decided to walk back to the bus station. I saw him standing at the far end with a long face. One of the buses had been delayed by over an hour, and after the wait, that driver didn't recognize her. The other driver wasn't due in for several hours; the manager assured Horne he'd show him the photograph.

Horne thanked him, hustled me out to the car, and drove off fast. When I asked where we were going in such a hurry, he handed me a sheet with directions to Dr. Murray Epstein's office. He'd spent the last week calling almost every doctor in Chester, trying to locate Lilah's physician. It wasn't easy, given patient privacy laws. Some told him they didn't have a patient by that name (assuming she used her real name); others refused to respond. He finally found one who made him think she was hiding something. Just a sheriff's hunch, he told me. He'd tried pulling rank as a law enforcement officer, but she told him he could be Jack the Ripper for all she knew over the phone. He suggested she call his office to verify, but she wasn't having it.

When we entered that office, we had no doubts that Dolores Lopez, according to her desk nameplate, was a no-nonsense woman. I looked forward to seeing how Horne handled the situation.

He didn't do too badly, showing his badge and using a courteous tone. Ms. Lopez studied his ID and said, "I can confirm that she had an appointment that day—but didn't show up for it."

Which threw Horne's theory into a tailspin. Why had she missed her appointment—one she'd gone to great lengths to get to? Maybe she'd arrived too late and didn't bother to stop by. But the appointment time she'd circled in her calendar was1:30 p.m., and if Dibble had dropped her off at noon, she could have made the appointment in plenty of time, even with a long walk in from the outskirts.

Horne and I talked over the case on the way home. I could tell he was as worried as I was about her not showing up. From the timing of her appointment, it appeared she'd gotten an early start on Thursday and likely wanted to get home before dark. I got the sense he still felt Dibble had done more harm than he'd admitted, but there was no denying the bus station janitor's recollection of seeing her on Friday. Dibble was long gone by the time Ralphine had coveted that suitcase.

Traffic was light, a break I needed because I'd been away much longer than I'd told Shiloh. I was relieved the store was still open.

But Horne wasn't ready to call it a day. When he turned off the ignition, I sensed something hanging in the air. He took off his somewhat creepy reflective shades and sheriff's hat—not quite cowboy, not quite fedora—and turned in his seat. Even his voice sounded different (and better) when he told me he enjoyed my company and hoped we could be friends. At first I thought *oh no*, that protective reaction every woman has. But then I remembered how Gregg O'Donnell, the Forest Service ranger, had turned me down years ago when I told him I wanted to continue to be "just friends." He'd said he couldn't do that, and I never saw Gregg after that except by chance a couple of times a year.

Horne rolled his hat brim between his fingers as he told me he needed someone he could relate to. "Lonnie just doesn't cut it. It gets lonesome around here. I know you've got your 'friend' (he added air quotes, awkwardly juggling his hat in the process), so it's nothing like that. I just appreciate your intellect. And when I see you with your family, it looks so …"

He couldn't find the right word, so I filled in the blank. "Nice. And it is. Though it's small and an unusual one, at that."

"Well it looks like a big one when you're a family of one."

Once I understood he really was looking for "just a friend," I felt, well, honored. Maybe because I understood that kind of loneliness—and the courage it took to do something about it. We shook on it, as though we'd just signed a contract.

"I'm sorry I'm so late!" I said as I stepped through the front door. Shiloh was busy stacking cans of tomatoes, beets, and kidney beans in what appeared to be an everything-red pyramid. And the store reeked of patchouli. *Oh well*, I thought, *it was worth it to get away.*

"Oh, hello. I was just working on this display for you," he said, beaming at his sculpture. *Good thing I got back before he started in on the green and yellow pyramids,* I thought. I settled up with him, paying cash out of the register. There definitely seemed to be more bills in there than when I left.

"How'd it go?" I asked.

"Oh, you had quite a flurry of customers. We had a good discussion going, too, about why you were off to Chester and the Buddhist way of viewing criminal activity. I explained to everyone that Buddhists see punishing an offender only as a means to reform his character. We focused mainly on whether Horne saw it that way, and just what your feelings on this matter might be."

"Thanks, Shiloh," I said with only a hint of sarcasm. I agreed with his stance, but I wondered what my customers would have to say about all that. I was already dreading the mayhem he'd likely dredged up, something Mary Lou and I would have to deal with in the days ahead. I shuffled him toward the front of the store. "Thanks again," I said, trying to close the door, but he didn't take the hint.

"I hope you'll call on me again, Ms. Kincaid. I found I have quite a rapport with your clientele. Oh, and one more thing. I think you'll be getting some new orders." He punctuated that with a wink and a smile before turning to leave. I sighed. What in the world did that mean?

It was right at quitting time, so I brought in the sandwich board (Shiloh had added two smiley faces to it), locked the back door (he'd put out a tin of imported Spanish tuna for the feral cat I was trying to discourage) and counted the till (it came out to the penny). I wondered to myself why righteous people could make you think such unrighteous thoughts.

17

Abit

I didn't feel much like working, but I needed to stay busy. I sanded a coffee table Della'd ordered not long after Fiona'd left me. She swore it weren't a pity order, and I guessed I believed her. I vaguely remembered her saying something earlier about an order. Whatever, I was glad to have a small project to work on. That was all I could handle.

I tried focusing on my dovetail joints, but I kept thinking about what I'd learned the other night at one of our concerts. Our banjo player, Tater Matthews, told me he'd seen Fiona out with a doctor from the Newland Hospital. They were in a restaurant up in Boone, not hanging out local, he said. I was trying to figure out what he meant by that when he added that his wife, who was also a nurse in Newland, had heard that the doctor had just separated from his wife. That meant neither one of them had waited long to jump in each other's arms. I made myself stop picturing it happening *before* we split. I just couldn't believe that.

Shiloh didn't complain about my mood that day, and he worked in merciful silence for a while. I switched jobs, carving some leaves and birds on the top piece of a hoosier. It felt good to make something pretty. The piece turned out so nice, I thought about keeping it for myself—but what did I need with a baking cupboard?

About three o'clock, Shiloh brought over a thermos of mu tea, some herbal concoction he drank most days, and offered me a cup. Not bad, really, though that seed loaf he shared tasted like sawdust. (And believe me, I knew what *that* tasted like.) But he was trying to cheer me up, and I appreciated that. When he asked about Fiona, I told him about her and that doctor.

Just like that, he was doing his goddam standup routine. The joke was so bad—something about a second opinion—I just tuned him out. I knew he'd meant no harm. That strange brain of his heard a cue like "doctor" and whirred through his bank of jokes to find one that worked. Only it hadn't.

I got through the day, and at quitting time I met Duane Dockery out back of Della's store. We were looking over the old Rollin' Store bus. Della heard us talking and joined us, holding out two cans of beer.

"Do you think she'll work for Abit's band?" she asked, patting the side of the bus. "By the way, Abit, what are you guys calling yourself these days?"

"Rollin' Ramblers."

"Well, this old Rolling Store bus seems fitting for a band with that name. What do you say, Duane?"

"Oh, we can get her on the road again," he answered after taking a long pull on his beer. "But what about the outside paint job? I don't know if either one of us has time for a major overhaul of that." We talked a while, and then Duane's eyebrows shot up. "I've got an idea," he said, smiling.

A couple of days later, the bus had a fresh coat of paint in the spots it needed. Duane had played round with the flowers and vines, making them look like exhaust coming outta the bus he'd added on the side, like it were riding on flower power. Della was clapping her hands, and I was as happy as I'd been in some time.

Then Shiloh stopped by. "What is a Rollin' Rambler? The opposite of a Stationary Rambler?" he asked. It took me a minute to follow his logic. I saw his point. It *was* kinda repetitive, but for a guy whose name meant peace, he sure could stir up trouble. Besides, the band had agreed we wanted to keep the Rollin' part in honor of the bus's history.

That evening I signed Duane on to be our driver and roadie. It didn't pay much, but it got him out. He and I made a sorry duo—pining for our former wife and girlfriend. The only good thing that came from his divorce was he'd lost a lot weight and had been working out. Later on, oncet he was working with the band, he got invitations same as me, women asking us to join them after our gigs, but our hearts just weren't into that.

Not that I didn't *notice* pretty girls. They'd be sashaying to our music, and I wasn't blind to how nice they looked. When I was growing up, everyone from Mama's church—and plenty of others—made a real fuss over the evils of dancing. I could never make out what they were so worried about. Then one night while we were playing, I looked up, and I swear you could see clear as day what was on their minds as those boys and girls swayed close to one another and then back, close again, making eye contact and sharing a knowing smile. For the first time I could see what those church folks were talking about. Not that I thought it was evil, just as natural as the sun coming up.

Since Fiona'd left me, I'd had a lot of time on my hands, so I put them to work writing songs for our band. I'd been listening to Ricky Skaggs, and when he sang "Memories of Mother and Dad" by Bill Monroe, something just blew open inside of me. Something good. Like I had things to say and music I wanted to write.

We had a gig coming up at my old school, The Hicks, in Boone. I went back from time to time to play on Dance Night, which they held every Saturday night except for Christmas, if it fell on a Saturday. It was amazing how the Keefe House, the main building at the school, woke up from its sleepy weekday vibe. Even with school in session, that place had a comforting hush about it, pine tongue-and-groove walls absorbing over sixty years of sounds and handmade rugs quieting every footfall. And all them black-and-white photographs of people lining the hallways. Doris Ulmann had come through these parts in the 1920s and '30s taking pictures of Appalachian crafts makers and musicians, among others. They looked back at you so weary you couldn't help but feel it, too. And yet she'd captured them in a way that had dignity. Those portraits on the walls were a shrine of sorts, a tribute to what our ancestors had created outta nothin'.

But come Saturday night, that building rocked in its big community room where they held the dances. On that particular Saturday, I planned to perform a song I'd just finished. During our practice, all the band folks told me they liked it. Mr. Monroe had awakened the songwriter in me—I wasn't stealin', just inspired in the way artists had always done—and I wrote a nice solo for the mandolin in his honor. Gina Rodgers played it so good during our practice, I could imagine Mr. Monroe nodding his approval.

Tater drove us to Boone in the bus (Duane couldn't start 'til the following week), and we got set up in plenty of time before eight o'clock when the dance got in full swing. The weather had turned especially hot and humid, so the doors were wide open, letting in the night air and, as the evening went on, light from the full moon, which added something electric. I couldn't exactly hear the crickets and katydids sawing away out there, but as I stroked that bass, I felt we were all in harmony, inside and out.

The deal was we'd play country dance music for a while, and when those mostly young folks needed a break from all that flirting and cavorting, we performed a few bluegrass numbers. That was when I planned to premier my song, at the beginning of that set. Then we'd close the evening with about six more dance numbers, ending with "Dargason," an English folk tune so grand to dance to I even felt the urge to sashay a bit.

I always got nervous performing other people's work, but playing my own was somethin' else altogether. When I started to introduce it, my voice croaked. I swallowed hard and carried on. "I wrote this song a few weeks ago when my life took a bad turn," I said. "But these notes brought me some comfort, the way only music can. It's called 'My Thorny Irish Rose,' and I hope you enjoy it."

> *You oncet were my rose*
> *As bright as the stars*
> *Then you left me with nothin'*
> *But a heart filled with scars*

Where oncet you did bloom
Like light from above
There's nothin' but thorns
Where oncet there was love

My thorny Irish rose
How could we be foes?
My thorny Irish rose
Now I've nothin' but woes

When we started playing, even the dancers, who could be unruly, all hepped up with them hormones, stopped to listen to my melancholy tune. I liked the way it sounded and felt something close to happiness when Gina joined me with her mandolin as I played my bass, deep and mournful.

Until.

I looked up and saw Fiona swaying in the fourth row next to some handsome guy with his arm wrapped around her. When I missed a beat or two, Tater gave me a look, and I got back on track. I put my head down and played with all the heart I had left. When I looked up again, Fiona was gone.

We went right into "Ashes of Love" and a couple more heartbreakers: "I Wonder Where You Are Tonight" and that favorite of mine "Little Cabin Home on the Hill." I mean, what else could I have played? I nearly lost it during that last one, but I got through it. By the end of that set, I was beat. We took a break.

Women came up to me, telling me how much they loved my song and my bass playing. But I'd never heard of anyone having a thing for the bass fiddle, except those of us who played it. I knew they were just putting me on.

It felt like forever, but we finally finished our gig. When they passed the hat, our take was better than usual. I think they liked the new song and everyone's playing.

I didn't say much on the trip home. The rest of the band were all whooping it up, happy about the take and the beer Ed bought before we headed home. I was driving, so I didn't drink any. Besides, I didn't feel like it. I preferred looking out at the kind of night the full moon created—strange looking critters and objects flitting past, outlined in silver. And I got a lift from driving the bus. It might have the Rollin' Ramblers painted on its side now, but it would always be the Rollin' Store to me, offering me a chance to get out of my life and do something good.

18

Della

"I can't go back."

We'd just finished a late breakfast, and I overheard Alex on the phone. After he'd filed his stories on the L.A. murders, he'd driven back down to Laurel Falls for a little R&R. When he hung up, he told me he'd just refused to go back to L.A. "That O.J. trial—and the busy lead up to it—would take over my life. I don't want that to happen."

I was stunned. I'd never heard him say no to a big story. I recalled how when we were married, I'd begged him to turn down a story now and then so we could travel more or do something fun in D.C. But back then, he *wanted* stories to take over his life. They *were* his life.

We both had the day off, so we puttered around the apartment all morning, doing our own things. Later, Alex pulled together a lunch of prosciutto, baguette, and green salad. We finished up with coffee and late-season strawberries. As we sat there enjoying the simplicity of the meal, Alex said, "You do know I love you, don't you?"

He'd never said anything like that before, not even when we were married. I wondered what was going on with him. All the time I'd known him, he'd held everything inside, so I'd had to learn to read his actions. I must have missed some cues. When I faltered, not prepared with a ready answer, he looked stricken. "I do *now*," I quickly answered.

"Please don't bring that up again," he said, referring to his wayward years back in D.C. when his ego got the better of him.

"I'm not, and actually, you brought it up. Obliquely. It's just that I have a natural, understandable caution. That's all."

"Do you love *me*?" he asked.

"I've always loved you. Even when I hated you." I started clearing the table, just to have something to do. And time to think. After a painful, prolonged silence, I suggested we go for a walk. "Seems like ages since we spent time outdoors."

As we hiked around and past the falls, nature did its soothing thing and eased our sorrows, at least the ones close to the surface. For two old reporters, it was hard not to talk about his latest story and the Holts' troubles, but we managed to leave them behind. We listened to birdsong and stopped talking altogether when we chanced upon a small field—a sanctuary, really—filled with yellow lady's slippers.

Even so, I couldn't help but wonder what was bearing down on Alex. His mood lifted some while we were walking, and I looked forward to a nice evening together.

Then his work got in the way, after all. A different editor called with a new assignment—this time in D.C., so at least he could sleep at home. That home.

I was feeling blue about his leaving unexpectedly when the phone rang. Horne asked me to join him the next day for another trip down the road to Chester. The thrill of that search was fading, but I said yes. It was better than the alternative.

After Alex left the next morning, a sadness took hold like I hadn't felt in years. Something wasn't right. When I turned back toward the store, Mary Lou and Horne drove up at the same time, so I didn't have time to explore what was bothering me.

"You're not going to believe it, but the leads keep coming in," Horne said as we drove south. "Not only do we have the bus driver to interrogate, but some woman says she gave a lady hitchhiker a ride on Thursday—that first day, when Dibble was driving through. When I asked her what took her so long to contact us, she said she'd only just seen the newspaper story. She sounds older than my mother, so unless she's the Ma Barker type, this could be a solid lead into what went on with Dibble."

We got behind every tractor-trailer on the way to Chester, and I asked Horne if he could pull out the bubble light and put it on top of his car. He wouldn't. Just as well.

We managed to arrive in plenty of time to talk with the bus driver who'd recognized Lilah's picture.

"You were going *to* Laurel Falls? You sure of that?" Horne barked at him. There was no need for his tone, but the driver—Wm. J. Fowzer was embroidered on his uniform—could hold his own. He'd likely earned his stripes dealing with rowdy passengers.

"I believe I still have enough sense to know where I'm headed," Fowzer said as he ran sausage-like fingers through snow white hair before replacing his driver's cap. "I remember because she had one of them suitcases on wheels. Harder to squeeze them into the under-coach storage. The wheels get caught on everything."

Horne showed him his makeshift mug book, and once again, Lilah had a finger pressing on her face. "But she didn't look that good, not with all them scratches on her face."

"Did that make you question taking her on the bus?"

"Sheriff, if we held a beauty contest before letting people on our buses, these coaches would be empty, and I'd be out of a job."

"So you were headed out to where? Raleigh? New York?" Horne asked.

"No, that run was just to Roanoke. I remember letting her off in Laurel Falls because I had to tug at that suitcase to get the wheels out of the handle of another suitcase. Just one of those things that sticks in your mind."

"And you're sure this was the Friday in question?"

"Yes, I know I'm right about that because it was the day before a long weekend I had coming. In my business, you don't forget breaks like that."

When we left the station, Horne surprised me by turning the car around and driving in the direction of the doctor's office. "I have an idea I want to ask Ms. Lopez about," he explained.

He didn't exactly barge into the office, but he sure looked official. "Why didn't you tell us Lilah Holt came back for an appointment on Friday?"

"You didn't ask," Ms. Lopez snapped back at him, "and besides ..."

"Patient privacy," Horne interrupted, removing his hat and wiping sweat from his forehead. "Yeah, I know. Patient privacy."

He stormed out, but I could tell he felt good that his hunch had proved right. For some reason, though, when we got back in the car, he didn't want to talk. "Just read the directions to Flora Pearce's place," was all he said. A man on a mission.

When Ms. Pearce opened the door to her trailer, I agreed with Horne. No way she'd harmed Lilah. She and Aunt Bee could have been sisters.

"Yes, that's the woman I took to her doctor's office," she said, pointing at the photograph. "But she had scratches on her face. I was so worried about her safety."

"Now tell us, did you pick her up on Thursday out near Highway 221?" Horne asked.

"Yes to Thursday, but no to Highway 221. It was along county road—a shortcut I like to take. Say, you haven't told me. How is she?"

"We don't know. She's missing."

"Goddammit. That poor woman." Flora stopped to let out a sizeable belch, patted her stomach, and carried on. "She seemed troubled, not just from the bastard truck driver who scared the hell out of her, but from what she told me, that sumbitch husband of hers, too."

Well, so much for stereotypes. Horne and I shot looks at each other, and he wrapped up the interview. In spite of her surprising demeanor, Pearce seemed like a reliable witness. Lilah *had* been scratched up and Dibble *didn't* let her out where he'd said. And according to Fowzer, she'd been heading *home* on the bus on *Friday*—not Thursday—confirming Ralphine's statement.

As we drove back, Horne was swearing as bad as old lady Pearce. I'd barely heard him say as much as damn before, but the case was getting to him. "Goddammit, that just burns my biscuit. I hate it when these idiots don't tell the truth and waste my time and my gasoline—all of which is really the people's. They pay the taxes outta their hard-earned money so these bastards can fuck around with me."

I let him vent. He deserved it. When we got to his office, he ran inside to call Potash 3K. Bud Maguire told him Dibble was on the road but promised to have Dibble call him back, probably in about an hour.

It was only two o'clock, so I agreed to wait. We sat around for a while, awkwardly trying to chitchat the way friends do. (We were both working at our new arrangement.) Horne made a fresh pot of coffee, and bad as it was, I gratefully accepted a cup to have something to fiddle with. Finally, the phone rang.

Horne put it on speaker so I could listen. After he revealed what Fowzer and Pearce had told him, Dibble confessed. "Okay, okay, I didn't tell you about all that. I knew it wouldn't sound right." He paused, getting ready for what he was about to say. "I was running late, and I took a shortcut. When I turned onto a county road, she just freaked out. Screamed at me that I wasn't going to get a chance to rape her. No siree. That's how she musta gotten them scratches, because she was never hurt while she was in my truck." I could almost see Dibble's Adam's apple bob as he took a big gulp.

After few moments passed, Horne had to ask, "Okay, what happened next?"

"She jumped out while I was driving slow. I called out to her, but she ran in the opposite direction, and I didn't have anywheres to turn that big truck around."

That was pretty much it for the interview. After that, every question Horne threw at him got a simple *no sir* answer. Horne told Dibble not to leave the state and slammed the phone back in its cradle.

Horne had to take me back to Laurel Falls, and on the way, I felt so sleepy, I asked him to pull over at the next café; I needed coffee.

"Didn't like mine, eh?" he said, but he was smiling. No response necessary. "You know," he went on, turning the car around, "I think we're close to this place I overhead some guys talking about. A little espresso bar out in the woods."

I looked at him like he was crazy; in these parts, that sounded more like a wild dream that reality. But sure enough, when he turned down a narrow dirt road, a small shack sported a sign for Bottoms Up Coffee. He pulled next to the window to order, and a young woman, who couldn't have been more than nineteen, kind of blanched when she saw his uniform and cruiser. She quickly recovered and leaned out the little window, flashing a smile and more décolletage than her black bikini top was designed to handle. After she took our order, she asked if we wanted anything extra, and I looked around for a menu of some kind. We'd skipped lunch, and I was starving. I couldn't find one and said no thanks. When she turned to make our coffees, I noticed her red bikini pants (revealing more flesh than I cared to see) matched the "bottoms up" logo on the side of the building.

As she made the espressos, I could see Horne taking in the surroundings—small trailers circling the shack, men hanging around, out in the middle of nowhere. It didn't take a genius to figure out what extras she was selling.

"Well, shit. Some other goddam thing I'll need to investigate," he hissed.

When she brought our coffees and leaned out the window again, Horne couldn't pay fast enough. He was about to pull away when I asked him to stop. The woman's eyes got big as I held out a twenty dollar bill. "Here's something extra for *you,*" I said. When she grabbed the bill, I added, "Maybe you could put it toward some clothes."

We rode along silently for several miles after that, just sipping our coffee (which was remarkably good for backwoods espresso). Finally I said, "I guess Ma Barker picked her up after she'd 'escaped.'" I used air quotes because Horne wasn't good at picking up on sarcasm.

"Yeah, seems that way. By the time they got to town, I guess she'd missed her doctor's appointment and scheduled one for the next day. But where in the hell did she spend the night?"

I thought about that for a few moments. "Does it matter? I mean we know she was safe the next day when she went to her doctor and rode the bus home. What matters is she came back to Laurel Falls on Friday. Thanks to that much-discussed suitcase and its wheels, I suppose she walked home from our bus stop."

"Maybe that Dibble guy's shortcut scared her enough to return home—if she wasn't planning to anyway. But she didn't take any clothes and ..." He scratched his head as his words trailed off. His theory wasn't making much sense.

"Hard to say what someone that unstable was thinking."

Horne nodded. "I knew that husband was hiding something. I'm telling you, husbands lie and cheat better than some hardened criminals I've met."

I knew that firsthand, but I didn't want to comment. That had been in my past, right?

19

Della

Horne planned to go straight to the Holts', but I told him I wanted to stop by home first. I needed to let Jake out and get my own vehicle. Enough togetherness for one day. He agreed, but made me promise I'd head out to the cabin; he was worried I'd skip out on him. I had thought about it—but I knew he wanted me along because of the kids. You know, a woman's touch. He dropped me off at the store and sped toward Hanging Dog.

Mary Lou joined me while I watched Jake trot around the meadow behind the store. "I had two women asking for mu tea and one who wanted quinoa," she said, pronouncing it qwin-oo-ah, but then who wouldn't? "Oh, and something called adzuki beans."

"Just ignore them." I knew that was Shiloh's doing—the new orders he'd teased me about. "If anyone asks again, tell them we can't get them. Blame it on the distributors who aren't willing to deliver this far out." Mary Lou smiled, looking relieved.

Jake and I piled into the Jeep and headed back to Hanging Dog. When we parked at the cabin, I had no trouble finding the sheriff; I could hear him arguing with Enoch on the back deck. I looked for the kids, but they were nowhere around, likely stuck in their rooms again.

"We *know* she came back home before she disappeared," Horne shouted. "The poor woman went through hell and high water to get to a doctor's appointment, trying to get well for you and the kids." He looked at Enoch with disgust. "Or at least the kids."

Enoch's face contorted as he struggled to find the right words. "Okay," he finally said, "she *did* come back. When she got to the house and saw Maddie was here, she got furious. She ranted on and on about that and said she was leaving us. That's the God's honest truth. She was shouting so loud, I was afraid the kids would hear her."

"Yeah, and pigs fly," Horne spat. "Come on, buddy, that just doesn't make sense. She makes a long trek home, then suddenly decides to leave you and the kids, taking nothing but that tiny suitcase? And heading where? Back to the goddam bus stop? On foot? At night? Are you kidding me?"

"No, it wasn't like that. She came back and went wild. I knew she hated Maddie, and I knew I'd been wrong to take up with her, but Lilah was so hard to live with. I got mad and told her to go away and leave us alone. I was sick of the upheavals, and the kids were all torn up by her tirades. I said she was welcome to come back if she ever got it together."

"I'm not buying it, son. Something's happened to that woman, and you're the last to see her alive." Horne left that hanging in the air. Enoch looked over at me for help, but I didn't have any to give. I didn't know what had happened; this would have to play out Horne's way. "I need you to come down to the station with me. I want to go over this again, and this time get at the truth." Horne started dragging Enoch toward his car.

I stood in front of the steps leading off the deck. "Wait a minute, Horne. We need to figure out what to do about Astrid and Dee."

Horne restrained himself while Enoch and I talked. I noticed two scared kids creeping outside to watch, so I tried for a cheery voice when I told Enoch they could stay with me. There was no one else to call on, and Jake would help take their minds off the nightmare unfolding in their lives.

When Horne began pushing Enoch into the backseat behind the metal grid, Dee started crying. I picked him up while Astrid ran to the car window to tell her father that the "authorities" were wrong, she just knew it.

Jake did make the ride home easier. I could hear both kids in the back, patting him and talking gently to him. When we got to the store, we all scrambled up the steps. As soon as I opened the door, their moods lifted, as if it were all a big adventure. The home above a store!

I pulled together a simple dinner of soup and cheese, whole wheat bread and apple—not all that different from the first meal Astrid and I shared. Then I made the bed in the guest room and asked if they wanted to stay together, or did one want to sleep on the couch in the living room? "Together," they said in unison.

The next day, I was on duty at the store. I couldn't afford to take more time off, so I took the kids with me. Astrid acted like a twenty-something sales person and talked with all the customers. It was fun for her to play store, like I used to do at her age. *Give her a couple more days of it*, I thought. But I had to admit—I enjoyed her company and the customers seemed to get a kick out of her, too.

Dee colored in the back with crayons and books Cleva brought with her. She helped keep an eye on him, drinking coffee and eating anything she wanted from the store (and taking more home with her). It was a good deal for both of us.

That evening, I was glad for the chance to get to know Dee better. He wasn't as impish as Astrid, but he seemed like a happy little boy, playing with some toys Cleva left for him. And, of course, Astrid helped me with dinner.

I couldn't imagine what would happen to those kids if Enoch were sent to jail for any length of time. More than likely, they'd get caught up in the family services bureaucracy. Horne seemed hell bent on making a case against him, and I had to admit it wasn't looking good. He was convinced that after Lilah told Enoch she was leaving for good, Enoch harmed her somehow, pushing her and that suitcase Otis Cale's dog discovered down the cliff and into the water.

While the kids stayed with me, I could tell they enjoyed the relative quiet at my home. They played together with an innocence that was both sweet and heartbreaking. They were too young—even twenty-something Astrid—to know how serious things were for their father.

The next evening, just after dinner—I'd made spaghetti and meatballs, which seemed a hit given the red smears on both the kids' faces—I was washing dishes when I saw Lonnie's cruiser pull up and park in front of the store. Enoch got out and said something to him before shutting the car door.

"Your daddy's here," I said. Both kids jumped up and opened the door just as Enoch got to the top of the stairs. He hugged them and murmured something only they could hear. He nodded at me and looked at the mess in the kitchen.

"Smells good. I don't suppose there're any leftovers."

I smiled. "You're luck has finally changed."

After Enoch finished dinner, I drove them home. Astrid and Dee were sound asleep in the back, so Enoch talked freely. Something about riding in the dark, the warm interior lit only by greenish dashboard light, must have felt safe as a confessional. "I begged for a lie detector test, but the sheriff just scoffed; said it wouldn't stand up in court. After a while, though, I think even he knew he didn't have anything to hold me on. He left Deputy Parker to watch over me while he drove to Spruce Pine to interview Maddie again. Thank God she described it just like I had, with Lilah storming off on her own."

I waited a beat and asked why he or Maddie hadn't told Horne about this earlier.

"We'd talked about it, and in twenty-twenty hindsight, we should have. But at the time, we believed the confession of an adulterous relationship would just make matters worse. It didn't happen all that often. I knew it was wrong, but sometimes I got so lonely. Haven't you ever felt that way?"

I nodded. I'd felt lonely much of my life. "Okay, but what was she doing at your house that night?"

"Great timing, huh? Maddie'd called and asked if she could come over. I thought Lilah was gone on one of her jaunts, so I said yes. She said she'd make us dinner, which sounded great; I don't need to tell you I'm not much of a cook, and Astrid said she was 'unavailable.' While we were alone in the kitchen, Maddie started harping on me to push out Lilah so *she* could move in. I guess a lot of people get to feeling awful lonely out here in the mountains. But I couldn't ask the kids to just forget their mother—crazy as she was—and throw Maddie a housewarming party. We were arguing, and I told her it was over. I was sick and tired of women telling me what to do.

"Then the door flew open, and Lilah went haywire. She ranted a while, took off her barn coat, changed into something warmer, and ran out. I swear I don't know where. After she left, I told Maddie she could spend the night—on the sofa. I'm damned glad I did, too. I wouldn't have an alibi without her." He paused before adding, "I feel guilty as hell, but I don't miss Lilah. The kids aren't as edgy, either. We could never figure out how *not* to piss her off. We're better off without her."

20

Abit

I'd moved on, best I could, after Fiona told me to get lost. Not that she'd had the decency to tell me to my face. No, she'd used my answering machine, just saying that same thing about not having kids would be like cutting off a limb. I kept hoping she'd call back so we could talk things through. After more than a month went by, I gave up.

Things like that change you, as surely as a scar on your face makes you look different. But a scar on the inside does even more damage. It runs deeper, out of sight. You're never the same person after somethin' like that. How could you be? Those old-timers I sat with outside Della's store—I used to wonder how they got so broken. No more.

Just when the hurt was easing some, damned if that man I saw Fiona swaying with at a concert didn't show up at the shop. *Dr.* Gerald Navarro, he said as he shook my hand (his hand so cold and limp it reminded me I needed to cook that trout Tater Matthews brought over). The Doctor was taller than me and so out of my league, I felt like a real hick, what with sawdust in my hair and them baggy overalls. At least he'd taken off his white coat, but his shoes were shiny, his shirt pressed and unwrinkled late in the day, and his suit perfectly tailored. Even his beard looked clean shaven, not creeping up on five o'clock shadow like mine.

He walked all round my shop, running his hands over works in progress, like I needed his damn fingerprints messing up the finish. Finally he said, "Fiona speaks so highly of your woodworking skills," beaming like a preacher blessing his flock. "I want to order a dining room table for her new apartment."

New apartment? That meant I didn't know where she was living anymore; I couldn't even picture her sitting on her couch or easy chair, looking out at that big oak tree shading her front window. And *Dr.* Gerald Navarro seemed to have no idea I'd been her true love, oncet upon a time. I didn't tell him she was still mine.

He asked a bunch of stupid questions before ordering a curly maple table, four-foot by three-foot rectangle with curved legs. I had trouble writing up the order form, my hands were shaking so bad. And I did somethin' I'd later feel ashamed of: I charged him extra. Maybe that went against my notion of "be kind," but it helped take some of the sting out of the order, at least at that moment. Not a lot, but enough to ease my pain. Like Della'd said, I needed to be kind to me, too.

I was glad The Doctor was already heading to his car when Shiloh came back from meditating, though he seemed to know exactly what had just happened. We both looked out the window as he drove off in a Porsche. "Figures" Shiloh said as he squeezed my shoulder. "Sorry I ever told that joke."

I wished he'd left it at that, but he went real quiet-like. "What?" I asked.

"What do you mean 'what?'?"

"You're pondering somethin'. I can tell."

"We're getting like an old married couple," Shiloh said, pulling on his mustache. "I was just thinking about the Second Noble Truth: According to Buddha, the basic cause of suffering is 'the attachment to the desire to have and the desire not to have.' That's why you're suffering. You want what you can't have."

I was so heartsick, I just ignored him. I didn't have the stamina for two jerks in one hour.

After that, I went over to Della's, saying I needed to buy some milk, but we both knew I was after somethin' besides groceries. I told her about my afternoon.

"Did you tell Shiloh to go fuck himself?" I could tell Della was mad; her face had turned bright red. She got that way when folks dumped their judgments on me—or really anyone she liked. "First the so-called Christians did a number on you while you were growing up, and now the laughing Buddha is having a go. What's next? You don't know any communists do you?"

126

I chuckled a little and answered both questions. "I didn't say anything like that to Shiloh, and I don't know any commies."

"Opportunity lost," Della said as she priced some funny looking spaghetti.

"Yeah, but I have to work with him. I need his help."

"Well, there's that," she said, though I could tell she hated to admit it. "I have a lot of respect for Buddhists— real ones," she went on, "but Shiloh has grasped just enough to be dangerous. I hate it when any convert, be it Christian, Buddhist, or whatever, uses tenets like weapons against someone trying his best. That's not how they're meant to be lived."

"Well, when he started up again, I did tell him to take a long walk offa short pier."

She smiled. "Of course you'd find better words."

By then it was closing time, so she invited me up for an easy supper, as she called it. She'd poached some salmon that she put atop lettuce with an amazing creamy dressing. Said it had avocado in it, but I couldn't figure where she'd got ahold of one of them round here. We focused on eating for a while, but after a spell, she asked, "What kind of table are you making that damn doctor?"

"I'm not making it for *him*, Della. I'm making it for *Fiona*."

I didn't know which of us was more surprised when, all of a sudden, Della started to cry. I couldn't recall when I'd seen her broken up like that. She excused herself and went into the bathroom. I could hear her blowing her nose and all, and when she came back she said two things: "Abit, I'm proud to know you," and "All I've got for dessert is chocolate ice cream."

As if that were a problem.

I put everything I had into that table. I chose my best curly maple boards and sanded the table as smooth as Fiona would've. I worked so hard, I started dripping sweat into the wood. After a time, I realized they were tears. I tried sanding them out, but they were as stubborn as my heartache. Under the table, I carved the initials RB + FO for Rabbit Bradshaw + Fiona O'Donnell. They were tucked up near one of the leg joints. You'd have to look hard to see them.

I got a good photo of the table before some men The Doctor hired loaded it into their truck. I was glad I didn't have to see him again. Any satisfaction I'd gotten from charging him extra was spent.

Late that day, I was finally finishing up Della's table when a shadow fell across my workbench. I turned and saw Daddy standing in the doorway, looking kinda ghostly with the low sunlight shining behind him. It startled me so bad, I was glad I wasn't working on the table saw, or I'd've been short two or three fingers. He'd never just stopped by in the two year I'd made my woodshop there. That didn't surprise me, given how I was raised, but I wondered why he was coming round. I already felt down, what with my last connection to Fiona gone with that table, so I didn't want him heaping his shit on me.

"Daddy, what brings you over?"

He kinda hemmed and hawed for a little before saying, "I just wanted to say that I really liked that girl, Fiona." I braced myself for some lecture on how I'd fucked up. "And I'm sorry she disappointed all of us. You especially."

I couldn't remember when Daddy had shown me any sympathy, and I was grateful for it. You'd've thought that might've made my heart hurt even more, but it eased it.

"Thanks, Daddy. Won't you come on in?"

"No, no, you're busy."

"But I could show you what I'm working on."

"Oh, I see plenty from the window—when you load it onto that Sherlock's truck." I'd always known there weren't much that got past the big plate glass window at the front of the house, and maybe somehow he knew that table was for Fiona.

"You could still come on in," I said as I put down my chisel. When I looked up, he was gone.

21

Della

"Honey, we ain't seen each other in too long. How 'bout I cook for us tonight? You could bring some wine and spend the night. What do you say?"

Cleva. Best friend anyone could have. She had an uncanny way of calling at just the right time. "I say a great big, grateful yes. Can I bring anything else?"

"Just that old hound."

The Holt case had gone cold, and I'd gone back to being a shopkeeper. During August, the store had been busier than ever—people gathering to speculate about our crime wave. But once school started after Labor Day, everything returned to business as usual, and my sense of plodding through life reared its head again.

I didn't close early, much as I wanted to, but I locked the front door at six on the nose. Jake didn't require any convincing, hopping into the Jeep before I was ready to leave. We drove to Cleva's, about five miles from town. Her home perched atop a ridge, not far from the falls; the rush and rumble of its waters made me relax almost as much as the friendship.

I was looking forward to watching the sunset from Cleva's ridge, but when we arrived, the sky seemed reluctant to give up on the day. Barely a hint of color registered along its sun-kissed horizon. When I got out of the Jeep, Jake scooted past me to stare down a squirrel. I didn't worry about him; he'd prowl around for a while before he'd head back for his dinner, which I'd remembered to bring along.

After we got ourselves settled, I poured two glasses of Grüner Veltliner and we carried them to Cleva's porch, where we watched the sun offer up a few rosy rays before finally slipping away, eliciting some oohs and aahs from both of us.

"Praising the heavens is about the only thing I feel good about these days," I said. "I've seen too many sad stories. Not just living here, but in D.C. where I wrote all those articles. I know I told you about earning the nickname Ghoulfriend—because I seemed to attract the most violent assignments. And I can't even imagine the misery you've seen as a teacher and later a principal."

"Honey, I don't want to go there," Cleva said. "I will say this might be the best wine I've ever had." We clinked glasses and sat quietly.

Jake came over, looking at me with those big brown eyes. "Dinner?" I asked in a sing-song voice, and he twirled twice. When I put his dinner down, Cleva asked if I were ready for ours. "Let's sit a while longer," I said as I settled back in my chair.

No words passed between us until I broke the silence. "Funny how they lived here fifteen years, but no one knew Lilah Holt enough to miss her. Though at the store I've heard murmurs about 'those poor kids,' which is always followed by 'and that good for nothin' father.' But you know, over the weeks since I first met Enoch, I've come to appreciate him. Our rocky start has leveled off into respect for one another. He's even stopped by the store, asking his own cooking questions."

"Yep, that's a strange case. Do you still think they feel relieved that Lilah is gone? The thought of that breaks me up."

"I do. Of course, I haven't seen Astrid in a while, but Enoch seems happier as a single dad. And Astrid was more relaxed the last time I did see her. Bipolar is such a wicked condition." I told Cleva about my friend walking up the middle of Connecticut Avenue, and she shook her head.

"Well, on that happy note, let's join Jake and have some dinner." She said it in the same sing-song I'd used with Jake. We stood and hugged each other, trying to ward off the sadness that seemed to have enveloped us.

I'd hoped Cleva would make one of her signature dishes, and I lucked out. Chicken and dumplings with an array of fresh vegetables from her garden—tomatoes, zucchini, and green beans—on the side. At seventy-nine, Cleva hadn't slowed down much, at least not when it came to her garden. We finished off the bottle of wine with chocolate cream pie compliments of Lonnie Parker's mother.

"Good thing you're spending the night, honey, if you feel even half as stuffed or drunk as me," she said, dragging a chair back to the porch. I joined her. The evening was still warm and the sky clear enough for some mesmerizing stargazing. After a while, she asked, "Why do you reckon that little girl turned her back on you?"

"I really don't know. Maybe misplaced blame or crushing memories. She sure is a charmer, though I guess her mother didn't feel that way." I was going to stop there, but all the wine and good company urged me on. "I like having people to care about. I want to feel as though I'm helping out in this mean old world. But I'm at a loss now. Astrid's gone. Abit's grown up. I'm feeling restless, or rather, lifeless. I don't even know what I want anymore. I've written more than a thousand stories as a reporter, but I can't seem to get my own story straight."

"You've done a lot right, if you could see it from my viewpoint. But I know that's not how it works. But I …" She stopped short.

"What?"

"Oh, I just ain't seen Alex around lately, and you didn't mention him just now. I didn't want to bring it up, but it seems like the right time."

"He's playing hard to get. I've been leaving messages for him, and he's returned my calls—except he waits until he knows I'm at the store and leaves messages at my home number. At least, that's how I see it."

Oh, I saw it all right. I knew his ways. How he'd shut me out rather than talk about what was bothering him. Or hide from me because something about me, maybe the part that attracted him in the first place, made him face things he could ignore by himself or in the company of others. We made one another stretch, challenging each other to confront our darker sides. I liked the way he calmed me down, showed me a gentler way to react to issues. Maybe I was lucky—the things he taught me were mostly pleasurable. The things I reflected back on him stirred up the kind of issues he wanted to avoid.

"I'm sure there's a good reason," Cleva said, breaking through my thoughts. "He loves you. I see it in his eyes. And I know he likes visiting down here. It does him a world of good."

"I hope you're right, Cleva," was all I could think to say. I couldn't help but compare this time to those awful days before we separated. I didn't want to think about that—but spending so many nights with an old dog that snored made it too easy to imagine the worst.

22

Della

The next day, I invited Abit and Millie over for lunch. Abit brought the coffee table I'd ordered for the living room, and, of course, it was gorgeous. "Shiloh taught me some joinery tricks, so this all come from my hand," he said as he set it down.

I could see how much he'd put into the table. "It's beautiful, honey. I couldn't be more pleased." He nodded, grateful for the praise but without much enthusiasm.

After lunch—nothing fancy, just ham sandwiches, leftover roasted potatoes, and his favorite apple cake for dessert—I perked some coffee. While it bubbled and popped, I reflected on our life together in Laurel Falls. "You know, Abit, we are one sorry lot, you and me. Filled with sorrows and consoled only by a couple of dogs. And we've lost our detecting skills. We can't even find a missing woman."

"Yeah, which makes me wonder if we've got a killer on the loose. Someone who pushed her down that cliff. Remember how Mama and her friends used to try to scare you outta walking in the woods? They'd carry on that there were men lurking out there, ready to pounce on you? Well, maybe they were right."

"I have to admit I've had thoughts like that, too. I find myself imagining what happened to Lilah Holt—and who among us might have done her harm. It's like one of those old-time mountain murder ballads I've heard you perform. I believe you could write a song about this. It has all the sad ingredients required for a heartbreaker."

"You're probably right," he said, "though I doubt I could make one original note."

I hated that we were both feeling so lost, but it was hard to ignore. Alex was MIA, Fiona was MIA. Lilah was MIA. And possibly a killer was in our midst.

When I sighed, Abit said, "Well, being a loser may be new to you, but I'm used to it."

"We were both doing good there, for a while. I'm sure glad I still have you and Jake."

"And Millie," he added, pulling some brambles from her wiry fur. She acted like she wanted to bite him, but neither one of them even considered that a possibility.

"Wouldn't you know it?" I said. "Mary Lou has been a godsend. She spruces things up when I'm away and adds touches I hadn't thought of—at least not in years. But now that I've found someone I can count on in the store, I don't have anyone to play with much. Cleva and I are going to Asheville next week—before the leaf-peepers descend on us. Want to come along? "

"Thanks, but I've got a lot of orders to get out. And Mama wants me to show Little Andy the ropes. She thinks I ought to hire him to help me instead of Shiloh, for god's sake. Surely she knows he ain't old enough—or good enough at woodworking."

"I thought I saw him hanging around last Saturday."

"Yeah, I've hired him to sweep and clean up the shop on the weekends when he comes down to visit. But I don't think I could handle much more. She's practically adopted him. Do you know Daddy and her took him to county court to officially change his name from Andy to Andrew? I always thought Andy was a nickname, but that's the name his parents put on his birth certificate. His mama called mine from Italy or somewheres they were visiting, and they got all the details worked out so he could make that change. My folks never oncet drove up to see me at the Hicks in all the five year I was there, but they go regular-like now. That kinda rankles me when I ..."

He stopped suddenly. I looked over at him, and we started to laugh, even if there wasn't much mirth in it. We'd heard ourselves carrying on when deep down we both knew how much we had to be grateful for. Abit's business was booming. My store was in the best shape since I'd bought it. And Abit was thriving with the Rollin' Ramblers. I went to a concert not long ago and marveled at his playing—and how the girls fawned over him. He didn't seem to notice, but someday his heart would heal, and he'd pay attention. He had plenty of time for that.

1996

23

Abit

"Are you ready to head out tomorrow?" Della called out, her hand shielding her eyes against the bright springtime sun.

Shiloh and I were struggling to get a sideboard onto his truck. "Yep, that's why we're loading this now. Shiloh can deliver it tomorrow and hold down the fort while I'm gone."

We were taking another road trip to D.C. I hadn't been up that way since my trek through Virginia, and I was looking forward to our time together in the car—plus all the stops along the way.

Della had gotten it in her head that I *had* to go to the Smithsonian Craft Show. I trusted her judgment, though I had no idea what to expect. I'd seen plenty of crafts while at The Hicks, especially during its Fall Festival, which attracted a fine mix of artists. And I always went to the big show in Asheville that the Southern Highland Guild put on. Even so, Della claimed the Smithsonian show was the *best*.

It'd been not quite two year since Fiona left, and I'd put all my time into my woodworking. I'd moved my home to what had oncet been the hayloft above my shop, which made it easy (sometimes too easy) to work. I'd decided to give up my cabin on the lake since it was so big and lonely on my own. Besides, no need to get away from it all. I already was.

Back when I was making the loft livable, I couldn't get that little Astrid outta my mind. I could just hear her, sitting in that passenger seat of our bus, accusing me of moving right back home. In a way, I reckoned I had, but I kept my distance from Mama and Daddy—not in a mean way, just the way grown people naturally did.

Astrid and her brother seemed to be doing pretty good. I only saw them now and then in town, but from what any of us could tell, they'd adjusted to having just a daddy. And no one else had come to any harm in a strange way, so we were all breathing easier that we didn't have a maniac roaming our hills.

As things turned out, all that extra time I had on my hands was good for my business. I was selling all I could manage to make. Good to be that busy, so I didn't have time to think about what was missing. Until nighttime, anyways.

Working on the same things over and over spurred me on to try my hand at something different. Della and I spent time brainstorming, and she helped me get beyond the usual. Like all those dining tables I'd made—I wasn't so keen on them anymore, especially after Dr. Navarro ordered that one for Fiona. I'd branched out into coffee tables and side tables and other pieces.

I'd also increased my use of inlays; I'd found someone to make small marquetry panels that told stories about our mountains and trees. And I'd been spending more time with Jack Harper to learn how to carve better. He was the one who carved crèche figures so real looking you halfway expected to see a halo glowing above the baby Jesus's head. We got a fair price for anything that included his carving, and later mine. All the rich people coming round seemed able to afford—and appreciate—them.

Though that didn't sit quite right with me, selling just to rich people. I felt bad that no one who grew up round there could afford to buy my work. From time to time, I'd hold a sale for locals only—or sell them the ones that had a little something wrong in the wood. Still, that whole situation bothered me, but I knew I needed to make a decent wage, too.

The next morning, Della and I, along with Jake and Millie, headed up the highway toward D.C. As we drove north, I told her I wanted to stop at the exact same places we did almost seven year ago.

"Don't you want to try something new?"

"Nah. I've got too much new in my life. I'd like to revisit pleasant memories."

We rode along quiet-like; even the dogs went to sleep after the first few mile. Both Della and I were likely thinking about the main reason we were traveling—and it wasn't the craft show. Alex had been through a hard year with some kinda cancer. That was why he hadn't been calling her back; he was avoiding her. Crazy, if you asked me, at a time when he especially needed loving. But I knew plenty of men like that—Daddy and Wilkie and Duane, just to name a few. They'd rather suffer in silence than come out with how they were feeling. I didn't know all the details, but I got the impression Alex was gonna be okay. Something about better than a fifty-fifty chance. As strong as he was, I just knew he'd beat the odds.

Della had spent a lot of time over the past year up in D.C. She'd nearabouts turned the store over to Mary Lou, who oncet she got settled in was the perfect shopkeeper for our town. Business at Coburn's was up, and it was hard for Della not to think her absence had something to do with that. Not that folks didn't like Della, they just liked Mary Lou more. As they saw it, she was their kinda people.

While I knew Della was going up to D.C. to be with Alex, I also knew she was itching to get back to the kinda work she used to do. She told me she was helping Alex with his research and interviews, something she'd been really good at.

Oncet we were well into Virginia, we stopped at the truck stop we'd eaten at before, just off the highway on the way to Lexington. We even got the same waitress as last time. Don't ask me why I remembered her so clear, but I guessed that trip was burned into my brain. I couldn't remember what I'd ordered back then—maybe country-fried steak—but this time I went with the meatloaf and three vegs: mashed potatoes, green beans, coleslaw. Della got a salad. Big mistake. The lettuce was all brown round the edges. She looked over at me and started pecking at my plate. I laughed and pushed it toward the middle of the table.

Since we'd shared our dinner, we figured we deserved pie. That time she chose right: chocolate cream pie. I got rhubarb, and we pushed those plates toward the middle, too.

After we tanked up on coffee and gave Millie and Jake a break, we were off again. I thought all that coffee would wire me, but I was dozing pretty good when I heard Della ask, "Have you gone out with any of those women throwing themselves at you at your concerts?"

I kept my eyes closed and shook my head. "They just seem silly to me, kinda giggly. There was a time I'd've loved that, but that was when I was sixteen year old." She chuckled at that. I sat up and added, "But that's okay. I'm content in my woodshop. And, you know, now that my heart has healed some, I know I made the right decision. No regrets. If having kids was a requirement for being with Fiona, well, we are best apart. I feel real strong about that, Della. I'm not gonna bring any Abit Junior into this crazy world if he might have my traits. Couldn't bear it.

I'll always think of Fiona as the one who got away—and dammit, she seems to have spoiled me for other women— but that's the way it has to be."

She looked over at me, real sad-like. Time to change the subject. Besides, I wanted to know more about Alex. I figured since she'd just put me in the hot seat, I could return the favor. "How's Alex doing?"

"Oh, don't worry, honey. It's been quite some time since his treatments, and his energy is coming back. He looks even better than the last time he was down in Laurel Falls. It's just one of those things you never know about. The past year has reminded me about living one day at a time. I always believed that—just didn't live it very often. But now, every day feels like a gift. And having you along with me on this trip feels that way, too. It gets monotonous—and lonesome—on this highway."

I offered to drive some, but she shook her head. "Just tell me some stories. Or about your woodworking. No, I know—tell me some of Shiloh's jokes."

I begged offa that. I'd given up on telling jokes. Instead, we rode along talking like old friends. And before we knew it, we'd sailed past the exit for the Skyline Diner where last time we'd stuffed ourselves with biscuits and coffee. I was still full from our big dinner, and we were both eager to see Alex.

We pulled into Georgetown and parked in front of his house. Alex didn't greet me this time with a welcome banner, like he did on my first trip, but he didn't need to. I *knew* I was welcome. I gave him a big hug and headed inside with Millie and Jake. Millie'd never been there, but she knew just what to do—follow Jake. They drank a bunch of water, ate from the bowl of kibble Alex had put down, then raced round the house sniffing everything.

And Della was right—Alex looked good. His wavy hair was as full as ever, though like Della's, it had more streaks of gray than the last time I saw him. He had on a plaid sports shirt with the sleeves rolled up, and his face and arms were kinda tanned looking.

The weather was unusually warm and humid (a fluke for that time of year), so Alex'd made us a big salad with all kinds of vegetables, cheeses, and chopped chicken on top. My stomach forgot all about that dinner back at the truck stop as I plowed through salad plus some bread I thought I recognized from Firehook Bakery, the one Nigel, our forger pal, lived above. And cherry pie, more than likely from the same place.

While Alex went through all his coffee-making chores (he could make that espresso machine smoke, but it seemed to take forever), he told us about one of the stories he was working on. "I'm worried about what it portends. It's called Fox News Channel—a new television news network that doesn't concern itself with facts. It's so biased toward the extreme right, it skews important issues.

The channel won't debut until next month, but I've seen some of their media previews, and I've interviewed a couple of the anchors so the story can run just before the network launches. I'm struggling to maintain an even-handed journalistic approach. I want to rail and rant and use snarky words—but then, I'd just be succumbing to their tactics."

"Oh, surely that won't last. Not in the long run," Della said. "Democracy is tenuous enough with a *strong* Fourth Estate. I can't even think about something like that taking hold." When Alex finished serving our coffee, she picked up her cup and said, "Here's a toast to the abiding intelligence of people!" She looked at me and winked, and it felt good she was including me.

We took our coffee into the living room where the dogs had settled. We had to sit in chairs because they were hogging the couch and wouldn't budge. Out of the blue, Alex told me he wanted to order a hoosier. Della and I both gave him a funny look. All I could figure was maybe he just liked the looks of them.

"I've taken up baking," he said. Della motioned toward the kitchen in a sign language they musta perfected over the years, and he nodded. "Yeah, I baked that bread. And made the pie. I took a course at Firehook, two nights a week for six weeks, and I want to keep at it. It feels good to do something with my hands besides type. I'd like one with the marquetry inlay, like I saw last time I was down."

"Well, you're in luck. They never picked that up," I told him. "They're getting divorced and plan to sell their second home. They put down a deposit—which they'll lose. I'll let you have it for the balance."

"I'm not one to turn down a good deal, but I want to pay fair market price."

I told him we could haggle about that later. "I think you'll like the inlay—a wooded scene with the falls in the background. And the light maple wood in the hoosier makes it pop."

"I'll drive the truck next time I come down," he said. A few year ago, he'd bought himself a truck for trips to Laurel Falls (and gave me his old Merc), though I could tell he was partial to the new Merc he'd bought a few months ago.

"When's that?" Della and I asked almost in unison.

"Soon. Really soon. I miss being down there, and I don't want to waste any time."

24

Della

I seemed I'd always worry about Alex, for one reason or another. I was still dealing with the feelings I had after learning what was going on with him.

When he kept avoiding me, I drove up to see him, unannounced. On the long drive, I'd imagined a big showdown, like we'd had years ago. But I almost didn't recognize the gaunt man who opened the front door for me. When I asked him why he'd shut me out, he told me he had prostate cancer and he was embarrassed he couldn't "you know."

"You think *that* would matter to me, compared to *you?*" I said, tears smearing the makeup I'd put on trying to look nice for him. I went to the room I used as my office up there and closed the door. I sat quietly, trying to pull myself together.

After a while, I came out and knocked on his closed office door. When Alex opened it, I started to speak, but only a sob came out. Then more wet, messy sobs. He held me while I got that out of my system. I mopped my face and finally found some words. "I was afraid you were up to your old ways, but the truth is even more devastating."

"Unfortunately I'm not up to anything with anyone, at least for the time being." I could feel my face turn into a scowl. "I'm sorry," he added quickly. "I was speaking generally; I didn't mean to include anyone but you, Della." He kissed me, and we gave up on words and sat together for a long time.

Since then, I'd been working on living each day fully. When I stuck with that philosophy, I found a lot more to be happy about. Like having Abit and Millie with us. On that first day of our visit, we all just hung out together at the house. Alex and I worked some, and Abit took Millie on walks, like he did with Jake when he visited before. Jake wasn't up to such long treks anymore; he mostly stayed close to Alex.

In addition to the story about that dreadful-sounding news channel, Alex was busy with several breaking stories, including Ted Kaczynski, the Unabomber, and the '96 elections. I helped make calls and type up notes. But mostly I just wanted to hang out with Alex.

The next day, Abit and I got up early and headed to the craft show. Alex packed us a lunch, warning that food service during big shows was not only a rip-off but lacking in taste and nutrition. I could remember his Big Mac days—not unlike Bill Clinton's—and I was glad for his sake those seemed behind him.

When we entered the giant hall filled with row after row of booths, I wished I'd grabbed Abit's camera to capture the look on his face. I knew he'd seen craft shows before, but not like that one. A palpable hum pulsed throughout the space, an amalgam of creative conversations, professional lighting, and amazing wares. The show glowed with an incandescence from far more than kilowatts.

"Well, what do you think?" I asked.

"I could never imagine such a thing," he said. "And look—some of the craftsmen are wearing business suits." He pulled his jacket a little closer to cover his flannel shirt. A few booths later, though, we saw signs of more familiar hippie attire, some looking as though they'd slept in their vans and hadn't changed clothes in days. That seemed to put Abit at ease.

He started scribbling notes, and as his notebook filled, it grew harder to write on the go. We found a break area so he could sit down and finish his thoughts. He didn't say much the rest of the morning, which surprised me, especially since I knew how excited he was.

Around one o'clock, we returned to the break area and opened our lunches. Alex had created his own works of art in a couple of refrigerator dishes. Our sandwiches (on homemade bread) were cut into quarters and placed carefully along each side of the box, alternating with hardboiled-egg quarters. In the middle, carrot sticks radiated from the center with cornichons and olives filling the gaps. Sliced apples (dipped in lemon juice to keep them from turning brown) made the centerpiece with a few almonds scattered about. Somehow we'd carried them upright so they weren't jostled too much; I would've hated to ruin his creations. We bought coffee, which was surprisingly fresh, and enjoyed the two chocolate chip cookies from Firehook.

We spent the rest of the afternoon at the show. Abit eventually got up the nerve to talk to some of the craft artists. Not only those working in wood, but also tile makers and cloisonné artists. I stepped aside and watched as they exchanged professional courtesies and allowed Abit to take a few photographs.

When we were on the Metro train heading toward home, Abit started talking, and I just sat back and enjoyed his ramblings. I dozed a little, knowing if I missed anything, I'd get another chance to hear it again with Alex.

The dogs were elated by our return, and after we greeted them properly, I told Abit I needed a lie down. Upstairs in our bedroom, I drifted off to his telling Alex all about the show.

"Man, there was furniture that looked like food—chairs shaped like celery stalks and tomatoes. I saw a couch built and painted like a whole cake with a slice out of it—and the slice was an ottoman. Others were painted in so many colors, you'd think it would look a mess, but they were cool together. I even saw a chest of drawers shaped like a fat carrot. ... Mostly, though, I loved the simple but perfect craftsmanship, joinery that put mine and Shiloh's to shame. Well, maybe not shame, but at the back of the line. Barn-wood stools with legs painted shiny red, in contrast to the wood ..."

25

Abit

Della and Alex were knee-deep in work, so I called Nigel to see if Millie and I could stop by. We retraced the same path I'd taken with Jake on my last trip. As we walked, we passed a bunch of men who looked like they were living rough. I didn't remember seeing so many homeless people last time.

Back home we had folks who didn't have much, but they always seemed to have somewhere to sleep. At least round where I lived. And people were fed, even if just beans and cornbread. Our barn had some old hobo signs carved into the logs, markings hobos used to leave to help others know what kind of place it was. I asked Daddy about it, and he remembered when they roamed round the area, especially when he was young (though he didn't live in our house then).

I reckoned whoever owned it before had done a good turn for them. There was an odd kinda cross carved into the barn and something resembling two eyes with a smile below it. I got a book from the bookmobile that said those signs meant "talk religion get food" and "can sleep in barn." It felt good working in a place that had sheltered people in need. I also found something carved into one of the barn logs—down low where the owner might not see it but someone sleeping there would: "The Bible is a book of instruction on how to be a hobo with style and joy." I would give that a lot of thought over the years ahead.

As Millie and I walked on, I stepped over the outstretched arm of a man sleeping on the sidewalk. He'd used his bedroll as a pillow and lay flat on his back, a soft snore rattling his lips. Millie kept sniffing round, so I tugged her away, but not before I noticed his hand tightly clutching, even in sleep, a black plastic bag I figured held everything he owned. I wanted to slip him some money, but I was afraid he'd wake up and think I was trying to rob him. I felt bad just walking away; I'd have to ask Della what to do next time.

Nigel greeted us with his usual "Hello, hello, hello" and some behind-the-ears rubs for Millie, which helped me shake off images of that lost man. After we caught up on our news, Nigel said we needed some refreshment. I thought he was gonna run downstairs to the bakery for scones, but instead, he put on a suitcoat over his crisp white shirt, took a fedora off a hat peg, smoothed his already-slicked-back white hair, and set the hat at a jaunty angle. "And not those bloody scones again."

"I thought you liked tea and scones—and *curd*," I said, kidding around because that word sounded so awful (but tasted pretty good).

"I do, dear boy, but I'm more fond of a pint." He ushered me out the door muttering, "My treat."

We walked down Connecticut Avenue to a place called Churchill Arms. Even somebody from Laurel Falls knew that was likely an English pub. We settled in a nice booth near what appeared to be a fireplace with glowing coals. As warm as it was outside, I couldn't imagine sitting there for long, but then I realized it was just lights and fake coals; the heater was turned off.

I was surprised Millie got to join us, but Nigel assured me he was a regular there, and because he was from the homeland, they played by *those* rules. From that, I figured dogs were allowed in pubs in England. Sounded like a good idea to me.

Nigel came back with two pints of Guinness, black as those fake coals and creamy on top. "I thought you might have taken to Irish brews, Abit." I wasn't sure where he was headed, but I hoped we weren't gonna talk about Fiona. I changed the subject and told him about the Smithsonian Craft Show.

Nigel let me go on about that some, but all the while he was kinda twitching, like he was waiting his turn to say somethin'. After a time, he took a big slug of the dark brew, licked his lips, and said, "Now, look here, Abit. Della told me *not* to mention this, but I was very sorry to hear about your Irish lass, Fiona. I so enjoyed meeting her last year at Christmas." Ever since that first Christmas together, he'd been coming to Laurel Falls every other year; the rest of the time he went to his daughter's.

When I didn't say anything, he went on. "A lot of Englishmen don't like the Irish, but I have a fondness for them. Some of the best forgers in the business. Like Stumpy the Scribe ... 'er, hang on. Let's not get into that. Suffice it to say, they're a good lot when they're not blowing up London pubs and such."

"Well, it's over."

"No, my boy, I'm sorry to say the Troubles have started up again, breaking the ceasefire. They're still blowing things up over there."

"No, I mean Fiona is over. And I don't really want to talk about it."

"Yes, I can imagine it still hurts," he said, patting my arm but not taking the hint. "I know I shouldn't be giving out advice, but I really wanted to tell you about something that worked for me. You can imagine that relationships, marriage in particular, are difficult with my, er, profession. My *former* profession." He took another big drink and kinda winked at me. This wasn't the Nigel I was used to, but in spite of his dwelling on Fiona, I was getting a kick out of him. I was beginning to see another side to the guy and, for the first time, could imagine him getting up to no good with his forgeries and God only knew what else.

"Anyway, my wife had given me the boot, and after a year or so, once I'd gone to work for the Treasury Department, I wanted her to know I was doing well. I honestly believe that was why I called her. Not so much to get back together, but to say, 'Hey, I'm not a loser. Look at me now.'"

"What happened?"

"We got back together, for a few more years, anyway. She loved it that I called her. And even though we eventually broke apart again, we're still friends. When I see her at my daughter's, I'm genuinely delighted."

"Thanks, Nigel. That's a nice story."

"Hang on, I'm not telling you *stories*. I'm giving advice. You should call that lass—just to tell her you're not sitting round with your thumb up your arse. You're a fine craftsman, and according to Della, you're making some wonderful music at those bluegrass concerts you play at. What do you call yourselves? The Rambling Rovers?"

"The Rollin' Ramblers."

"Hmm, that's a lot of moving about, but I imagine your music warrants the name. Anyway, give it a try—but promise me, when you talk to Della, not a dicky bird, all right? She'll have me guts for garters."

I promised, mostly to get him to stop talking. (Besides, I didn't know what he was on about with dicky birds and garters.) We sat staring at the fake fire for a while, the beer taking effect. I almost started laughing at how much I felt, well, grown up in a way I'd never done before. Out with a friend, having a beer, in Washington D.C. Not a six pack in the back of the bus in the middle of nowhere, but a real pub in our nation's capital with Millie at my feet. I was feeling pretty happy when Nigel spoke again.

"Well, are ye gonna do it?" he asked, his words a little slurred. He was working on his second pint; I was only halfway through my first.

"Do what?"

"Oh, for crissakes, man. Call the woman!"

26

Abit

Something came up, and Della needed to stay on in D.C. for a while longer. I paced round Alex's house, nervous-like because I really needed to get back to my woodshop.

I guessed Della picked up on my fidgets, because after lunch she told me she'd booked me on the Southern Crescent. That was the name of the train that headed close to home; I knew about it because I'd taken her to Gastonia a time or two to catch it. "We'll need to leave just before suppertime, but you can get a fine meal on the train," she said, knowing that would be on my mind.

When I turned to go pack, I nearly tripped over Millie. "What about …" was all I got out before Della added, "I'll bring her in a few days when I come back." I reached down to pat my furry friend and figured I could cope without her for a day or two.

Union Station blew my mind. After Della dropped me off, I went into the main hall and stood there staring up at the plaster ceiling and all them statues. People kept bumping into me, some of them glaring, most of them not caring. Even the platform where I caught the train was awesome, in an industrial kinda way. I heard a guy dressed in a railroad uniform shout, "All aboard," and he didn't have to ask twicet.

I made my way to my seat, which was surprisingly comfortable, especially for a big guy like me. Not long after the train started rollin', I swayed with its rhythms down the aisle to the dining car. Moving between cars, the wind roaring and couplings clattering, I felt a jolt of excitement go up my spine.

When I found the dining car, right away I could tell how special it was, what with the waiters dressed in white shirts, black ties, and black jackets with brass buttons. Their crisp uniforms were matched by their kindness as they served me a fine dinner, just like Della promised: fried chicken with green beans and a flakey biscuit. I finished up with apple pie and coffee. The silver coffee pot reminded me of all that room service we'd had in Atherton, Virginia, when Della and I were closing in on them cons.

I rocked my way back to my seat and after thinking about the craft show for a while, started feeling sleepy. But something about that seat—the way it had a rolled cushion at the top—reminded me of that poor homeless feller. I felt bad I'd forgotten to ask Della about that—but I would when she came home.

I musta fallen asleep because next thing I knew, one of the uniformed guys was shaking my shoulder. "Gastonia," he whispered, trying not to wake the other passengers. I dragged myself off the train and finished sleeping in the station; there weren't no buses that time of night. I didn't get home till late the next morning and was grateful Shiloh had taken the day off. No saws buzzing while I crashed upstairs.

When Shiloh showed up the next morning, I shared some of my notes from the show with him, then poured myself into my work. Lots of orders to catch up on. I looked forward to getting them out, because I wanted to design some new furniture Alex and I had talked about— and some I'd conjured up on the Crescent before I fell asleep. Something about traveling on that train really made my mind pop.

Over the next coupla weeks, I sanded and sawed and polished until my arms ached. I told myself that show gave me a real kick in the butt, but deep down I knew most of that energy came from trying *not* to think about Fiona. My heart had started to heal, and then Nigel and his damn story had gotten my mind working on her again. I gave some thought to calling her. I even tried a time or two. I gathered enough courage to pick up the phone, but each time, I put it back in the cradle before I dialed. I just couldn't do it.

Until I did.

I waited 'til I knew she'd be at work and I'd get her answering machine. I'd written out what I wanted to say so I didn't stumble and say stupid things. But then I found myself going off script, just the same. It went something like:

> *Hi Fiona, it's Rabbit. Just wanted to check on the table and make sure it's holding up.* [Why did I start like that? Of course a big wooden table was holding up!] *My business is going good, and I just got back from the Smithsonian Craft Show in D.C. where I saw lots of things that blew me away. Not just furniture. Oh, and I'm thinking of taking up the mandolin.* [I'd decided that while I was with Alex and Della in D.C. We'd heard a great band at an Irish pub my last evening there.] *It gets old lugging ol' Bessie round. I'll still play her, but I'd like to have a smaller instrument, too. Gina left the band, and we need more string players.* [I regretted saying that, but it was too late. What I really wanted to tell her was the big hole in the band was the loss of *her* fiddle playing and singing.] *Well, that was all I wanted to say—just hi, and I'm doing good—and I hope you are, too.*

I hung up without saying goodbye and immediately went to the fridge for a beer.

She didn't call back.

Instead, she came walking into my shop the next afternoon. Man, she looked even better than the last time I saw her. When I felt my heart kinda melt, I realized just how brittle it'd become. We were both acting awkward, and I didn't know what to say after hi. She was holding something that looked like a mandolin case, so I asked, "Whatcha got there?"

"Oh, me da sent this."

"All the way from Ireland?" She nodded, and just like that I felt like a fool. As if you couldn't ship things round the world.

"It's been in the family, and he thought I should have it," she said. I'd almost forgotten how sweet her voice was. "I love the fiddle too much to give this mandolin its due. If you'd like to borrow it to see if you want to learn it, well, that would be fine with me." She held the case out for me.

I liked the idea of borrowing something, because at some point, that meant I'd have to see her again to return it. I took the case and walked over to the workbench to open it. What a beauty. The peghead was carved pretty as Jack Harper would've done in a leafy design, and the fretboard had inlaid mother of pearl. While I was admiring it, and trying to think of something clever to say, she asked, "So the bus is still rolling?"

"Yeah, we've gotten a lot of gigs since you left."

"Well, thanks for that vote of confidence, Rabbit."

I started to protest that wasn't what I'd meant, but then I saw she was kidding me. And I just about lost it. What a sight for sore eyes she was, smiling at me. I asked,

"How's the table?" just to have something to take my mind offa that smile.

"Oh, I love it. It's beautiful."

"Notice anything about it?"

"Well, I couldn't have finished it better myself. Smooth as silk."

I guessed she hadn't seen the carved initials. We hemmed and hawed a while longer, and then she left. I felt kinda empty, all over again, but at least I had her mandolin, something of hers to hold.

I wasn't up to much the rest of the day. Shiloh asked me what was wrong, but since he'd been off meditating while she was there, I didn't have any explaining to do.

Later that evening, I called Della up in D.C. She'd brought Millie home like she'd promised, but then she went back a week later because Alex had a doctor's appointment.

"Hey, Della. It's me Abit."

"I thought it was you, Abit. I was just thinking about you—I'm coming home tomorrow."

"How'd Alex's appointment go?"

"Pretty good. The doctor told him things looked okay. For now."

"What does that mean?"

"That we take it day by day."

"Well, I'd like to live this day over and over."

"Oh, yeah? Did you get a big order?"

"Not exactly."

"Well, what then?"

"Fiona came by." She was quiet for what felt like forever. "Don't you believe me?"

"I believe you, honey. I just hope she wasn't toying with you."

"Oh, come on, Della. Don't rain on my day." I could hear her mumble something like *sorry*, and I went on to explain about the mandolin.

"How'd she know you wanted to learn that instrument?" Dammit. I was caught. I hadn't planned on telling her about my phone call, but then I had to explain about Nigel and all. "*Nigel* told you to call her?" she asked. I swear I could smell the smoke coming outta her ears.

"Yeah," was all I could manage to say.

"I'm going to have a talk with him."

"Why's that? Somethin' nice came from it. You of all people should appreciate a reunion, what with how you and Alex got back together. And it made my heart ease a bit. Ease a lot."

"Well, that little Irish shite better not break your heart again, or else."

"Or else what, Della? Have you been drinkin'?"

"No, I haven't been drinking. And I don't know what else, but she's got me to contend with if she pulls any funny business again where you're concerned."

I hated the idea that Della was mad at Fiona, but I shouldn't have been surprised. Man, Della could be a hellcat sometimes, especially when it came to looking out for me.

27

Della

When I got settled back in Laurel Falls, I felt all sixes and sevens. Not home there, not home in D.C.

A while ago, Mary Lou and I'd worked out a schedule that honored her need for regular hours (especially with four kids at home) and my need to keep the budget in line. So when I was in Laurel Falls, I worked two days a week plus one while Mary Lou was there. The store seemed more like hers than mine, but she'd earned that. She'd done a good job improving sales; I'd be crazy to upset that rhythm.

And it no longer felt right spending so much time in D.C. I'd left after I got the distinct impression Alex was just making work for me.

I didn't know where I belonged anymore.

The day didn't brighten till late afternoon when I saw Abit and Millie heading up the steps to my apartment. But even he came through the door with a worried look. While I made us some fresh coffee, Abit asked me about the homeless in D.C. I'd sensed something had been troubling him since his last visit up there.

"Yeah, I feel that way myself. Homeless, in a way," I said.

He stared at me for a few moments, growing agitated. "Are you crazy?" he finally said. "You've got *two* homes, for crying out loud. I can't believe you just said that. You've got it great next to them guys lying on the cement, all their possessions in a goddam bag."

I could feel my face flush. I poured us more coffee, mostly to avoid looking at him. "You're right, honey. I shouldn't have said that. Just a weak moment."

"How do people get in such a bad situation?"

"Well, what can I tell you? The world can be a hard place, and some folks don't have anything or anyone to fall back on."

"Man, that sucks. I mean, is anyone doing anything about those guys?"

"Not just guys. Women and children, too. Almost as many of them are living rough."

"Stop. That's even more depressing." Abit went on to tell me about one man in particular, holding his possessions while he slept. "He haunts me. I wanted to give him some money, but I was afraid he'd think I was attacking or robbing him. I wish I knew how to help."

"Most relief comes from churches and leaders like Mitch Snyder—who got so depressed by the situation he hanged himself." The look on his face made me regret my lack of finesse. "Sorry I was so blunt, but it's difficult to paint that situation any way but as bad as it is. People act all sad and wring their hands—until it comes time to build housing near their property or raise taxes to pay for shelters. And I couldn't tell you how many times I've heard sanctimonious people say 'those people just need to pull themselves up by their bootstraps.'"

"If they even have boots."

"Good point, Mister. And most of these complainers are white and male and so-called Christians, which means they had three big things going for them as they tugged at their bootstraps."

We both looked around for something else to talk about, and our eyes fell on Millie and Jake tussling on the rug. We both smiled, and I suggested we talk about this issue another time. Not to gloss over it, but my state of mind at the moment wasn't right for this discussion.

"Okay, but it feels so big, and I can't get that guy outta my mind."

"Then do something. Contribute a percentage of your profits one month or put a piece of furniture in an auction. I bet Alex could find some charitable auction for the homeless in D.C., and next time I go up, I'll take it. You can't fix that mess, but you can do *something*."

A week later, I found out I'd be going to D.C. sooner than I thought. Alex called and asked me if I wanted a job. His editor needed help with election coverage. The race between Bill Clinton and Bob Dole was heating up (even though Dole couldn't seem to ratchet his rhetoric past tepid), and Ross Perot and Ralph Nader were trying to stir things up with third- and fourth-party challenges. Plus all the House and Senate races. Washington goes electric during election years, and I surprised myself with how eager I was to get back in the game. And get paid. Not that Alex hadn't been generous with me, but that was more like wining and dining. This would be like the old days.

28

Abit

It'd been more than a coupla months, and Fiona hadn't called or come by again. Like a fool, I'd taken her loaning me that family mandolin as a gesture of lasting friendship—that we might get to know one another again. But I reckoned she'd just felt sorry for me.

While I waited and hoped, I dove in and got mandolin lessons from Gina. She'd quit the band because she had to get a fulltime job, but she made time for me. I already had the finger calluses I needed from the bass, so it was more a matter of scaling my technique down to size. Pretty quick-like, I learned to play some fine tunes, including "Bluegrass Breakdown" and "Jerusalem Ridge."

Trouble was, a day didn't go by that I didn't think about Fiona. I mean, how could I not when I cradled that mandolin in my arms? But I couldn't call again. I'd stuck my neck out for her earlier, and I wouldn't go beggin'.

Thank heavens I could still count on Della to keep me straight. Like one day when I was feeling low and she told me how having *too much* self-confidence wasn't good, either. I'd been hard on myself about not being, well, *more*. Hiding out in the barn both day and night, still not sure I was good enough at anything.

"Okay, maybe it *is* time to get out more," she said over one of our midday dinners of pulled pork and coleslaw. "But don't discount the way you keep learning how to make your woodworking even finer—and how you reached out to Jack Harper and improved your own carving. Confident people don't do that. Most of them just rest on their laurels. But you? You keep perfecting yourself. And in my opinion? You're already 'nearabouts' perfect." Then she ruffled my hair like she used to when I was a kid.

Della had a point about how I kept working at getting better. Like my special orders, which were my favorites to work on. I'd made some for clients who actually clapped their hands when Shiloh and I delivered their order. One woman, after seeing what I'd done for her neighbor, told me I had card blonsh, or something like that. (I had to ask Della what that meant.) A lucky break, especially since I was all hepped up after the Smithsonian show. I couldn't quit thinking about that stool I saw using barn wood set side by side with smooth, shiny wood stained red. I'd decided to make her table along those lines.

A week later, the phone rang, but I let it go to the machine. My hands were covered in red stain.

"I've been such an eegit, Rabbit."

Fiona. Red stain be damned, if she was callin' me, red fingerprints on the phone would be a fine reminder of that day. I rushed over to my desk to grab the phone before she hung up. When I picked up, my mouth had gone dry and I couldn't find my words.

"Are ye there, Rabbit?" she asked after a long moment.

I swallowed hard. "I heard you, and I agree with what you just said." I wasn't joking, neither. Hearing her voice without seeing her face helped me keep my wits about me. She *had* been an eegit. And just like that, I felt all kinds of hurt come up. I wasn't ready to go easy into a new conversation, one that might hurt as bad as the ones before. But I had to admit a part of me wanted to slip back into her life faster than a band saw through pine.

"I'm in the middle of somethin', and I'm not quite ready to talk to you," I said. I heard my voice quiver and cleared my throat to try to cover it.

"Okay, when could we talk?"

I didn't answer. I just held that phone so tight, the stain was making my hand stick to it. Finally, she said, "I know you're hurt, Rabbit, but there's no point in digging all that up again. It was so good to see you."

"Yeah, it was, if you can remember it. That was two month ago."

"I had some figuring out to do. And some goodbyes to say," Fiona said.

"Well, so do I. Goodbye." And just like that I hung up.

Maybe the way I handled that was colored by spite, but I had some figuring out to do, too. And it stung that she thought she could just call up and tell me to forget about all that past stuff. I fumed round the shop the rest of the day, part of me wishing I could invite her over right there and then, and anothern knowing I needed to wait.

I worked hard for the next week, late into the evening, sanding things to a fine sheen. I finished up the barn-wood table, and the customer loved it. Didn't even blink at the cost. I also finished a new hoosier and a special-order black locust bedside table. That damn wood was the hardest I'd ever used.

I tried to act like nothin' had happened, but Shiloh could read people. One afternoon he asked me what was going on, and I tried to cook up some excuse. Before I could, though, he said, "Save your breath to cool your soup. I can figure it out for myself." I musta given him a funny look because he added, "I read that one somewhere. It's not original."

As if any of his jokes were.

The next evening I finally picked up the phone. I'd been right about one thing—the phone was now permanently colored with red stain. If Fiona gave me the cold shoulder again, I'd need to buy a new one. I wouldn't want a memento of *that* phone call.

This time I waited 'til I was sure she'd be home; I was sick of answering machines. And she picked up. Turned out, her story was right out of Mama's soaps. The doctor she'd hooked up with was married, but he left his wife not long after he and Fiona took up with one another. Then he turned out to be a hitter. That was all she'd say, but that sent such a surge of rage through me, I scared myself. How could a big man like Dr. Gerald Navarro hit her? Well, really, hit anyone, but especially someone small boned like Fiona. She finally got the gumption to throw him out, and he went back to his wife. I was relieved when she told me they'd left town. I didn't want to be tempted to take a two-by-four to him.

We talked for what seemed like no time at all, but when I hung up, it was almost one o'clock in the morning. I was too keyed up to sleep, thinking about what Fiona'd said. I pulled Millie close and stroked her furry head, which helped calm me down. I hoped this weren't just one of Fiona's weak moments.

29

Della

My new job got the adrenaline coursing through my veins again, and I began to appreciate what Abit had said about my having two homes. I loved being in D.C. for weeks at a time, and then I felt happy back in Laurel Falls. Good to have roots in both places.

While I was at Alex's, Abit called from time to time to fill me in about his business—and Fiona. She wasn't in the clear with me yet, though it did sound like she was ready to make a life with Abit. She'd better be good to him was all I had to say. (Well, I always had more to say, but I was trying not to.)

The work for Alex's editor—phone calls, congressional interviews, emails—proved mostly mundane, but that was fine. I enjoyed being involved behind the scenes with little or no pressure. It sure beat worrying about writing and editing the stories, something I once loved. Fussing over commas and misplaced modifiers just didn't matter to me anymore.

You would have thought with a presidential election looming—it was already August—I'd've been more hepped up, as Abit would say. But even the election story was pretty much business as usual. Sure, someone was always trying to rake up more dirt on the Clintons, but the economy was booming, so in my humble opinion, Bob Dole didn't stand a chance. Nor did Ross Perot. His newly formed Reform Party was still making noise, but I doubted he'd do as well as he did in 1992. And Ralph Nader? What damage could he do?

After meeting with an aid to one of the more colorful senators facing reelection, I hurried to catch the Red Line Metro train to Dupont Circle. As I raced down the escalator, I found myself blocked by a large man taking up the entire width of the escalator. When I heard the whoosh of the incoming train I was sure was mine, I craned my neck and caught a glimpse of it coming through the tunnel and into the station. I bent down for a better view, which put me face-to-face with the folks riding the up escalator. As I did, my heart started thumping, even before the information of what I'd just seen made it to my brain.

Somehow I caught that train, though I fidgeted all the way to my station, as though that helped the train move faster. I hailed a taxi instead of walking home, and after tossing too many bills in the front seat, I ran to the house.

Alex was on the phone, but one look at my face, and he said, "Listen, Paul, I'll have to get back to you. Yeah, soon." He hung up. "What is it, babe?"

"You won't believe what just happened."

Somehow, I managed to wait a week before I called Abit at his woodshop. I explained that I needed him up in D.C., ASAP. "I've got a caper I need your help with."

"Della, you know I'd help you any way I could. But why me? I mean, what can I do that Alex or somebody else up there can't do?"

I kept forgetting I was no longer the center of his world. Okay, I knew that was as it should be, but it still stung. I'd even stopped before I called him to ask myself if I really needed his help, or was I just making up excuses to hang out with him again? (I'd been in D.C. a while, and I was missing *our boy*.) I came down on the side of needing his help. "I'll tell you all about it when you get here. Trust me. You'll want to work on this."

"How will I get there?"

"You could drive the Merc. It knows the way here by itself after all the trips Alex made in it. Or I could pay for another ticket on the Southern Crescent. Why don't I do that? You could even leave tonight—it departs Gastonia around midnight. You'd be here in the morning. Bring your camera and please go in the shop and tell Mary Lou I sent you." I told him what I needed, and I kept rambling on, thinking he was following along.

Until I sensed he wasn't.

After a few moments of silence, I said, "I suppose you have a date with your horny Irish rose."

"That's *thorny*, Della. *Thorny*."

"Sorry, that's what I meant to say." Dead silence.

After several more long moments, he asked, "Why do you hate her so?"

"I don't hate her. I just don't like how she's treated you—twice! I'm holding out until I'm sure she's behaving herself." He tried to interrupt me, but I went on. "Abit, can you come up here? I need a second." Silence again. "Come on, Abit. Say something."

"I'm just waiting. You said you needed a second."

"Sorry, honey. I need a second, as in duels. Someone at my side, working with me."

"Okay, but can I come day after tomorrow?"

"No, it's urgent. Get Fiona to drop you off in Gastonia. If she won't do that, she's not worth it."

"Della, that's not your say."

Oh, man. I was fucking this up royally. "I'm sorry Abit. You're right. I'm talking gibberish. It's just that I'm all tangled up inside. *I found Astrid's mother.*"

30

Abit

I'd been thinking my life was finally going along regular-like, and then just like that, it turned upside down again. I had to stop work, catch a train, and tell Fiona I had to cancel our date to go help Della.

"What's the rush?" Fiona asked, finishing her afternoon tea in my loft. (I could set my watch by her teatime.) I felt especially bad leaving her behind because I really wanted her to join me sometime and have tea with Nigel.

"She found Astrid's mama. Up in D.C."

"You mean that woman who disappeared a coupla years ago? I thought the sheriff closed that case."

"Well, not exactly. He didn't have any real evidence of anyone doing her harm—just that messed up place down by the creek and the fact that she'd gone missing. And now she's found." I left it at that.

It wasn't a great time to leave, what with furniture orders and getting reacquainted with Fiona. But I had to admit the idea of another train trip, spending time with Della, and finding Astrid's mama was making the trip sound better and better. I caught Mary Lou before she started to lock up and found the photo Della wanted me to bring—one of Astrid and her mama from three or four year earlier. I'd always wondered why she had that on a bulletin board in the back of the store, but I reckoned she liked remembering that little girl. She was a corker.

Back at the woodshop, I got Shiloh straight on what needed doing while I was gone. Then I took a shower before picking up Fiona, who'd run on home to change. One good thing about the middle-of-the-night train ride was I didn't have to break our dinner date after all. I'd made reservations at her favorite spot—McGregor's—to make amends.

The fine meal put Fiona in good spirits as we rode back to her home, where we spent some time together before I had to get home to pack my grip. While we were talking, putting off saying goodbye, Fiona gently scratched Millie along her shoulder, in that favorite place of hers, and promised to spend the nights I was away with Millie in my loft. (Shiloh said he'd look after Millie during the day.) I was grateful Fiona loved her as much as I did.

I drove the Merc over to Gastonia. The train was running late, so I didn't board the Southern Crescent 'til almost one o'clock in the morning. An attendant found the roomette Della'd paid for and showed me how everything worked.

He put my bag down on the chair, thanked me for the tip, and gently closed the door behind him.

Man, I loved that room. I felt like I was staying in a for-real dollhouse, the way the sink folded up and a private toilet appeared underneath and the two chairs by the window made into the bed. Reminded me of sleeping in Enrico and Lilian's Airstream at the Sunset Mountain Trailer Park in Virginia.

But unlike those nights, I barely slept. I was glued to the window. When you see trains flying by, you don't realize from outside how big the windows are. I couldn't stop looking at the houses and animals and trucks we sped past. And little towns we flew right through. I lucked out with a clear night and a gibbous moon, which cast a glow on everything. I finally fell off to sleep just after three o'clock. By half past eight, I was plowing through a big breakfast in the dining car, with those shiny silver coffee pots that had come to mean adventure.

31

Della

The next morning, I picked up Abit at Union Station. Once we settled into the Jeep, and after he'd greeted Jake sufficiently (if there was such a thing), I asked him if he'd like to go to the house and get some rest.

"I'm too wound up to sleep. All I need is some strong coffee."

"Not a problem. Nigel said to come over whenever you felt like it, so we can stop in Firehook first to get you loaded up with caffeine."

As we headed up Massachusetts Avenue, I asked about the photo I needed from the store. Abit reached into his shirt pocket and showed it to me. I could feel my hackles rise when I saw Lilah Holt looking back at me. I'd felt a modicum of compassion for her a couple of years ago, trying to understand the depths of her depression. But now? Just looking at her with little Astrid and recalling how both those kids had wondered and worried about what had happened to their mother made my blood boil.

"Thanks," I said as he put the picture back in his pocket. "I want you to give that to Nigel so he can create a mockup of what she looks like now—in her bluestocking getup."

"Could you start at the beginning? And how on an escalator could you even see her blue stockings?" He shook his head and added, "I told you I needed coffee."

"I don't have much more information to share. I just looked her in the eye as I was going down the escalator and she was going up."

"Did she recognize you?"

"I don't think so. She's living in such a different world now, I wouldn't be on her radar—even if I lived in D.C. Oh, and bluestocking is just an old term for rich people. Can you imagine that? From Laurel Falls to high society?" Abit looked at me like I was crazy. "What?" I asked.

"You got me to drop everything and come up here because you *might've* passed some woman who *maybe* looked like Astrid's mama on a moving escalator?"

"Not so fast, Mister. I haven't had a chance to fill you in. After I saw her at the Metro Center Station—and got over my shock—I spent the better part of a week back there, all times of the day, hoping to spot her again. I hung around the train platform, breathing in enough burned rubber and body odor to take ten years off my life. But I found her. And I followed her."

"So you got a better look at her?"

"Well ..." We rode in silence for a while. When traffic came to an abrupt halt at Thomas Circle, I caught

Abit's eye. "I know I'm right about this, honey. And I've been doing some research since we talked."

Finally he smiled. "I bet you have."

"Yesterday I followed her to the National Museum of Women in the Arts. She went right in, but by the time I got through the ticket desk, she was gone."

32

Abit

As Della and I climbed the stairs to Nigel's apartment, the smell of butter and sugar from the bakery below made my mouth water. We'd talked about getting coffee before we met with Nigel, but finding a parking place right out front was so exciting, we'd both forgotten. Tea would have to do. I could hear the kettle whistling through the open front door.

Nigel fussed over me and Della, then motioned for us to have a seat. "I'll get us some tea. Everyone up for that?" He headed to the kitchen and added over his shoulder, "We'll have a Guinness together another time, eh, V.J.?" Della raised her eyebrows like she did, but I knew she got a kick outta me and Nigel being friends on our own.

I reached in my pocket and laid the photo I'd brought from Coburn's on the worktable Nigel had all set up with pens, markers, and his Identi-Kit. Before he settled down to the drawing, we sipped tea and wolfed down something Nigel called Irish barmbrack. He told me he thought I should broaden my horizons and try something new. Then he winked and said it was something Fiona would like.

(He'd called me in Laurel Falls to congratulate me on taking his advice; I guessed Della had told him about all that.) The cake was filled with fruit that I thought might've been soaked in whiskey. I had a second piece, something that might broaden more than my horizons.

Then we got down to business.

"So, here's the photo with her daughter, from a few years ago," Della said. "But it looks so out of date when you compare her hair and clothes in that photo to what I saw at the Metro station. So rather than age her, I'd like you to give her the bluestocking look."

Nigel studied the photo for a while before getting to work. He sketched and erased and looked at cards from his old-fashioned Identi-Kit—line drawings on clear plastic sheets with a whole bunch of noses and eyes and chins and hairdos. Years ago, he'd wanted to be an artist, but that didn't work out for him. Later on, when he was using his artistic skills as a forger, he'd discovered the Identi-Kit while handcuffed to a desk in a police station.

Oncet he'd drawn the basic outlines, he worked on fleshing out the features. Della and I were both watching like a coupla kids as a real person slowly emerged on paper. I looked over at her to see if she thought Nigel's woman was the same as the one she saw on the escalator, but I couldn't read her face. After blowing off all the eraser crumbs, Nigel held up his drawing.

"That's her!" Della shouted, patting Nigel on the back. Then I started in, smiling and congratulating him. It was too hot for his usual waistcoat, but I could just imagine him tugging on its hem, real proud-like. Now we had something besides an old photo to show people.

"So that's what the old bat looks like," Alex said when we got back to his house. "Not bad." Della punched his arm. "Just kidding," he added, chuckling—and rubbing his arm. He'd already given me a big hug and welcome.

"Nigel did a great job," Della said. "Especially considering he's never seen Astrid's mother." I nodded, though I'd only seen her oncet in town.

When we'd come in, I'd noticed the lingering smell of fresh baked bread. Alex had come down a coupla months ago and picked up his hoosier; I was anxious to see where he'd set it. When he headed into the kitchen, he pointed at it with such pride of ownership, I felt a swell of pride myself. He'd set it next to a window that looked out into his small backyard. The wooded scene captured in the marquetry panel blended right in with the trees back there.

Over an early supper, we talked more about what Nigel had accomplished with his Identi-Kit. "So wonder what her name is now?" I asked.

Alex cleared his throat, like people do when they've got something important to say. "While you were away, I did some research. The Internet is getting faster and better all the time." He sounded so upbeat, I saw Della's face brighten. "But I could find only two-year-old stories about her disappearance. Sorry, babe."

"Oh, well. At least we've got this," she said, holding up Nigel's work.

The next morning, we hung out at the Metro station. When we got there, Della gave me a copy of Nigel's drawing to help me look for the right person. After a while, I could see the guards giving me the eye; I guessed I was standing in one spot too long and looking round too curious-like. They didn't seem to question Della doing the same thing, and I wondered what that said about me. Just after one o'clock, she came over to tell me the museum where she'd seen Astrid's mama go in—the National Museum of Women in the Arts—had one of the best lunch spots in the city. Sounded good to me.

We headed up 13th Street, turned onto New York Avenue, and walked to the museum. The Mezzanine Café, as it was called, wasn't what I'd say was frilly, but close. Lots of flowerdy fabric and throw pillows. Della ordered something called a Cobb Salad, and I got burger and fries.

"This place is nice," I said between bites. "The light is especially good in here." I was thinking ahead, hoping I'd need to take photos.

After splitting a peach cobbler a la mode, we killed time over coffee. I pulled Nigel's picture out again to refresh my memory, but no sign of Astrid's mama. We weren't really discouraged—we knew the odds were against us, but at least we'd tried.

And I could tell Della was loving the chase, as she called it. She got so excited, I had to laugh.

"Why do you do it?" I asked.

"What?"

"Get yourself all tied up in these things. I like helping out, but it sure is nerve-wracking."

"Why do I do this? It needs doing is the answer I usually give, but the real answer is I'm born to it. Like horses are born to run—they cannot *not* run—this feels like that for me. I thought working for Alex's editor was what I wanted, but *this* tops that by a mile."

We went back and looked for a while longer, but it was Friday and people were pouring in. The station was getting so crowded, it was kinda hard to breathe.

"No point in looking for her now," Della said. "It's the weekend, and there are too many tourists in town. Besides, everyone's schedule changes on the weekend, so I doubt we'll spot 'the old bat.'" She hugged me and added, "There's another woodworking show at the Renwick Gallery. We can go there tomorrow and anywhere else you'd like." I could tell she was trying hard to please me, not that she needed to work at that.

The next day, Alex dropped us off on his way to an interview. We headed up 17th Street to Pennsylvania Avenue. Della did that on purpose so I could finally see the White House; on my earlier trips, we'd never made it there. We walked through Lafayette Square and stopped in front.

All kinds of folks were milling around—people holding protest signs, others dressed in Uncle Sam costumes, and even more homeless. I looked at Della as I folded a twenty dollar bill. She nodded. I tucked it into a man's shirt while he sat on the grass.

After turning back onto Pennsylvania Avenue, we arrived at the gallery after just a block or so. We walked up the steps and into the cool, quiet calm of the museum, a pleasant contrast to the hubbub round the White House. Della sounded like one of them tour guides when she told me the museum was housed in a nineteenth-century building that was originally built to be D.C.'s first art museum and was based on the "loove's twirlies addition." (She made them air quotes with her fingers, though I had no idea what she was on about.)

I combed through the woodworking exhibit and loved it as much as the Smithsonian show. Wood that curled and curved against its nature, with lines that flowed like an old river. The museum didn't have a café, so we found a bench outside where I could finish my notes. When I closed my sketchbook, I sat quiet-like for some time. Della could tell I was thinking about Astrid's mama.

"Don't worry, honey. We'll find her."

I still had a coupla days before I needed to go home. On Monday we came back to Alex's feeling kinda low—again, no luck. I knew what Della meant about that burned rubber smell in the station. I was tired, but I took Jake for a short walk, just to get some better air in my lungs. That evening, we agreed to try one more time on Tuesday.

We walked round the neighborhood some, checked out the Metro station with no luck, and finally took a break at, where else, the museum café. We were getting sick of the same menu—I didn't think I could ever tire of burgers and fries, but I had. And it worried me how much all this was costing Della. Man, she'd gone through some cash. But it felt good to spend time together. Not since that summer had we hung out like this, and I reckoned we both sensed it wouldn't happen all that much in the future.

Those thoughts made me feel kinda sad, but I forgot all about that when I saw something to my right. "Don't look now," I whispered, "but over your left shoulder, I think we have one Mrs. Holt, or whatever she calls herself now."

"Oh, my God. What's she doing?"

"Eating lunch."

"I know *that*. Is she with anyone?"

"Yeah. She's head-to-head with a big guy in what looks to be an expensive suit."

"There are more of those in this town than in all of North Carolina and South Carolina combined," Della said. "Maybe that's her new hubby. Though we don't even know if she's married. I bet she is. How else could she while away so much time at a museum?" She wiped her mouth with her napkin and set it on the table. "What are they doing now—besides eating lunch?"

"Just talking. Oh, wait. They're getting up. But it doesn't look like they're leaving. His briefcase and her purse are still there. Trusting folk."

"There are plenty of guards around the museum, but you're right—it's kind of odd. Okay, Abit, you've got to follow them. She knows me, or at least knows what I look like. I don't think she ever got a good look at you."

I grabbed my camera and walked down a hallway real careful-like, not wanting to bump into them or a waiter from the restaurant. I had an excuse in mind—looking for the bathroom—though the thought of someone asking me why I needed a camera for that unsettled me. I waited a while and then inched closer to the area where I saw them go. I couldn't believe my luck.

Della was acting all nervous-like by the time I got back. "Oh, thank heavens you're back," she said. "I had to order more cobbler and coffee to stall the waiter. I could see a long line waiting for tables, and I knew he wanted to turn ours."

"Well, I think it was worth it. You won't believe the pictures I got. Like I said, the light in here is perfect. I followed them until they slipped into another room, off a hallway. I waited a beat and looked round the doorway. I lucked out with a coat rack near the entrance and hid behind it. That plus my long lens worked wonders."

"Did they see you?"

"They were so busy kissing, they didn't know what day it was. And they didn't look like hubby kisses to me." As if I knew about that, never having been married and never seeing my parents hug, let alone kiss. But I'd seen movies and the like.

As we waited on our check, those two came back in and sat down, apparently satisfied, and not because of the menu. I kinda chuckled when Della pulled out a compact with a mirror and watched over her shoulder. When she saw them gathering their things, she slapped down enough for our lunch and a whopping tip, and we followed them downstairs.

We held back just enough to stay out of sight—but close enough not to lose them. The guy gave Astrid's mother a public kinda kiss and went one way. Then she hailed a cab, and Della waited a beat to hail one for us. I couldn't help but chuckle again when Della told the cabbie to "follow that cab." Like in the movies. She added, "There's an extra twenty dollars in it for you." That really made me laugh, though I reckoned it was more from nerves.

While we were riding, I asked her something that had been on my mind. "Why did you ask me to come up? You could have done this on your own."

"Not really. I've never been good at photography—and I believe you've gotten something we can use. And, oh, I just wanted to see you. Moral support. Friendship."

Before I had a chance to respond, we noticed our cabbie had lost the first cab. "Dammit," Della said. "There's *not* an extra twenty in it for you." Della started to stuff the money back in her purse, but the cabbie had such a sad face when he looked over his shoulder, I could see her waiver. He was younger than me and so small that his head barely made it over the steering wheel. She told him to pull to the curb, and when we got out, she gave him the fare plus the extra money. "Good luck in America," she said. He smiled and waved goodbye.

"What?" she asked when I gave her a look.

"He could've lived here for years, Della."

"You might be right, but he'll still need good luck in America."

33

Della

We walked a few blocks looking for a one-hour photo shop I'd used before. The guy behind the counter promised our photos in *two* hours. I couldn't believe their deceptive name; Abit couldn't believe how fast the photos would be ready. Since we had a couple of hours to kill, I suggested we go to the National Mall.

"Lead the way," Abit said, picking up his pace.

Two hours wasn't much time for all the choices the Mall offered; stately statues, majestic memorials, and castle-like buildings beckoned. Not surprisingly, Abit pointed at the National Museum of Natural History, where we wandered past mastodons and stuffed birds, Inuit masks and Indian canoes. I'd seen the exhibits dozens of times—it was a favorite stop for guests—but I never tired of them. I had to tear Abit away from a stegosaurus so we could pick up the photos before closing time. Then I hailed a cab for home. Abit needed to pack.

As we looked over the pictures en route to Alex's, Abit got a wicked grin on his face. Something I hadn't seen before. "I think you got her," he said.

"No, I think *you* got her. Or them." The pictures showed the loving couple locked in an enviable kiss. Their faces were obscured in those shots, but when they came up for air, Abit got several photos that clearly showed Astrid's mother and whoever she was kissing.

"So what's next? Are you gonna turn her in?" Abit asked as the cab pulled onto Alex's street.

I didn't have an answer yet, though I'd thought a lot about it. I couldn't see the point of ruining half a dozen lives, only to rub those kids' faces in the fact that their mother had chosen a rich lifestyle over them. But I didn't want her to get off easy, either. I told Abit I needed to come up with a plan. He flashed that grin again.

We didn't have time for a meal together before his train home, but Alex gave Abit plenty of cash for dinner and snacks en route. And if he liked his overnight accommodations as much heading home as he had coming up (I'd heard dozens of details about that roomette), he'd be happy.

After I dropped him off at Union Station, I went home to meet with Alex. I apologized for blowing off my editorial work and promised to get back to it as soon as possible. He seemed to understand how much this meant to me, but still, I needed to make some progress with my work-work.

"Any idea who this guy is?" I asked, holding up Abit's photographs.

"Not at the moment, but I'd like a kiss like that." Easiest request I'd had all day.

When we got back to work, Alex said he was knee-deep in a big election story he needed to file, but he promised to check out Lover Boy soon. Off the top of his head, Alex didn't think he was famous or infamous, which in that town eliminated a lot of folks. But one way or another, those photos were the centerpiece of a blackmail plan I was still pulling together.

About midnight, we took up where we'd left off with that kiss.

Something told me that paramour of Astrid's mother must work around the Metro Center station. That would make meeting for lunch easier, especially at the Mezzanine Café. With all that chintz, it wasn't the kind of place men—at least burly men like him—frequented, so he was less likely to run into cohorts. I doubted she'd worry too much about seeing people she knew. The café was nice by my standards, but not chichi enough for her society friends.

And I chewed on another idea—she must live in the neighborhood. If so, that meant I might see her out shopping or getting her tootsies pampered. The next day, I took the train to Metro Station and headed toward the café. I was sick of the menu and wondered how she and Lover Boy could keep meeting there. But then I guessed the lovebirds weren't focused on the food.

It took a couple of disappointing days before I saw her again—walking down New York Avenue where I'd been standing for hours like a streetwalker. (Seriously, many of the working girls in D.C. dressed far better than me.)

I followed at a safe distance and could make out her once-lank blond hair, now shiny with expensive highlights and cut to just above her shoulders. She wore a dress made of some kind of soft fabric, also sporting an expensive cut that flowed as she walked.

Before long, she escaped into a swank condo building, The Meridian. My spirits sank. Those places were like fortresses. Impenetrable. Even if I stalked her, she could just blow me off with a shriek. Or accuse *me* of a crime. I kept running through scenarios of how to pull off this caper, but every idea hit a brick wall.

Until one didn't.

34

Abit

Fiona agreed I should keep my loft and she'd keep her place in Newland. No point in making too many changes at oncet. And to be honest, I wanted to be sure this thing between us was steady.

But Fiona refused to return to the band. She said real firm-like that she never would. All I could figure was she was embarrassed. I mean, everyone knew she'd had a thing with a married man—and it'd failed. But I also knew they loved her like I did, and who among us hadn't made asses of ourselves, at least a time or two? She just needed a way to ease back in.

After a few weeks, I found one. And somehow I talked Fiona into going along with it.

That weekend, the Rollin' Ramblers had a concert at one of our regular gigs, not too far away in Spruce Pine. All them fans had welcomed me when I'd had nowhere else to go. They'd nursed me through my broken heart for well over a year, cheering at the sad songs I wrote and played. So I wanted to thank them with a little surprise.

The band was all set up, but I took the stage with only Bessie. I started singing Buck Owen's "Together Again," a fetching tune that's both happy and mournful. (The solo bass really added to that feeling.) When I got to the end of the first verse, singing about long lonely nights at an end, Fiona came out from backstage, and we sang perfect harmony about her holding the key to my heart in her hand. That set the crowd off whistling and hollering.

It was just me and Fiona singing and playing together, sounding sweeter than I ever recalled. And then something came over me. Time just fell away, and the crowd noise faded. Like when of an evening I swam underwater at Chatauga Lake and floated in a perfect world of peace and harmony. I lost track of time—and yet I kept perfect time with the music as we sang about the love we oncet knew and how we were together again. When we finished, Fiona set down her fiddle and we moved closer, her arm round my back as I held onto Bessie.

I came back to the room and heard the crowd going wild. I could tell they'd already forgiven Fiona, maybe even faster than I had. I gave Fiona a squeeze and whispered, "Thank you for being the best sideman anyone could hope to have."

"Oh, Rabbit," was all she said, but she squeezed me back.

35

Della

"Is that you, Ms. Kincaid?"

"It is, indeed, Sammy."

When I followed Astrid's mother to her condo building, I'd recognized the doorman standing outside The Meridian—Sammy Feldman, someone I knew from my reporter days. I hadn't gone up to him that day; I'd wanted to think through how I could use that connection to my advantage. It took me a couple of weeks, in part because I needed to catch up on real work, and Alex and I had tickets for the theater and plans for dinner with some of his friends. Time together having fun. What a concept.

When I returned to the building, Sammy stood at the front doors of The Meridian. As I walked toward him, I had a big smile on my face. He recognized me straight away and smiled back.

"I haven't seen you in ages, but then it's a big city, eh?" Sammy said, grabbing my hand and shaking it like a long-lost friend.

I just kept smiling and shaking his hand. I didn't want him to know I'd moved away. Over the years, I'd gotten the sense that people often felt a twinge of betrayal if you'd left their town, and I wanted to stay on his good side.

I'd met Sammy more than twenty years ago, when he went by that nickname. (His brass nametag now read *Samuel*.) His mother, Pearl, was putting five children through college working three jobs, too many hours on her hands and knees cleaning other people's mess. I did a feature story on her, and I always got a good feeling remembering how that article sparked substantial donations for her boys' college education. Sammy and I stayed in touch for a while, even after his mother passed away. He apparently still appreciated how that story played out.

"How's Rosie?" I recalled his daughter's name, but not his son's. I hoped he'd mention it.

"She's in Cambridge. You know, near Boston? My brother who's got a teaching gig at Harvard lives there and keeps an eye on her for me. And Donnie's headed to American U next year."

"Gosh, that's great. They grow up fast." Trite, but I was winging it. "And how about you, Sammy? I thought you were a teacher, too."

"Oh, I am. They just don't pay enough for someone with two kids in college. This is a summertime gig for me with a few nights and weekends during the school year. It's not too bad, as work goes. Easier than taming those wild kids and trying to teach them something. You still telling stories?"

"As a matter of fact, I'm trying to get a story from someone I believe lives here—but she keeps giving me the cold shoulder." I showed him Nigel's drawing.

"Mrs. Overton?"

"Uh, yes, Lilah Overton."

"Wait a sec. Her name isn't Lilah. I have to call her Mrs. Overton, but her first name is Christine."

"Did I say Lilah? I swear I'm getting old, Sammy. Lilah is another story." Was she ever. Since her disappearance, I'd been saying that I never again laid eyes on Lilah Holt. And I'd been right. I was tailing Christine Overton. "Mrs. O. won't give me the time of day. I keep trying to get her to tell me more about this charity event she's involved in."

Sammy made a face. "I'm not surprised. She's a real snob. She and her lawyer hubby, Clifford, could start their own mint, and yet they complained about having to contribute to our—the staff's—Christmas bonus."

"So busy with charity, she forgot it starts at home."

"Isn't that the truth?"

I waited an appropriate amount of time and slipped him a hundred dollar bill. "What else could you tell me about her?"

He eased the bill into his coat pocket with a practiced motion, then looked around before answering. "Well, given how many bags I have to help her get out of the taxis, she spends most of her days shopping." He thought for a few moments and added, "Now that you're asking, I have noticed that on Thursdays, she goes to a salon for her hair or nails or whatever. She comes home all coifed and perfumed."

"Well, that doesn't narrow it down much. There are probably a million salons and spas in this town."

"Not called Chez Perry."

I laughed. "How in the world do you know about Chez Perry?"

"Oh, those women talk in the lobby like I don't exist. I heard one of them recommend Perry or whoever the hell actually works there. I pay attention to things like that." He patted his coat over the pocket where he'd stashed the cash.

"Well, as long as I'm breaking all the doorman rules, could you tell me what unit number is hers? And more about her hubby?"

Sammy didn't hesitate. "Clifford's a pretty nice guy. He's lived here for several years, and she joined him after their wedding last year. Kinda old and tame for her, I'd think, but he's a super-rich real estate attorney." He gave me a wink that said money beats personality. I slipped him a twenty, and he told me their apartment number. As he pocketed that bill, he whispered, "This must be some story."

I thanked him and left. I wanted to get out of there before he asked me what any of that had to do with a charity event.

When I got home, I did some research on both Christine Overton and Chez Perry. The Internet sure made research faster and more informative than the phone book. The salon was easy—just a few blocks from her home. Christine, on the other hand, didn't have much of an online profile—though in those days, not many people did. But I found a few mentions on charity sites, and she was definitely the same person.

I spent the next few days working for my editor. Like a clock-watcher on the job, I had my eye on the calendar, anxiously anticipating the next Thursday. Finally it rolled around. Sammy had told me Christine rarely left home before eleven o'clock, so I made breakfast for me and Alex with enough time afterwards to linger over coffee.

As I approached the salon address, the vague but distinct smell of polishes and pomades let me know I was in the right place. I crossed the street and grabbed a stool in the window of a coffee shop facing Perry's. Sure enough, just after eleven o'clock, Christine walked into the salon, dressed more casually this time, though even her silk apricot-colored jumpsuit looked as though it cost more than my weekly take at Coburn's.

I sipped my espresso and waited. When the jolt from the caffeine mixed with my already elevated adrenaline, I felt ready to pounce. But a minute later, I felt more like the dog that caught the car. What in the world could I do with my quarry? I couldn't go charging in on her, at least not yet. Too much explaining about who I was and why I was cornering her. And this was her turf, too many people around. I needed to confront her somewhere more private. I ordered another espresso and drank it slowly. By the time I finished that one, I had my plan.

36

Della

I waited until the following Monday to go back to the Mezzanine Café. I figured Christine's weekends were likely spent with hubby. I didn't want to waste my time chasing—but not finding—her when I could spend that time with Alex.

I decided not to buy lunch again—my editor wasn't paying me *that* much—but I started to feel conspicuous just hanging out and wandering around the block. The miserable heat and humidity didn't help matters. (Summertime in D.C. drove out everyone who could wangle a trip somewhere else. I could only hope Christine and Lover Boy *wouldn't* leave town.) When the temperature and humidity climbed into the nineties, though, I broke down and bought a museum ticket. I saw a fine exhibit of Frida Kahlo's work, taking breaks to check on the café. No luck.

By one o'clock, I was starving and my resolve was shot. I headed for the café.

"Good to see you again," my waiter said. I'd tipped him plenty the last time, and he'd deserved it. I'd been hogging his table for weeks. "The usual?" he asked. *Oh, brother*, I thought, *was I that predictable? Or was he that good?*

"No, I think I'll have the burger and fries." In honor of Abit, who'd called last night and told me all about Fiona's return to the stage.

"Ah, like your son ordered." I smiled and nodded. That guy *was* good.

But they never showed. Not that day or the next. I had work piling up, so I gave up and transcribed four interviews on Thursday. I got through that and even had time to do more research for my editor.

On Friday, I chose to skip the café, which left only The Meridian. I knew I couldn't stakeout her building with Sammy standing out front, so I decided to move a couple of doors down and across the street to avoid his spotting me. Trouble was, that was far enough away that I needed binoculars. Not a great idea in a hoity-toity residential area. If they suspected a spy in their midst, rich residents would call the cops faster than a lousy politician forgets his constituents.

All I could come up with was an (embarrassing) impersonation of a birdwatcher. An old fellow sporting binoculars and guidebook used to stalk back gardens in Georgetown with knee socks pulled over his trousers and a long-sleeved shirt to protect his arms from briars and branches. I rummaged through old clothes and found the right gear. Alex's laughter still rang in my ears as I made myself comfortable in the shade of a large maple tree.

I didn't have to wait too long before I saw Christine saunter out of her building. She looked radiant. She deigned to give Sammy a little toodle-oo wave and started walking in my direction. A bit of luck, since I wouldn't have to walk past Sammy, and I didn't need to hide any longer—she was too self-centered to recognize me (especially in that getup) after a couple of years and in a radically different venue. She walked to the Hay-Adams Hotel, where she appeared to be a regular, nodding at the staff with that rich-person familiarity that made my teeth ache.

When I walked into the lobby, something came over me; I felt dizzy. As I steadied myself on a nearby railing, I thought *this must be how the women meeting Alex felt. Or when Fiona had her head turned by that doctor and hurried to meet him.* I pushed those thoughts away and followed Christine into the restaurant.

I wondered why the maître'd gave me such a strange look—until I sat down and put my napkin in my lap. My ensemble. Oh well, stranger people wander the District every day. I ordered a club sandwich and coffee for a mere thirty-five dollars.

Within minutes, Lover Boy showed up. He was a galoot, but a well-manicured, well-tailored one, and he looked almost as radiant as Christine. Young love does that, even when you're well into middle age, before the arguments over important stuff like socks on the bathroom floor or whose turn it was to empty the dishwasher takes its toll. Though from the looks of those two, they had maids to help them avoid such petty differences.

After cooing at one another for a while, they finally ordered. While they waited for their lunches, Lover Boy pulled some papers out of his briefcase. Maybe they really were having a business lunch, and I was just a cynical snoop. But then I recalled Abit's photos. And I caught the gleam of shiny, color brochures. They were going away together—Hawaii or Tahiti, that kind of place.

After an hour or so—and the need to order a ten dollar molten chocolate cake to hold my table—he looked at his watch, kissed her on the cheek, and left. No nooner in a backroom this visit.

Christine had just pulled out her lipstick and mirror when I slid into the seat next to her.

"Greetings from Laurel Falls."

37

Della

"Who the hell are you?" Christine demanded as her eyes ran up and down my creative couture.

"Don't recognize your daughter's cooking advisor from Laurel Falls? Hell, maybe you don't even remember your daughter."

It took a few seconds before what I'd said registered. Her face went white. Well, whiter. She already had that pale look—not like when she lived in Laurel Falls, but a fashion statement some women thought made them look younger, hipper.

"Leave me alone or I'll call security," she growled.

"Fine with me," I said, fanning her with the photos and report. "Maybe your rich lawyer husband can get you out of all the trouble these could cause you—that is, if he doesn't dump you. And I know all your society pals would love to learn how you abandoned your children so you could raise money for starving artists."

"I don't know what you're talking about," she said, floundering.

"Sure you do, Christine. You know, Astrid and Dusk—those poor kids you stuck with names they hate?"

"What are you playing at?" she hissed through gritted teeth.

"Oh, I'm not *playing* at anything. But I'm about to I'll tell you how this is all going to play out."

We bantered like that for a good ten minutes before she looked around furtively and muttered, "We need to leave." When she stood, I could tell the cheapskate wasn't going to leave any tip. I put a bunch of bills on my table and followed her. Closely. I didn't trust her not to run off.

Once we were out on H Street, she stopped and looked around. When she didn't offer any ideas about where we could talk, I suggested her apartment. "It's so close," I added, letting her know I knew where she lived.

She scoffed. "You think I'd have *you* to my apartment? And possibly run into my husband?"

"Listen, Christine. You're acting as though you've got the upper hand here. Trust me, you don't. I've made copies of all my research, and if you skip out again on me—or rather Astrid and Dee—those copies are going straight to the sheriff *and* the *Washington Post*. I know reporters there who'd love the opportunity to knock some art maven off her fucking pedestal."

She got a desperate look on her face, and I fully expected her to jump in a cab and flee. But the fight seemed to have gone out of her; she agreed her apartment was the best place. Apparently hubby was off fleecing clients for outrageous billable hours—or she had a gun waiting for me there.

Christine hailed a cab, even though her apartment was just a few blocks away. I was surprised she'd sit in the backseat with me, which made me worry about what she had in mind. We arrived in a matter of minutes. When we pulled up, she looked at me as though I should pay for the cab. This woman had gotten used to the princess life. With a sigh, she forked over a tenner, but I could see there were still plenty more bills in her wallet.

I was relieved Sammy was busy with a trio of women who looked like clones of Christine. I didn't want to get sidetracked, and I couldn't remember all the lies I'd told him. We took the elevator to the penultimate floor. Inside, the long views of the Potomac and Virginia landscape were breathtaking. Christine pointed at the couch, and I sat. We had a lot of logistics to work out. At least, that was the way I saw it. She saw it as a shakedown.

Christine headed straight to a drinks table and poured herself a hefty scotch from a crystal bottle. I guessed it was the maid's day off. After knocking back a half glass, she topped it up before she sat on a stiff-looking Queen Anne chair and started to talk.

She and Enoch (though she called him Jonathan) had met in an underground group back in the seventies. Mostly rich kids playing at being domestic terrorists. She tried to justify the riots and bombs with the old line that they were "responsible terrorists," as some of her compatriots had dubbed their actions. I scoffed. Those two words side by side were a joke.

"We were just tagalongs. Misspent youth and all that," she said, floating her hand languidly in the air as she warmed to her old story. Given her surroundings—brocade-upholstered furniture, brass chandelier, mahogany sideboard and tables—I doubted she'd uttered a word about this in ages. "We escaped from the group. They were cultish and didn't want anyone leaving, but we managed to get away. We headed to the Virginia mountains and had to move around a lot."

"Hold on a minute," I interrupted. "You sound like those Japanese soldiers on some Philippine island thinking World War II was still going on thirty years later. Didn't you know the FBI screwed up so badly they'd had to drop most of the charges back then?"

In what I guessed was a moment of honest reflection, she said, "We were so self-absorbed, we thought we were on the 10 Most Wanted. Later we learned that was only for the biggies in the movement like Bill Ayers and Bernardine Dohrn. At the time, though, we were running scared. We went from a cabin outside of Roanoke to that godforsaken Laurel Falls. A few years later, I had Astrid."

I had Astrid. Like the kid was a disease. I'd never *had* children because I didn't think I'd make a very good mother. Compared to Christine, I'd've been Mother of the Year. And I wasn't buying their innocent bomb throwing.

She picked up on my attitude, leaning closer. "We never hurt *anyone* back then—and we didn't *want* to hurt anyone. That's why we fled. Why else would we move to that hellhole, away from civilization?"

"So what's with the folksy names—Enoch and Lilah?"

She raised her eyebrows and shrugged her shoulders in a "what else?" gesture. "We were running from the law, so we needed aliases. We took a common surname to blend in, though of course we never did or never could. Or ever wanted to." I must have looked confused, because she added, "Fit in. We never could or wanted to *fit in*. And now look at me," she said, motioning around her stuffy old living room. It may have cost a lot to decorate, but it was as cold as her intentions. "You think I'm going to confess to anything like this to my upstanding husband, Clifford Overton, Esquire?"

"Except he's not your husband, is he? You're still married to Enoch, which nullifies your current arrangement."

"Ha! You don't know everything, even though you think you do. Jonathan and I never married. Like everything we did, we just played at it."

I thought that little victory would invigorate her, but she seemed spent. I just let her stew in her stinking story. Eventually, she stood up and poured herself another glass of scotch. No offer to me, but I wouldn't have accepted. I had too many other things I wanted from her.

Something struck me while I watched her guzzle alcohol and wallow in self-pity. "You are such a piece of work, you know that? You think I'm concerned about your checkered past, don't you? I don't give a flip about your political escapades. I'm not here to hold you accountable for *that*. I want to know what you're going to do about your *children*. Remember them? I met them. I cooked for them. I consoled them when you'd run off and left them. When your husband was accused of murdering you and was carted off to jail. Do you have any idea the kind of scars that leaves? In your twenties, you were busy playing at revolution—in theirs, they'll be busy dealing with their fucked-up psyches."

No reaction other than topping up her drink before sitting again. I went on. "But you know, I've written too many stories about parents who beat, starved, or even tortured their children, so your leaving them behind probably did the least damage. You were a lousy mother— and once they got over the trauma of those first few weeks, they seemed a lot happier *without* you."

I expected at least a frown, a wince, something. She just shrugged again. "I wasn't any good as a mother."

"You don't have to convince me of that. I first met Astrid when she was cooking for *you*. An eight year old in charge of the kitchen.

"Oh, fuck off," she said, baring her teeth. I was afraid she was going to throw her crystal glass against the wall—or at me—Hollywood-style. "You act as though you got everything right, but I came in your store early on and saw you lying to yourself. Oh, that surprises you, does it? I thought you knew *everything*. But you don't remember me from back then. I watched you, trying to get along where you didn't belong. I knew the signs too well myself not to notice."

I let that pass. This wasn't about my shortcomings. Or hers, really, except for one. "We've all made mistakes, Christine. You, me, my ex-husband. Even Clifford—I know because I'm looking at one of his right now. I tried, I really tried to cut you some slack, but then I asked myself why you should be living this life. Have all *this*"—I borrowed her game-show-hostess wave—"while Astrid and Dee get their clothes from Goodwill and have never known a mother's comfort."

She just sat there, simpering. I took away her scotch glass, and said, "Okay, let's get down to business."

Christine slumped deeper into her chair. Not easy in a rigid wingback chair, but either the alcohol or her conscience had finally kicked in. More than likely the alcohol. "I can't go back," she whined. "I've got a good life now. You can't make me." She sounded about the same age as Astrid.

"Don't kid yourself. No one wants you back in Laurel Falls," I said. "And I'm glad you've got such a good life, because you're going to pay for your kids' lives to get a lot better. But you're too drunk right now to listen to reason. I'll see you tomorrow—and you'd better be here."

I waved the copies of the photos as a reminder and let myself out.

38

Abit

Life carried on normal-like for a while, but just about the time the Queen Anne's Lace turned the roadsides snowy white, everything started to change again.

First, Jasper O'Farrell stopped by Daddy's and asked if I'd be interested in a small place out Hanging Dog way. Seemed a widow woman, Addie Compton, needed to move fast and asked O'Farrell to help her sell her place. Fiona and I went to look at it the next day.

A small farmhouse, surrounded by two acres of meadows and trees, sat atop a knoll overlooking the valley below. One of the prettiest scenes I'd seen since the meadows at The Hicks. When Fiona stepped inside the knotty-pine paneled kitchen, I knew what her heart was doing because mine was working like bellows, too. Same with the chestnut-log barn. (Chestnut trees had been wiped out by a blight early in the century, so them logs were precious.) I saw myself working in there, as real as if I had a twin brother standing at a band saw, making fine things.

Within a coupla weeks, the bank approved us for a loan. Mrs. Compton sold at a good price, so we didn't haggle with her or nothin'. She seemed happy, and we sure were. We just needed to close on the deal and figure out when we could move in. Mrs. Compton did ask if she could come back and dig up a few dahlias when she got settled in her new place. We said sure.

"Rabbit, pinch me. I can't believe I'm this lucky," Fiona said on the way home from the closing.

"And if things work out the way they said," I added, "we could move in as early as next month." Fiona didn't say anything, so I went on. "Right? You *are* moving in with me?" I smiled and looked over to her side of the car. She wasn't smiling, and I lost mine. "Wait a minute. You're not planning another runner, are you?"

"No, it's just that we aren't married."

I had enough sense not to mention that she'd overlooked details like that when she was hanging out with her married doctor. And we'd been living like a married couple, just under her roof one night and mine anothern. After a mile or two, I finally I got it. Even though she considered herself a so-so Catholic, she didn't want to *live together* 'til we were married. Somehow, messing round but having your own place didn't make her feel as guilty as living together.

I wasn't keen on the idea of getting married right then, and I didn't see why a piece of paper from some clerk made much difference. But I knew we'd marry sooner or later, so why not sooner?

"Are you proposing to me?" I asked. She started laughing, which I took as a good sign. I went on. "So, I reckon you want to get married quick-like?

"I do."

The next day, Daddy stopped by my woodshop again. I reckoned Mama had told him Fiona and I were getting married, and he wanted to know when he'd get his barn back. Well, I planned to move my shop out to my new place as soon as possible. Them chestnut logs were calling to me.

"Daddy, thanks so much for finding that place for us. We can't believe our good fortune."

"I didn't have nothin' to do with it. I was just getting that O'Farrell offa my back."

Man, you couldn't say anything to him without getting some sorry reaction. That was why I kept putting off telling him something else, but now seemed as good a time as any. "Daddy, I want to ask Nigel to be my best man. I know it should be you, but if it weren't for him, we wouldn't be having a wedding next month."

"Son, I don't know about all that wedding stuff. Never made sense to me, so go ahead and ask that man to do it. I'd be obliged if he would spare me that."

I was glad he wasn't upset, but his comment kinda stung. I started some busy work on a hoosier and asked, "Will you come to the wedding?" He didn't answer right away; when I turned my head his way, his face carried a world of hurt. I didn't know what to say, so I went back to sanding. Pretty soon, I heard him leave.

39

Della

Christine kept giving me the runaround, wasting a lot of my time. After a while, I'd had to let my plans for her go while I spent a week down in Laurel Falls tending to some store matters. I'd just returned to D.C. the night before.

Alex was already at his desk when I got up. "Hon, I finally had a chance to research that Christine character's husband. He's loaded. One of those D.C. lawyers whose quietly raking in the money." He handed me a sizeable file.

"So she can afford the plan I've got in mind," I said, sipping his coffee and leafing through his report. "You know, what I'm planning to ask for those kids, she probably blows on facials and pedicures in any given month. I'm done with letting her drag her well-groomed feet any longer."

I didn't want to ask too much of Alex—he had plenty of his own work to worry about—but I needed to know more about Christine's burly boyfriend. Alex had tried searching in some photo database he subscribed to, but nothing had come up.

I still had a few contacts from my reporter days. The last I knew, Howard Pinzer was at *The Hill*. While Christine's galoot didn't appear to be in politics, reporters like Pinzer had tools to find almost anyone. I dialed the only number I had for him and was surprised when he answered. Then again, given the state of journalism, few reporters had the luxury of job-hopping.

"Howard? It's a blast from the past—Della Kincaid."

"Hey, Ghoulfriend, how're you doing?"

Just like that, I was back in. When I gave him a brief overview of what was going on, he suggested we have lunch. "I want to hear all about you and Jed Clampett." Journalists think they're so funny (and generally they are).

We met on Wednesday at the Old Ebbitt Grill, Washington's oldest bar and restaurant. A great place for people-watching, at least for us political junkies. Howard looked the same, only without as much hair. With his tie askew and dark circles under his eyes, he gave off a weary vibe.

After we ordered, he said, "Tell me what it's like to get away from it all."

"To tell you the truth, I haven't gotten away from anything. I'm embroiled in something that landed me back in D.C." I brought him up to date with a CliffNotes version of the Holt/Overton ordeal. When I showed him a photo of The Couple enjoying their steamy embrace, he whistled the way people do when remembering a kiss like that. Then I showed him the one that captured their faces.

He removed his glasses and held the photocopy close to his eyes. "Can I have this?" he asked. He put his glasses back on and added, "He looks mobstery. I've got some connections I can show this to."

I paid for our lunch, and we left. Out on 15th Street, Howard gave me a kiss on the cheek and promised to get back by day's end or the next day at the latest. True to his word, he called around nine o'clock that evening. Just what I'd figured. Roscoe Cohen, a major mobster in the construction business.

40

Della

My foot was caught in the Overton's front door.

I'd been calling Christine for over a week, but I couldn't get past her maid. The next Monday, I decided not to call but to show up on her doorstep at seven in the morning. Sammy was back to teaching, and I caught a break when his replacement was out front helping an old woman out of a taxi. I slipped into the elevator without anyone calling upstairs to announce me.

A young Nordic woman answered. The maid, I presumed, though mercifully they didn't make her dress in one of those black-and-white uniforms. "Would you please tell Christine I'm here?" She started to close the door in my face, which was when I stuck my foot in the door the way I'd seen private eyes do on TV.

"She's not here." She sounded mousy, afraid even.

"What is it, Hilde?" a mellifluous male voice called out. A tall man with perfectly sculpted gray hair stepped around the corner, dressed impeccably in a four-thousand dollar suit. The Hermès tie alone would shoot my clothes budget for months. I could easily picture him holding court around the conference table, but I couldn't imagine his being very exciting to live with. Not compared to her construction goodfella, all muscles and swagger. They were polar opposites.

Hilde held her hands out in a "I don't know what to do" stance, but before Clifford could offer any counsel, I announced through the crack in the door, "I have a breakfast date with Christine."

He nodded at Hilde to let me in. "I'm sorry, *Miss?*" He motioned with his hand, implying I had rudely not given my name and should proceed. Ever the lawyer.

"*Ms.* Kincaid. Della Kincaid."

"Well, *Miss* Kincaid. You must have gotten your dates mixed up. She's out of town."

"But we made our plans just last week."

"She was called out of town to help a sick friend in New York. I'm sorry, but you'll have to contact her when she gets back. Unless you'd like to join *me* for breakfast." He motioned toward the kitchen area, but I knew the sly old bastard was just being cocky.

"Thanks you so much, Mr. Overton. I seem to have lost my appetite."

The doorman was dealing with a stack of FedEx packages when I raced through the lobby; he didn't even give me a glance. As I walked to the Metro station, the fresh air revived me; the stink of that expensive but prison-like building had started get to me. I thought about Clifford falling for Christine's lame excuses. Sick friend, my ass. I was certain she'd gone on that trip to Hawaii or Tahiti she and Lover Boy had planned at the Hay-Adams—with the added benefit of getting away from me.

I got the impression she'd be away for a week or more. Just as well, I supposed. I'd let it all ride a little longer, until I got back from Laurel Falls. I needed to drive down there again to check on some things that Mary Lou couldn't and shouldn't have to handle on her own. I was just about caught up with work for my editor, and Alex seemed in good spirits. I wasn't even dreading the long drive with Jake. Some of my best thinking happened on the highway.

Over the following week, Mary Lou and I worked our regular schedules. On my next alone day, I heard the bell over the door ring and looked up, hoping someone enjoyable like Abit or Cleva was stopping by for coffee and a chat. Or Astrid. I missed the little imp.

Instead, I saw a hunk of a guy turning the *Open* sign to *Closed*.

"Hey, wait a minute," I said, more from instinct than logic. He pulled a gun and motioned me toward the back. It took a moment before I realized the scene was for real. He motioned again. Figuring I'd have more luck out front,

I moved as little as possible. And started talking. Jabbering, really.

"There's nothing to steal yet. It's too early in the day. There *is* the forty dollars I start the day with, but that's hardly worth gunpoint. Armed robbery, you know, is a far worse crime that just robbery. Put that gun away and here's the forty." I held out the bills, even though I knew that wasn't what he was after.

He scared the shit out of me, reminding me of the kind of guy I used to write about. Souls lost to poverty, abuse, drugs, war, greed—take your pick—doing desperate things to fill the emptiness of their lives. Any way you looked at it, America was becoming the land of too many opportunities for ruining your life.

"Hand over the papers and photographs," he said, moving closer with the gun, his voice deep and menacing.

"What papers?"

"Cut the shit, girlie. You know." He did that thing again with the gun that means *move it.*

"No, I don't." We went back and forth like that for a while, until a customer came up and knocked on the locked door.

"Tell 'em to get lost—and make it convincing," he grunted.

"Sorry," I called out. "We're closed, er, for inventory."

The Goon nodded his approval when he turned his head enough to see the customer head back to her car and drive off. "Now get in the back and find those papers. I'm not leaving till I get them—or I use this," he said, waving the gun for emphasis. "Then I'll find them on my own."

"They're not here."

"You better hope they are."

"They're upstairs. My office is up there. That's where I keep them."

He looked confused about what to do next. His back was to the door, so he didn't see Sheriff Horne walk up and look in the window, curious about why the store was closed at this hour. I pointed in a frantic sort of way, and The Goon turned. That gave Horne a view of the gun, and he kicked down the door, weapon drawn. A hail of gunshots rang out before The Goon ran out the door past a wounded sheriff.

Horne had a flesh wound in his upper arm. Not life-threatening, but still, it needed professional attention. I couldn't lift him, so I had to wait until he sat up and then stood up so I could help him into the back of the store. I kept a sizeable first-aid kit back there and found what I needed to clean and bandage his wound for the time being. I figured he didn't want an ambulance and paramedics roaring to his rescue. Maybe for a shot to the gut, but for a flesh wound, he had his pride. He'd get around to reporting the intruder and gunshot wound in his own time.

While we sat there, both of us getting our heart rates down to reasonable levels, I realized Horne had saved my life. I did have copies of the papers here, but they *were* upstairs in a hard-to-get-to space. I didn't want to think about the logistics of going up the stairs to my apartment, pulling the bed away so I could get at the box underneath, Jake growling and carrying on. Maybe The Goon wouldn't have shot me, but he would have hurt me, for sure. And Jake, too.

"Remember our talk on friendship?" I asked. He nodded, wincing. "Well, you're my friend forever. You saved my life."

"But I just needed some milk," he said before passing out.

41

Della

I called Lonnie Parker at the county office. By the time he arrived, Horne was awake again and talking. I kept telling Horne he was looking better and better—good as new once that wound healed. After a while, he asked, "Are you trying to get rid of me? I thought we were friends for life."

When I laughed, even I thought it sounded theatrical. But I wanted them gone. Customers would be flooding the place once word spread about the shootout at Colburn's—and I had a call to make. Finally, Horne dragged himself out to the patrol car and waved gingerly as Lonnie drove off.

I grabbed the phone and dialed Christine from memory. Lover Boy must have put a tail on me, because they knew I was back in Laurel Falls. And of course they knew I'd just had a visitor. What they didn't know was what I was going to do about it.

I was surprised when Christine answered. I managed to keep my voice even, but I could hear how strained it sounded. "You are one breath away from my handing these papers over to the sheriff, who suffered a bullet wound at the hand of your thug and who would love to throw both of you in jail. *And* your boyfriend, Roscoe Cohen, the mobster."

Unfazed, Christine shot back, "Yeah, but Jonathan would go, too." Not *I'm sorry*, not *I didn't know anything about it.* Just more attitude.

"Not necessarily. I wrote up my report in a way that keeps Enoch/Jonathan out of it. It will be your word against mine."

"Oh, come on, Columbo. You think you're such a hot-shit writer that the police won't dig further into his past? The FBI may not be looking for him, but I'm sure he's broken some kind of law—or laws. Then what happens to those kids you're so fond of? Are you ready to risk that?"

"Yes, I am. Because I know it won't come to that. If it does, that means *your* world will have already turned upside down. Say goodbye to Clifford's money. Say goodbye to all those secret trysts with Lover Boy. I don't care what you have to tell either of those arrogant sons of bitches—by next week, I want confirmation from Enoch that the first installment for those kids has arrived in his mailbox. I've got those damning packets ready to go, and I've told our local sheriff—the one who is in pain right now thanks to your goon—where one is in case anything happens to me. And I mean anything. So you damn well better pray I wear my seat belt and look both ways when I cross the street, because you're going down if *anything* happens to me."

I slammed the phone down. It wasn't a sure thing, but I felt better. For a while. Then I changed my mind. I called Alex and asked him to have a courier deliver a sealed envelope with copies of the photos to Christine—and only Christine. I wanted to remind her how easy it would be to have them delivered directly to Clifford.

42

Della

I waited until I got back to D.C. to contact Christine again. Of course, the deadline I'd demanded had passed, and she wasn't returning my calls. I was sick of the drama, but I needed to talk with her. I decided not to press my luck trying to slip past the new doorman; I took a different tack.

The next Thursday I waited at the coffee shop across from Chez Perry. I saw Christine sauntering down I Street around eleven; I gave her time to get settled in and covered in goop or polish or whatever she was having done. As I entered the spa, I could hear Chopin playing on a first-class sound system, though the thought of the delicate composer enduring competition from dryers and gossip—and noxious fumes in his delicate lungs—made me sad. The smell was the same as any beauty shop, though I was sure the word *spa* added at least one decimal to fees for services rendered.

"May I help you?" asked a stiff-necked young woman, her shoulder-length earrings likely the cause of her limited range of motion.

Her smile changed to puzzlement when I answered, "I'll help myself."

The salon was divided into semi-private cubicles dripping with silver lame and tinselly things hanging from the ceiling. Somehow through the shimmering miasma, I saw Christine, who was enrobed in her own world of silver—the shiny salon cape and foil-wrapped spikes of hair sticking out all over her head.

I stood behind her chair and shrieked, "You stole my husband, you, you ..." I wasn't faking the stammer. I honestly couldn't find words harsh enough to describe that woman.

Dryers turned off. Stories ended. I believe Chopin even stopped playing. For once, Christine didn't have a quick retort. She stared at me, at first with incomprehension, then recognition, then rage. Like a personal performance of Dante's Medusa and the Furies.

I considered some physical tussling, but even I thought better of that. Just a little embellishment. "He's leaving me and our three children practically on the street."

Christine stood so fast she knocked over the tray of hair color. When the manager threatened to call the police, Christine barked at her, "I'll handle this!" Without a thought about her appearance, she ushered me out the front door. Even in the flurry of activity, it wasn't lost on me that Mrs. High and Mighty Overton was standing on I

Street NW in a getup no woman ever wanted to be caught wearing.

"You got it now, Christine?" I asked before she could say anything. "No goons, no out of town trips, no gatekeeper maid will get me to stop. I'm like a dog with a bone. No, make that tick on a dog. I won't let go."

"Ah, but you can be poisoned," Christine said.

"Fine, think up all the stupid plots you want, but don't forget the packets—like the one I sent you. If anything happens to me, they go public—and directly to Cliffy."

She stormed back into the salon. She wasn't in any position to go home, not with all those chemicals on her head. I hoped they'd burn her hair off like in that "I Love Lucy" episode when Ethel and Lucy watched their perm-rodded hair pop onto the table as they played cards.

I went back to the coffee shop and waited, enjoying an espresso and a celebratory croissant while Christine finished getting coifed. Finally, she came out and hailed a cab. I ran out and trotted along behind it. For once, I loved D.C. traffic—so slow I could keep pace on foot. When we arrived at The Meridian, the doorman asked if he could help me.

"Just waiting for my friend, Christine Overton," I said, pointing to the cab that had just pulled up. But the words were barely out of my mouth when the cab speeded away and turned the corner. I smiled sheepishly at the doorman and headed to a bench across the street.

Two hours later, Christine got out of a black car with dark tinted windows. It sped away after she closed the passenger door; I got the license number, just in case. I jogged across the busy road, dodging between cars. As the doorman opened the front door for Christine, I scooted through.

When he called out "Mrs. Overton" with an inquiring tone, she waved him off.

"Well, I see the tick is back."

"Never really left."

"You might as well come up."

I wanted to tell her that her hair looked a little over-processed, but I decided not to push my luck.

In a reprise of my earlier visit, she started hitting the bottle pretty hard. The more tipsy she got, the more she spilled the beans. Like the fact that she *wasn't* bipolar. All that had been part of her ruse to get away from Laurel Falls and her family. She *was* depressed living there, she told me, but that was because, well, she was living there.

"I staged the whole disappearing act," she told me with slurred words. "I saved pennies for a couple of years from that stingy bastard and finally had enough to get away."

"So the trip to Chester and doctor's appointment were part of your getaway plans?"

"Mostly, except for missing the bus and catching a ride to that godforsaken truck stop. And then that truck driver scaring the shit out of me." She went into detail about the shortcut the Potash 3K truck driver took and confirmed that she'd thought he was heading somewhere remote to rape her. After she jumped out, Flora Pearce gave her a ride into Chester. But by that time, she'd missed her doctor's appointment. With a brittle laugh she added, "That doctor wasn't treating my so-called bipolar condition; I'd been seeing him because he gave me some cool drugs for my depression."

"And what about that diary of yours?"

"I was hoping someone would find that. I needed a little help from Stephen King, but it added a nice touch, eh?"

I hated that woman. I got it that living in the middle of nowhere could get to you, especially when you were accustomed, as she'd bragged, to a life of money and privilege. But she was so glib about what she'd done to three other family members, not to mention all those volunteers who traipsed through hot, buggy fields to try to find her.

I had a lot more questions, and I needed to get to them fast before she passed out or got violent. "Why don't you start at the beginning—that Thursday when you left home?"

I could tell she hated being interrogated by me, but she cooperated. Maybe she'd finally grasped what a tight corner she'd backed into. "I got out before dawn with that tiny suitcase. I bought that thing mostly because it was cheap and small. I figured that would throw people off—

no one would escape with none of her clothes, right? But I didn't want any of that crap. I planned to buy everything new. Start over. Anyway, it was small enough I thought it would be easy to cut through some fields to get to the highway the shortest way. But the wheels kept getting tangled in brush. That's when I cut my hand on barbed wire. Goddam stuff is everywhere." From there, her account matched Dibble's latest story, except for her take on his shortcut.

"What about that old suitcase of yours strewn above the creek?" I asked.

She laughed. "I told Astrid I was taking that suitcase to Goodwill, but I stashed it in the house where even that nosy creature wouldn't find it. When she was off at your store one day, I packed it with some of my clothes and hid it near the creek to throw suspicion on Jonathan. That weasel deserved it.

"I was planning to leave soon, but not for a few days. I needed those drugs first from that doctor who didn't ask a lot of questions. Chester was only supposed to be a day trip, but when I missed that appointment, Dolores managed to squeeze me in the next day. I'd been gone before without Enoch knowing where I was, so what the hell? I got a room and stayed over. It felt luxurious, even in that hick town."

So Dolores Lopez, who'd been so vigilant about patient privacy, worked for a drug-dispensing doctor. And she'd withheld information about the second appointment, throwing Sheriff Horne off track for days. So much for pristine professional ethics.

Christine asked me if I wanted any coffee. I said yes, only to keep her busy and talking. And maybe it would help sober her up. While she fussed with a fancy Rancilio espresso machine, she told me more. "I didn't get home Friday until after seven. Jonathan was there with that Earth Mother, Maddie Something-or-other, who was fixing dinner. I didn't give a flip about Jonathan, and I actually saw Earth Mother as my ticket out. I figured he'd hook up with her and the kids would be better off. But I was hot and tired and seeing them in that little domestic scene pissed me off. Just like that," she added, snapping her fingers, "I decided to leave early. Leave *then*."

To make things look more suspicious, she went back to where she'd stashed the old suitcase and messed with the slope—breaking some branches, rolling a log down the steep bank, and tossing a few pieces of clothing from the suitcase. She had enough daylight left to make her way along the creek bank to the Blue Ridge Parkway, where she caught a ride with a couple heading to Lynchburg, Virginia. From there, she took the early-morning train to D.C. "After that, things just fell into place. My cousin helped me at first, and then …"

I interrupted her reminiscing. "I'm glad you mentioned buying new things. I have a plan that lets you buy all kinds of stuff."

When I finished explaining, she just nodded. "I need time to think this over."

"You still don't get it, do you? There's nothing to think over. This is happening—or else." I reminded her of the photos.

"Okay, I should have said I need to make this work without Clifford knowing. Give me a month."

I glanced over at the crystal scotch bottle—almost empty, and I doubted she'd remember what she'd promised. But *I* wouldn't forget. "Okay, one month," I said. "Besides, I'll be busy with a wedding. You know, when people actually love one another."

43

Abit

I'd carried the dread around with me for more than a week. I'd been so happy that Fiona and I were back together, I hadn't mentioned anything troubling—like about having kids. But I couldn't get married with something like that hanging over us. I finally got up the nerve.

"Do you still want to have children, Fiona?" My heart was thundering.

"Of course I do, Rabbit."

I felt like she'd punch me in the gut. "Why'd you come back, then? You know how I feel."

"Yeah, I do." She paused, like she was thinking of the right thing to say. "I decided I'd rather have a life *with* you without kids that a life *without* you."

I didn't know what to say. How do you thank someone for giving up a dream?

After that, we started planning the wedding and figuring out who to invite. I was surprised how long that list grew; I never imagined I'd have that many people who might come. Or for that matter, that anyone would want to stand next to me in a wedding—let alone someone like Fiona.

Mama acted all prudish at first. I knew she was thinking *about time* or something along those lines. She'd told me she knew we'd been *sleeping together*, in a way that made it sound all ugly-like. But oncet she got over that kind of foolishness, she dove into planning the food and all.

Fiona was a ferocious list maker; she took a full inventory of our furnishings and other stuff. Then she told me which things of mine she just couldn't bear to live with. Fine by me. They didn't mean a thing to me. Just something to sit on or sleep on. She also made what she called a "short list" of things she'd like me to make in the woodshop, including a hoosier with carvings along the top. I musta sighed, because she added that I didn't have to make them before we moved in. I chose to think she was kidding.

When it came to things she had that I couldn't live with, I thought about the table I'd made for her that Dr. Gerald Navarro ordered. I didn't want to get rid of it, but it sure had bad memories. Then I remembered the initials I'd carved underneath, and I felt that was a kind of blessing, making that table ours all along.

I had one other thing I needed to mention: garden gnomes. We hadn't even moved in yet, but she'd already bought a dozen or more of them things to put all round the garden. I guessed it was an Irish thing. Trouble was, I didn't trust myself not to run over them with the lawnmower oncet we moved in. Later on, though, I looked at it another way: If gnomes were the biggest sore spot for me, things were going good.

Eventually, we got rid of a lot of stuff, but it still took a bunch of trips in Shiloh's truck to get our belongings out to the new place. One evening, we went out after Fiona got off work. As I drove, we both commented on how pretty the sky looked—big pink clouds catching the sun's long rays. But then, in the blink of an eye, like someone flipped a light switch, they turned gray; it was coming up dark fast.

As we crested a small hill along the road to our house, I could just make out some people digging in the yard. "Hey, what's goin' on here?" I asked when I got outta the truck. Millie almost never made a peep, but she barked at them.

Addie Compton stood off to the side while what looked like a coupla grandsons were digging deep holes in the yard. They'd taken a lot more than dahlias—including a big lilac bush and at least a dozen rose bushes. The yard wasn't safe to walk in with all them holes.

"You said we could take some," she fired back.

"Yeah, some dahlias. Not all this." A noise at the side of the house made me look over thataway, where yet another grandson was loading his truck with the firewood she'd promised us. Cold mornings weren't that far off, and

I'd looked forward to having a ready supply. "And just where are you goin' with that wood?" I asked.

"Home," he said, as if that cleared everything up.

"Well, I think you need to run along. Take your flowers but leave the wood." I looked to Addie and said, "You promised that. Said it was a housewarming present because we'd been so nice to work with."

There was a tense standoff, but finally she nodded, and the grandson threw a few pieces of wood back on the pile. They loaded Granny in the backseat, strapped down the trunk lid to hold in all the plants, and roared down the driveway. Halfway down, Granny stuck her head and arm outta the back window, clutching a piece of firewood. "I hope you'uns burn up with that wood!"

I had to console Fiona. She was awfully superstitious, what with all them Irish curses running round in her head. I assured her we'd be happy there. But we rode home quiet-like. I had to admit Mrs. Compton's curse sent a chill down my back, too.

When we got back to my place, that seemed like the least of our worries.

44

Della

I had just hung up the phone after a busy day of calls and interviews when I heard Alex step into my office. I was about to ask him how his day had gone when I noticed how pale he looked. "Della, the doctor says I need another treatment." Not *what for* or *why*. *Treatment* said it all. "I'm so sorry this comes right at the wedding."

I hugged him and whispered, "Not right at. You've got a couple of weeks yet, and as strong as you are, you'll be fine."

Only he wasn't. He had a bad reaction to the radiation and needed to stay in D.C.

I couldn't sleep, trying to figure out the right thing to do about the wedding. *He's still my husband, in my eyes, and the only man I've ever loved. No divorce decree could sever that tie.* But I couldn't pretend that wedding didn't mean the world to me. *Abit is our boy.* I tossed and turned until I finally convinced myself to let it go. I'd know in the morning what to do.

I could tell Abit was disappointed we couldn't come to the wedding, but he asked all the right things about Alex and acted as though he understood, which on one level I knew he did. Then I called Mildred and Cleva, who agreed to fill in for me. We'd already planned the menu, and I told them I'd pay for anything they couldn't make in time.

Earlier, we'd arranged to hold the wedding in the meadow behind the store. At first, getting married in a meadow—rather than a church—conjured Fiona's Irish Catholic guilt, but Abit won out. He wasn't so lucky with Mildred when he told her the Episcopal priest, Father Max, would conduct the service. Apparently she had a most unchristian-like fit and demanded her fire-and-brimstone preacher, Corky Cochran, officiate. No doubt the guy meant bad memories for Abit, but Mildred prevailed. Things evened up when she lost her argument against dancing. No way would Abit stand still for that.

Over the next week, we burned up the phone lines with details like how to get the string lights in the trees out back and when to hire Duane to mow the meadow and put down some pallets and plywood to make a dance floor. After a dozen phone calls, I felt satisfied the wedding could go on without me.

Once I'd made my decision, I poured myself into my work. At that point, I didn't care much about who won in District 18 in Virginia or District 12 in Maryland, but it took my mind off things. And I fielded a slew of phone calls from Wedding Central. Abit: Was he supposed to get a gift for Fiona? Cleva: How many bratwursts did she need to order? Mary Lou: Would Abit mind if she brought a guest?

Even though I'd made my peace with what had to be, my sorrow ran deep, showing up in troubled dreams. All kinds of weird scenes and consequences that kept me awake in the darkest part of the night.

A few days later, I was drinking coffee in a losing battle with boredom as I transcribed an interview with a senator who was behind in the polls. When I put the mug down on my desk, I noticed Alex standing in the doorway. He was dressed and freshly shaved. A good sign from someone who hated his razor. "Babe, if you'll drive, I'm up for riding along."

A rush of feelings swept over me. Mostly relief that Alex felt better (at least I hoped he did and wasn't faking it for me). And relief that, well, that was obvious.

The next day, I finished loading Alex's Mercedes around Jake, who'd already been in there for a good hour while we packed. We headed south, and when we crossed the Virginia/North Carolina line, Alex let out an uncharacteristic whoop. It sounded so good, I joined him.

45

Abit

Della beep-beep-beeped her horn and jumped out as soon as them Merc tires stopped turning. Millie and I flew down the steps to the store. We musta been a sight, all hugging and laughing and carrying on.

We had three days before our wedding day, and they were full up with chores. Alex brought some of his baking pans and set up in Della's kitchen. I couldn't imagine what all still needed doing; Mama had already filled her freezer and fridge with food she could make ahead. But she'd invited Alex over to the house for a meeting, and they musta put their heads together about who was baking what.

The next day, I went to the store to talk with Della about a few things before I headed upstairs to check on Alex. I felt a jolt of fear when I saw how pasty his complexion had turned. Then I had to laugh; it was just flour on his face. I brushed it off with a towel and started in on what I wanted to tell him.

Once again, I needed to explain why Nigel was my best man. I didn't know why this kinda thing got my gut in such a knot, but I wanted Alex to know that he'd always been—and would likely always be—my best man, so to speak. "Della told me about you slipping and calling me *your boy*, and I want you to know you can call me that anytime you want."

We both hemmed and hawed a while, clearing our throats and all. Finally, he changed the subject. "Abit, I know you don't go in for all the wedding shenanigans like bachelor parties and such, but I'd like to take you to lunch today as a sort of pre-wedding special occasion."

"I was just wondering what I'd have for my dinner."

We headed up the Blue Ridge Parkway to the Inn at Jonas Mountain, like we'd done all those year ago. I recalled that being one of the best times in my life.

I drove this time. I was sorry Alex didn't feel up to it, but I loved driving his new Merc. Well, new compared to mine. It was a little quieter (though that diesel engine still rattled), and the leather seats didn't look like old catcher's mitts. As we headed up the Parkway, we talked about this and that for a while. During a quiet spell, I started thinking how marriage was a marker of sorts. Life before and life after. Della and Alex were an important part of my life before. And I knew they'd always be in my life, at least I hoped so, but it would be different from then on. Even so, part of me wished Alex could just keep on buying me new clothes and taking me to Mystery Mountain, like he did when I was a kid.

At the restaurant, we lucked out and got a table next to one of the big plate glass windows. Alex sighed real big as he looked out at a view that drew thoughts away from anything else. When we got round to studying the menu, Alex couldn't believe I remembered what we'd ordered that first time we came there. "You got steak, and I got a burger," I said. "I think we should do the same."

He laughed. "Now that you mention it, I *do* remember that evening, and I believe you only ordered that burger because it was the cheapest thing on the menu. And you kept staring at my steak." Oh, man, he had me there; I could feel the red crawling up my neck. "So let's both get a steak *and* a beer. You couldn't do that last time. Besides, this isn't just about the past—it's also about our future together."

That got me kinda choked up, and while I was kinda blinking, Alex said, "Hey, that's okay. I cried before my wedding, too. And I cried after my divorce. So mind your ways so you don't ever have to do *that*."

Alex was good like that, making you feel comfortable with yourself. We went on to have a fine meal together. It even felt okay to ask about his health.

"Oh, I had a few follow-up treatments, which I hope worked." I knew I had a worried look on my face. "You know, Abit, I'm at an age when I can accept I won't live forever. I've spent my life trying to be in control, even thinking I *was* in control. And it's an illusion. I've made my peace with that, for the most part. And besides, I'm going to be fine."

I reached down and brought out something I'd snuck into the restaurant. I handed him a box, which I'd wrapped in some comics from the newspaper. "I'd planned to wrap it nicer, but our lunch together came up too fast," I said. "It's just something for when you come to Laurel Falls. I figured you don't wear these much in D.C., but maybe you could use anothern for when you come to Laurel Falls. Remember how you bought me all those clothes that *weren't* denim and flannel? It seemed fitting to turn the tables. And to be honest, in the hopes you can spend more time down here."

He looked at the box like it was filled with gold, and I swear he was about to clutch it to his chest. Then he opened it and pulled out the flannel shirt. After a moment he said, "Thanks Abit. I love it. It's just that I'm supposed to be buying the groom presents."

"Yeah, but you always have. Besides, it's only a shirt, and you've bought me whole wardrobes. I just wanted to say thanks for all that."

Then he did something so unlike himself. He put his new shirt on over his other shirt, right there in the restaurant. He buttoned it up and with his hands tried to iron down the creases that went up and down it from being folded in the package. Finally, he patted his chest, like he was giving full approval of my choice. We laughed when people started looking funny at us, and we carried those good feelings all the way back down the mountain.

46

Abit

I still had loads of things to get straight before the wedding. Nigel was coming in on the train in the middle of the night, and I'd offered to pick him up. My other guests, besides Mama and Daddy, were just Della, Alex, Cleva, Duane, and Mary Lou, and they all knew what to do.

It was Fiona's family I was fretting over. Her Auntie Chloe had already come down from Galax, and she wasn't any trouble. But Fiona's father, Quinn O'Donnell, and her sister, Elodie, had flown in from Ireland by way of New York and Asheville. Fiona had driven down there to fetch them. They'd all be staying in her apartment, thank heavens. I wanted to be a good host, but I wasn't clear on how to treat them yet. Or how they'd take to me. I reckoned that was what was really bothering me.

When they drove up, at first I thought Fiona had let her father drive because I saw Fiona get out of the passenger side. That seemed strange. Then I took a closer look. Sure enough, it was the same red hair and freckles, but this person was about six years younger. Had to be Elodie. Next I noticed a white-headed feller struggling out of the backseat, where he'd been lying down. When he got straightened up, I sensed Mr. O'Donnell had lived a life on the rough side, though not one with a shortage of food. Fiona and I both coulda fit in a pair of his pants. But he had a jolly way about him and gave me a bear hug right off the bat.

There was one more guest on my list, at least Mama thought so. Little Andy. (I was still having trouble calling him Andrew.) When we first started planning the wedding, Mama told me she not only wanted me to invite him but she wanted him *in* the wedding.

"What?" I asked, "and stand in as my best *boy*?" She told me there was no call for that kinda lip. "Well, he's *not* my little brother," I said and headed out to my woodshop to get away from her and her crazy notions.

Come to find out, she'd invited him anyway. "Well, that's fine Mama," I told her one evening when all the wedding commotion was bearing down on me. "He can come and eat cake—in fact, I'd like to push his little weaselly face right into the wedding cake—but he's not going to be *in* the wedding."

That set her off crying. I went out to my woodshop again, that time to finish packing up my tools and all, getting ready for the move to my own place. I fumed about why I wasn't enough, not even on my wedding day. She just had to have *Andrew* there. I went on like that for a while, throwing sandpaper and small stuff into boxes, when, as if the hand of Jesus reached down and rested on my shoulder, I felt done with that. I'd held that grudge long enough. I recalled how I used to mentor that kid; I even *liked* him. It wasn't his fault Mama seemed to latch on to him in ways she never could with me. And I liked his spunk in changing his name and all. So *Andrew* was coming on Friday before the wedding and staying all weekend in my old room. And he didn't need to worry about eating his wedding cake any way but with a fork.

Thank heavens all the wedding goings-on didn't seem to ruffle Fiona. We'd been getting along fine and even taking time to practice our music together. My favorite new tune was something for just the two of us: "Liberty." An old fiddle tune Fiona could play without even looking at the music, and I could follow along on my mandolin. I especially liked it because it sounded so merry, like a little bird singing. So many of those old fiddle tunes were mournful, but this one had such sweet notes. Took the edge offa all we had left to do.

We'd spent the better part of the next day moving the heavy stuff into our farmhouse. Including *the* table, which we set down near the front window. (I've always taken to looking outside during mealtime.) I didn't want to think about how it came into being, but I couldn't shake the memory of that day The Doctor showed up at my door. Fiona came over and hugged me. "I saw our initials, Rabbit, when I was polishing the table, getting it ready for *our* home." She gave me a little peck on the cheek, and we went back to the truck for more.

After we'd emptied everything, she could tell something was still eating at me. I told her it was just the wedding commotion and Alex and too much family and I didn't know what else. She went into what would be our bedroom after our honeymoon and came back holding something behind her back.

"I know you've picked up your suit and all, so you're clothes are all ready for the wedding, right?" I nodded. "Well, I believe this will be just the accessory to set everything off." She brought her arms forward and put that flowerdy hat of hers on my head, the same hat I'd borrowed the first day I'd met her, when I thought them con artists were after me. And just like that, I was back at the storytelling festival, reliving that day and how taken I was with her.

"Would you like to borrow it again?" she asked, fussing with the hat on my head to see which angle looked best. "We could add a veil so you could lift it when the preacher says we can kiss." She started laughing at me, and before long, she was laughing *with* me.

47

Della

Mary Lou closed the store early on the wedding day. She'd made a cheerful sign, which she hung on the door before hurrying home to change in time for the four o'clock service. I worried customers would get angry (they'd done that plenty of times before) or feel bad they weren't included, especially with the ceremony and reception in the meadow behind the store.

As guests started to arrive, I noticed a few I didn't know. Likely Fiona's friends from work. And I barely recognized Sheriff Horne in his civvies. *Wonder who invited him? Surely he wasn't crashing,* I thought to myself. Oh well, thank heavens that wasn't any of my business.

The dancefloor Duane built served double-duty for the ceremony. Mildred had dug out a large rug (looking surprisingly new) she'd stored in the barn and lined the perimeter with pots of chrysanthemums—adding color and a modest safety barrier to ensure no one fell off (which just might work given Mildred had forbidden any alcohol before or after the wedding).

Preacher Corky Cochran showed up well ahead of time. With such a perky name, I'd pictured a young man, but he had to be pushing sixty. In spite of the ill-fitting suit, he had a winning smile that put me at ease. Nigel looked striking in his tuxedo; needless to say he was the only formally clad guest, but he was taking his best man duties seriously. Fiona's maid of honor was adorable, but then what else would you expect from the blessings of youth paired with a pretty silk dress?

And, of course, the bride and groom looked stunning—until the ceremony ended. Their faces registered nothing short of horror as Preacher Cochran grabbed one of them under each arm, turned them to face the guests, and pronounced, "Everyone, I'd like you to meet Mister and Mizzruz Vester Bradshaw Junior." He was so proud for them, I doubted he ever realized how appalled they were. And whether out of prudishness or forgetfulness, he didn't tell Abit he could kiss the bride. Well, the joke was on Corky; they'd started a couple of years ago without him.

After the ceremony, the band members rolled up the rug, took over the preacher's place, and by five o'clock, the party was in full swing. We'd lucked out with perfect autumn weather.

I was glad Fiona and Abit hadn't had a chance to change yet. I didn't know when I'd get to see Abit again in a perfectly tailored suit. Hard to believe that was the same kid who'd sat so woebegone out front of Coburn's when

I'd first arrived in Laurel Falls. And Fiona—her hair in an elegant updo with white and orange flowers tucked here and there—looked lovely in her slim-lined ivory linen wedding dress.

In short order, Fiona dispensed with the traditional back toss of the bouquet—a large assortment of meadow flowers with a plump Joe Pye Weed poking out of the center—to all the women interested in marriage. Cleva and I stood well out of range. When Mary Lou caught it, she winked at Sheriff Horne, and it finally hit me—he hadn't been buying milk that day he saved my life; he was coming to see Mary Lou. I'd wondered at the time why he was suddenly buying groceries; he'd never paid for even a soda.

Cleva had borrowed back her old camera from Abit so she could make the rounds and capture the day for him. She was an old hand at getting people to stand together so she could take posed pictures; she also shot plenty of candids.

Finally, the feasting got underway. I was starving; I'd skipped lunch to help Abit find the ring, tie his tie, and calm down a bit. I headed over toward Alex, who was manning the grill, where juicy brats sizzled and Shiloh held court.

"What did the Zen Buddhist say to the hot dog vendor?" he asked the folks crowded around the grill. After a big bite of a brat, he had to swallow hard to get out the punch line: "Make me one with everything."

He was high fiving everyone and laughing, a good bit more than they were. Elodie stood close by, acting (unconvincingly) as though she'd gotten the joke. I figured she was young and sheltered. Or so I thought at the time.

Everyone was howdy-doing and circling the tables Abit had constructed from sawhorses and plywood. The wedding cake sat in the middle of the largest table. Mildred had decorated a two-tiered chocolate cake with creamy white icing and real flowers tucked into green tendrils of piped icing. The rest of the table was filled with a variety of cheeses and cured meats I'd ordered, a smorgasbord of salads from Mildred's kitchen, and breads and party sized-biscuits Alex had baked.

At some point, Nigel decided it was toast time. Something about his demeanor made me think he'd gotten ahold of some whiskey, but I saw Mildred looking at him rather lovingly, so he must have passed her sniff test. (She'd grown fond of Nigel over the years. His old-world politeness exonerated anything untoward from his wayward past.) He gave a robust whistle, and everyone stopped talking.

Nigel spoke to the beauty of transatlantic romances and raised what I assumed was a glass of sparkling cider to the next generation of that tradition. Aunt Chloe shared a story from Fiona's life that was so moving, even that rowdy crowd went quiet for a few moments. Then she livened things up again with an Irish blessing: *As you slide down the banister of life, may the splinters never point the wrong way.* Alex offered a bittersweet toast about "our boy" and how he was looking forward to getting to know Fiona.

The rest of us chose not to offer a toast, either out of shyness (Mildred), orneriness (Vester), or tendency to cry at weddings (me). And no one could find the father of the bride.

Shiloh finished things off with a laugh when he proclaimed, "Ladies and gentlemen, it's been a very emotional day. Even the cake is in tiers." Then he motioned for the band to begin, grabbed Elodie, and stole the dancefloor from the bride and groom. I could tell Abit was relieved he didn't have to do one of those bride-and-groom solo numbers in front of everyone. Fiona stood with her hands on her hips, radiating more than a little sibling rivalry.

The Rollin' Ramblers began playing "Roll in My Sweet Baby's Arms" (without Fiona or Abit but with Sheriff Horne on guitar and Chloe on fiddle). When folks started dancing (well, more like jiggling to the music), Fiona pulled Abit to the dancefloor. She must have given him lessons, because he hoofed it across the floor with remarkable ease. Fiona raised up her dress and let her feet fly.

After a while, Alex turned grill duty over to Cleva, who kept time with her tongs while we danced to "A Good Woman's Love," a sweet bluegrass waltz that was just our speed. As we slowly circled the dancefloor, I was amused by all the little scenes playing out. Fiona danced with Andrew, while Abit stood by looking pleased. Nigel moved gracefully across the floor with Fiona's maid of honor. And Shiloh locked Elodie in a tight embrace, even though the music didn't lend itself to *that*.

Pretty soon, Elodie was hanging all over Shiloh. When the band took a break, Fiona walked toward her sister, presumably to suggest a little propriety. In midstride, she shifted direction and started running toward Abit's woodshop. I could hear strains of singing and wondered if that were the source of her fury.

> *In aid of men like Connolly, Barney, and McCann to fight and die until they drive the British from our lands*

I couldn't believe how fast she made it up those mossy steps, two at a time, her dress pulled up again, this time well above her knees. Abit was right behind, and I wasn't far off. I heard him ask, "Who's Barney?"

"Not now, Rabbit. Help me get him out of here."

> *Young and old, side by side, fighting day to day there are The Army of the People. The Official IRA*

Before I reached the top, Nigel came puffing up the steps, muttering, "V.J., I told you I rather liked the Irish, but this is going too far."

By the time we'd all convened in the woodshop, Quinn O'Donnell was splayed on the floor, leaning against a table saw, drinking from a bottle of whiskey. He burped loudly and prepared to start another verse.

"Here, here, now," Nigel said, lifting Quinn under the arms with surprising strength. "Come on, mate, have ye forgotten about the ceasefire?"

"What bloody sheeshfire?" he answered. "Not on ye life."

"What was he singing?" I asked Nigel.

"The Official IRA song," Fiona spat through clenched teeth. "And where in the hell did he get this?" she asked, pouring the last from a bottle of Jameson on the shop floor. I heard Abit let out a big sigh, knowing it would reek for weeks to come. Fortunately (at least in that case), Mildred never ventured into his shop.

Abit and Nigel finished moving Quinn to an old sofa in the back of the woodshop. I looked around for Alex, who was nowhere to be seen. I knew he was the culprit who'd set up the small bar for guests who wanted it, and he was wisely laying low. But who could have imagined a scene like that? Good thing Mildred was too busy at the reception fussing over Andrew, or she'd've taken her broom to Quinn and Alex and likely me, ruining the rest of the day.

Mercifully, everything ended on a good note. I even danced with Abit, one slow dance. We were both awkward, all his earlier grace with Fiona gone. I didn't know about him, but it felt like sixth-grade dance class with Mr. Ellis. And yet that moment together seemed important, a rite of passage for two adults who loved each other, only now in a different way.

By nine o'clock, Abit and Fiona were driving to their honeymoon spot, and all the guests had gone home. (The Irish contingency had left not long after the IRA debacle.) Alex and Cleva and I turned our backs on the cleanup until the next day. In the meantime, the raccoons and deer were welcome to a fine feast of leftovers.

As we walked toward the front of the store, we stopped short. A strange sculpture loomed in the glow from the security light, rising from and surrounding the bench. I'd been concerned that customers would be angry about early closing, but after a closer look, I realized many had brought small gifts for Abit and Fiona and left them on the bench. *His* bench.

Elbert Totherow had shared a couple of jars of honey and one of sorghum syrup. Someone, I guessed Myrtle Ledford, had made two cornhusk dolls dressed as bride and groom. Homemade jams and piccalilli and potted herbs—even canned tomatoes—filled the bench. Some were wrapped in newspaper and twine, another in white typing paper with ivy vines encircling it. I turned on floodlights around the store and that plus the security light created enough ambient light for Cleva to shoot some decent photographs. They'd at least capture the moment. Alex wanted to help me box up everything, but I could tell it had been a long day for him. He and Cleva sat outside on an old bench while I carried everything inside.

I brought out a bottle of Champagne, and we sat on Abit's now-empty bench together, enjoying the lingering moments of a memorable day. As we sipped our wine in contented silence, I thought about those gifts. Abit was of this place, one of their own. Some like Elbert and Myrtle had believed in him, but too many hadn't given him much of a chance. Now that he had proven them wrong, it seemed as though they were admitting their mistakes and sharing in his joy. Those humble gifts were a shrine of sorts to human foibles and aspirations, misdeeds and forgiveness.

48

Abit

We didn't have the money for a proper honeymoon, but we were both happy enough taking the Rollin' Ramblers' bus to Lake Meacham up in Watauga County. Duane had cleaned it out and, to be honest, aired it out. (I saw him carry off a bucketful of empty beer cans.) It wasn't like one of those buses the big bands had, but we had a bed and a fridge and a little camping kitchen. Duane added some fresh flowers in a vase he'd screwed in behind the driver's seat (which would likely come to hold more than a beer can or two on future band trips).

I figured some fool would hide streamers with tin cans underneath the bus. Before we left, I did a quick check to see if I saw any tucked up there. I didn't find any, but we weren't a mile outta town when I heard cans clanking and banging against the highway. In that big bus, there was nowhere for miles to pull off. I drove on, kinda peeved, but when people started honking and waving, it was hard to stay mad.

We lucked out and found a spot on the lake with the mountains in the background. I took it as a good omen. I knew how easy it was to overlook the beauty I'd grown up with, but these days I wasn't taking *anything* for granted.

Later on, we saw where Duane had stashed a bottle of Champagne in the fridge, along with some leftovers from the feast. Potato salad and ham biscuits and even a coupla slices of our wedding cake. We also found a card from Alex and Della with a big check made out to both of us. We sat there together, man and wife, saying a prayer of sorts we made up on the spot, taking turns recounting all the good things we had going for us.

49

Della

That wedding had been a godsend, taking my mind off my troubles with Christine and my worries about Alex. I think it did Alex a world of good, too. The day following the wedding, after all that stinking cleanup was done, I talked Alex into taking a walk with me. Jake was already in the car.

I couldn't decide where to go, so I just drove. After a while, I found myself heading to the place where Jake and I took that fateful walk during the summer of '85. Maybe I wanted to expunge the bad memories it held, or maybe I just wanted Jake to see one of his favorite spots one more time. I didn't know how much time we still had together. For that matter, I didn't know how much time any of us had together.

"I've missed getting out in the wilderness like this," I told Alex. "D.C. and even the metropolis of Laurel Falls can't compare."

The size and quantity of trees always surprised me, the sun barely making it through their thick canopy. I breathed deeply as we stepped on the walkways padded with needles, their pine scent released with each footstep. And while spring claims to have the best wildflowers (as much because they herald the end of winter), late-summer wildflowers match their beauty, especially the brilliant red cardinal flowers huddled along the creek bank and the carpets of asters hugging the path. We didn't walk that far—neither Jake nor Alex was up to it—but it was long enough to revive our spirits. I hadn't realized how much nature had become a part of my life. The rhythms of the city had their merits, but they couldn't match those of the natural world.

We left Laurel Falls a couple of days later, Jake in the back, Alex riding shotgun. We didn't say much, both of us happy to cling to a fun time a little longer.

50

Abit

When we got back from the lake, I parked the bus where we always did between gigs. As I pulled in, I could see how folks had trampled the grass in the meadow behind the store. That brought up good feelings, remembering our wedding day and all.

It was late—we'd stretched our few days off as far as we could—so no one else was around. I was just as glad; I wanted this time together to last as long as possible. We headed home in the Merc, and everything looked grand as our headlights flashed on our new home. When we got outta the car, Fiona let out a howl when she landed in one of them damn rosebush holes. Millie and I ran over to her, but she said she was okay. We'd soon plant our *own* bushes.

The feeling I got being in my own house with someone I loved—and who loved me—well, I couldn't put words to it. After we unpacked the Merc, we walked through the house together, admiring each room and talking about our plans for making it even better.

The only thing I could find the least bit wrong with the house was the way it sat on the land, making it cold of a morning. The next day, when Fiona asked me to build a fire in the woodstove, I went out to the woodpile and kinda jumped back when I heard that old hag in my head, screaming her curses at us. When I finally got up the nerve to light that fire, we were both holding our breath. Then we started laughing, especially Fiona, who'd done some kinda ritual to cancel the curse. We enjoyed our morning coffee right by the stove, not a burn on us.

Della called from D.C. We spent time catching up, and she swore me to secrecy about the deal she'd worked out for Astrid and Dee. She never wanted them kids to know how it came about.

She also told me to go up to her apartment—I had my own key—because there was something nice up there. When I hung up, I got Millie in the Merc and drove over to Della's. We ran up her steps and went inside, where I saw she'd laid out some photos from the wedding in the same order as the day had gone. I got a kick outta reliving such a fine day, and I particularly liked the last photos—the ones of the bench full of gifts for me and Fiona. We hadn't seen them because we'd parked the bus outta the way and left for our honeymoon by a different route.

I took the boxes Della'd packed with all the gifts and drove straight back home, where I set them on my workbench in the barn. I pulled out each gift, one at a time, and imagined who'd given what. Not a one had signed their names, but I knew whose gift was whose as surely as if they had. Then I got Cleva's pictures out and set the gifts out in a way that mirrored how they'd done it on the bench outside the store.

It was mid-afternoon when Fiona came home from her early shift, and I made her come out, acting like I was having trouble with something in my shop and needed her help. When we got to the door, I put my hands over her eyes.

"What're you doin', Rabbit?" she asked, giggling softly.

I didn't say anythin', just guided her in closer and took my hands away. She looked at the workbench, then up at me, then at the workbench again. She handled each one real careful-like, gently setting them back down, respecting the fine things they were.

Later that week when Shiloh and I were finishing up a sideboard, he got this smirk on his face. "So, how's married life?"

That was such a stupid question, especially after only a coupla weeks, I chose not to answer and kept working. I could tell he was waiting for an answer of some sort, so I told him about the gifts people left us. He nodded in a way that said *go on*. Well, I sure wasn't gonna tell him about our honeymoon, so I mentioned how I was still trying to get Fiona to laugh at my jokes (short of putting on that stupid hat again). "She laughs at yours. Why not mine?" I asked.

He thought a minute, pulling on his mustache. "Well, maybe this one will do the trick." He started laughing before he even told it, so I figured it must have been one of his favorites. "This guy, Homer, goes to prison and in the mess hall, he notices that inmates are standing up and shouting out numbers. 'Twenty-one,' one guy says, and everyone bursts out laughing, cornbread crumbs flying across the tables. Another guy stands up and calls out, 'Eighteen.' Brought the house down, or I guess I should say brought the *big* house down. This goes on for a while, and finally Homer asks his cellmate what was going on. 'Oh, we've all heard the jokes around here so many times, we've given them a number. When someone calls out a number, we think about that joke and laugh.' Homer's eager to fit in, so the next day after someone called out 'Twelve' and got a big laugh, Homer stands up and shouts, 'Ten.' Not even a smile from the crowd. Homer's too embarrassed then, but later that night he asks his cellmate about it. 'Well, Homer, some people can tell a joke, and some can't.'"

Shiloh started laughing again. "V.J., I *know* you can tell that joke!"

51

Della

By the first of November, I hadn't heard from Christine. I was still up in D.C. on deadline with election stories, and I couldn't break away to go after her again. I knew she'd gotten my package of photos, so I figured she knew I meant business. I left a message with Hilde for her to call me and gave her Alex's number.

After a hectic day in the District, talking with a couple of hard-to-pin down House incumbents, I came home to a red light flashing on the answering machine. When I hit play, the caller didn't identify herself, but she didn't need to. I heard Christine say, "It's done. The money will start the middle of this month."

I went to bed feeling good about my plan, but in the night, I woke with a start: Enoch needed to be told his crazy common-law wife was alive in Washington, D.C. Early on, I'd thought about telling him, but with all the schemes and stakeouts and wedding plans, I'd put it off. Maybe the right thing would've been to tell him sooner, but I was afraid he'd overreact or go to the sheriff. I wanted my plan in place first.

When I got back to Laurel Falls after the election, I'd do it. This wasn't anything to discuss on the phone.

52

Della

Alex and I had both been working long nights. Even though we enjoyed the election hoopla (we got to go to one of the victory parties for Clinton), we were both ready for a break in Laurel Falls. Alex didn't whoop that time when we crossed into North Carolina, but our feelings were close to the same. He planned an extended stay until the new year.

I loved having him with me, but I couldn't help but worry. Especially after Abit mentioned he thought Alex looked awfully tired. I told him he was borrowing trouble. Or maybe I just didn't want to see what he was talking about.

I telephoned Enoch as soon as I got back, making it sound as though I just wanted to catch up. He must have heard the seriousness in my voice because he suggested I stop by late-morning, when the kids were in school. I was disappointed I wouldn't get to see Astrid, but I sure didn't want that precocious little girl picking up on my concerns.

When I arrived, Enoch made me a cappuccino—an excellent brew from a more modest machine than Christine's. We sat out on the deck, and I busied myself with my coffee, delaying the news as long as I could. Finally, I just blurted out: "Lilah is still alive, Enoch. And she's married to a very rich man."

His face did that strange thing I'd seen dozens of times when I was a reporter, racing through shock, disbelief, confusion, and then anger. In his case, he ended with relief. He sat quietly for a few moments before speaking. "I think I always knew on some level that she'd run away. I never pictured her dead. But I don't know what to tell the kids. They seem to have gotten over her. During that last year, it was hell when she was around. But I know they must wonder—and worry."

A few months ago when he came by the store, he'd mentioned that he'd taken the kids to a therapist in Chester for several sessions. I hoped they'd worked through some of their worst feelings of loss, because I didn't want him to involve them in the latest plans. "Given what I'm about to tell you, Enoch, I think the best thing is to leave well enough alone," I said. "I know telling Astrid and Dee the truth seems like a parental obligation, but think about it. Christine—yes, she's using her given name these days—made it clear she doesn't want them. Why should they be reminded of that?"

"Yeah, but they don't know what happened to her. That still has to weigh heavily on their little hearts."

I'd decided not to tell him her bipolar antics were made up. That seemed too wicked to share. And again, what good would it do? I just said, "It's your call, Jonathan."

His head snapped around, and he stared at me. I gave him some time. Once he was over yet another surprise, he didn't seem concerned that I knew about his past. "Listen, we didn't do anything but tag along. We were nobodies. Wannabes," he said. "And no one cares about that anymore; the FBI quit looking more than a decade ago. By then, though, we'd created all this," he said, waving his arm around the garden and cabin area, not unlike the way Christine had motioned in her baroque living room. "It would have been impossible to change everything we'd established. Our names, our lives—we'd even gone mainstream with Social Security. We'd never had that before, so once we started ..."

"How'd you get Social Security with fake names?"

"Easy. Lots of people around to help with false documents—one of the benefits of living in the underworld." He also confirmed that they'd never married, so she *was* legally Mrs. Clifford Overton.

"Well, what about your parents? Your family? Aren't they worried about you?"

"Oh, mine paid me with a trust fund to *stay away*. Christine's told her the same thing, only their demands came with no money."

"So if you tell the kids about Christine and your past, they've got a whole lot more baggage to process. And it would ruin my plans."

"*Your* plans?" he barked at me. I quickly explained my scheme involving Christine, and he grew agitated, pacing around the deck. "No way, I mean, *no way* am I letting her back into our lives. We can't take any money from *her.*"

"Only you and I know it's from her. And actually, it's from Clifford, her rich husband, who makes his money ripping off the rest of us as the price of real estate in D.C. skyrockets."

Enoch kept shaking his head no, and I kept making my case, pointing out that Astrid would soon be a teenager—clothes and nicer things meant more then. Dee could go to summer camp—and they could both go to college.

"Okay, okay. I get it." He stopped pacing and rubbed his face.

I explained how the plan worked and that I regretted we couldn't get a lump sum. I didn't trust Christine to keep up her end of the bargain, but I hoped the photos and records from her past would keep her in line. She really didn't want Clifford—or her society friends—to know about all that.

"The money will be doled out monthly," I said. "That way Christine can sneak it out of their joint checking account without Clifford noticing her withdrawals.

Besides, in their bloated budget, it isn't that much money. In all likelihood, he'll never notice—if he even checks their accounts. That's probably left up to some flunky who couldn't care less. Just the excessive expenses of a trophy wife accustomed to luxury. The money will be yours to share and save for the kids' college or whatever they need in the future. It's up to you to decide if a rich uncle died or you won the lottery."

"Oh, I'm not claiming her money as my own. No, *if* I go along with this, I'll tell the kids someone died. I'm not sure how I'd word it—*if* I agree. The kids don't know any kin, so I guess that works in my favor." He ran his fingers through his curly hair until it stood straight up on top. When he didn't say anything for a while, I got my hopes up. Then he added, "But I still don't like it."

"If she doesn't come through with the money, we can let it all go. I promise I'll never mention any of this ever again. I don't want to bring more trouble into your lives. I won't tell Horne a thing about your past—though I've got to warn you. I don't think he'll ever stop looking for that goon who shot him."

"How's that search going?"

"Nowhere. Horne still thinks it was attempted robbery, but he won't ever find him. That guy was a pro."

Enoch looked at his watch. "I've got to run some errands before I pick up the kids at school. I'll let you know something this evening."

He didn't call until the next morning. "Okay," he said without saying hello. "I guess that witch should pay for the heartache she's caused."

53

Abit

Some of the autumn leaves still looked good, coloring the view from our windows with copper and rust, even though Thanksgiving was just a week away. Fiona and I were having a big feast for Mama and Daddy, Della and Alex, Millie and old Jake. Our first.

I was looking forward to decorating for Christmas and spending extra time with Fiona and Millie. We were settling into a comfortable sameness, in a good way. Just leading our lives, without a lot of fuss or bother from others. Mama and Daddy nearabouts forgot me, now that I was leading a life so different from their own. And Quinn and Elodie seemed to think the Atlantic Ocean kept them from even letting us know they'd gotten home safely from the wedding. (We figured we'd've heard if they hadn't.)

But we were enjoying ourselves. I didn't see how life could get any better. I felt so full up with it, I even mentioned something about it to Shiloh, though as soon as I did, I knocked on wood. (Fiona's superstitions were rubbing off on me.)

The next day, I reckoned I hadn't knocked fast enough.

I'd fixed up my woodshop in the barn real nice, and I enjoyed working out there. More often than not, I found myself humming some bluegrass tune I'd been practicing on my mandolin. Shiloh was off that day, so I let it rip as I sang "Way Downtown." But I stopped cold when I saw Fiona standing in the doorway, looking like she'd lost her best friend. She held out something and started cryin'. I looked down and saw her birth control pills in her hand. It took me a moment, but then I got it. They'd failed.

"I swear, Rabbit, I took them faithfully. Just like I promised." She cried so hard I had to hold her up. At first, I couldn't say I didn't feel angry—though panicked was more like it. But then I felt as sad as I ever had, holding that lass who felt she needed to *prove* her honesty to me.

I took the container from her outstretched hand and set it on the workbench. Then I put my arms round her and held on for dear life. I thought about how this had torn us apart before, and I wasn't about to let that happen again. We loved each other, and we were a strong family of three. The only difference was we were gonna be a strong family of four. We'd deal with whatever came our way. I didn't know what Fiona was thinking, but likely it was close to the same, the way she was holding on so tight. There weren't no words for what was passing between us. Just a flood of tears trying to wash away our fears.

54

Abit

My religion was simple enough to say—be kind—but hard to do sometimes. I didn't mean it was hard to be kind to Fiona. I doted on her; I even learned to cook pretty good. And I let her know I didn't want her hiding her happiness about the baby, just because I was eat up with worries.

But I did find it hard to be kind to all the folks who came up and told me *I* should be happier about the baby, as if they knew what was going on inside my head. Or Mama, getting all teary-eyed and asking me if it weren't just the most wonderful thing in the world. All that kinda stuff stirred up something in me that didn't feel kind. Not sure where those feelings were coming from, but I wished I could've made them go away.

Fiona called the little baby Nixie after an Irish sprite. That was a lot better than calling it *it* until we chose a proper name oncet it came into the world. Then Fiona had a sonogram at the hospital where she worked; what with my issues and our curiosity that seemed like a good idea. After we saw it in her belly, we shortened the name to Nix to sound more like a boy. And so far, things looked good.

That test showed he was growing just fine. But it wasn't his outsides I had concerns about; it was more what was going on *inside* his head.

Something about knowing it was a boy got Fiona all worked up over naming him sooner rather than later. I wanted to see what he looked like first. Eventually I gave in, and we started playing with possibilities, narrowing the search down to Colin or Conor, both Irish names that worked in America. But then I put those names through my imaginary panel at the Laurel Falls Elementary School, and there weren't no way I was naming a kid Colin.

"Why not, Rabbit?" Fiona asked, stroking my hair and trying to calm me down. I'd gotten all worked up, likely some kinda flashback to being on the goddam playground myself.

"Because the kids at school would be off and running with that name, that's why. No way."

"Are you daft? What are you talking about?"

"No, I'm not daft. I'm *experienced*. And I can just hear all them names and jokes about bowels and bowel movements and any number of worse things. No way. Now with Conor, well, the worst that would conjure is Conman, and, after all, that's how we met. Seems fitting. You don't think Conor sounds too country clubbish, do you?"

She shook her head like I was crazy. "I like Conor just fine," she said, "and no, it doesn't sound country clubbish, whatever you're on about there." She paused a moment and added, "But what about religion? I came from a strict religion with more rules than I want our boy to grow up with."

"Let's try teaching him to be kind."

As I worked out in my shop, I tried to recall the Bible verses I'd heard as a kid calling on us to welcome all the little children. I couldn't remember the exact verses, but then I didn't need to. I knew it was the right thing to do.

I made all kinds of furniture for that young'un. I musta loved him already, because I put everything I had into his crib, sanding it smooth so he could grab it and gnaw on it without getting splinters. I made a changing table and some simple little chairs for when he could walk and needed to rest. I wanted to make a cradle, but I ran outta time. Fiona had me fixing plenty of other things inside the house, getting ready for Conor.

Fiona decided to keep on working, at least a while longer. She said we needed the money, especially for the baby. Hard to argue with that, but I hated seeing her come home looking so tired. I tried cheering her up with songs on my mandolin and stories about Shiloh and all. One evening, she seemed particularly give out, so I thought she might get a kick outta Shiloh's prison joke. I'd been practicing, and I'd gotten it down pretty good. I told it just like Shiloh did, but when I got to the punch line, Fiona was just like them damn convicts. Not even a smile. "Honey" she said, "just stick to what you do well."

I never could make Fiona laugh at my jokes. She tried to make me feel better by telling me I made her laugh plenty just being Rabbit.

"Well, thanks a lot," I said, kinda peeved.

She brushed the hair out of my eyes. "Oh, darlin', you know what I meant."

55

Della

In the new year, the months seemed to fly by. I could see how busy—even panicked at times—Fiona and Abit were, scrambling to get everything done before the baby was born. When we had coffee or lunch together, Abit often mentioned his long to-do list.

I wanted to do something for Fiona, but I was never keen on those silly baby showers with games and such I'd had to go to for colleagues at work. I was glad to learn the women at the hospital had given Fiona one of those because I just couldn't. Then I thought to myself, *why does it have to be silly?*

Cleva and I planned a simple get-together in April with just the three of us. Alex was back in D.C., but I found some of his scones in the freezer. Cleva outdid herself, making the prettiest carrot cake with little icing carrots indicating each piece. But really, we just wanted to wish Fiona well and make her feel special. I remembered how friends in their last months of pregnancy complained about feeling like beached whales.

We chatted a while, not exactly comfortably but pleasant enough. When Fiona mentioned how Abit refused to name the baby Colin, Cleva, who'd spent more time on playgrounds than all the kids in Laurel Falls combined, agreed. I could tell that put Fiona at rest; Conor really was the better name.

At some point in the afternoon, all my concerns about Fiona melted away. As we shared cake and presents, I knew she was the best thing to happen to Abit. I felt closer to her and wanted her to know how good I felt about their future together. Abit had shared all kinds of fears, and I knew all that couldn't help but affect her, too. I leaned over and said, "I hope you're feeling fine about the baby. Abit is so much more than he'd ever give himself credit for."

"I KNOW THAT," she shouted at me as she raced to the bathroom. Even through the closed door, Cleva and I could hear her crying. We started clearing up the dishes, barely saying a word to each other. When the bathroom door opened, I walked over to her. "I'm sorry, Fiona. Of course you know all that—way better than I do."

She blew her nose and shook her head. "No, I'm the one who's sorry. I guess I'm more tense than I thought. I look like a blob, I feel like shit, and Rabbit is a nervous wreck." She blew her nose again and added, "And Mildred was unkind to me today."

"Don't worry, honey, Abit won't let that happen."

"But it *did* happen," she snapped, then made that motion with her hands that said *I'm sorry*.

"Okay, but it won't happen *again*. You can count on that."

56

Della

I was working in the store when the bell over the door rang. I looked up. Astrid. Wearing new designer jeans and a stylish cotton sweater.

How Christine finally squeezed the money from their account, I'd never know. But I'd heard through Cleva that the school band had new uniforms, and both kids had new bikes. Enoch had come through, making the plan work in a way he could live with.

At first, neither one of us knew what to say. Like a wimp, I let a ten year old break the ice. "I'm sorry I haven't been by much, but it's been hard," she said.

"Honey, you don't have to explain to me. Just glad to see you." We settled in the back and shared some Earl Gray tea and Linzer cookies I'd recently ordered. She licked off the confectioners' sugar first, then ate the shortbread part, popping the jammy center into her mouth last.

"It's nice in here," she said, looking around the backroom. She acted almost her age again and seemed relaxed. "I couldn't come for a while, you know." I did know. Bad memories. Then she added, "I won't be needing to stop by much anymore. Daddy's hiring a housekeeper to do most of the cooking and cleaning."

"That's great news."

"Well, yes and no," she said, systematically dismantling another cookie. "Seems a distant relative died and left us some money."

I played along. "Did you know this relative?"

"No, but it's still sad, in a way, isn't it? I wish I'd met him so I'd know who to thank for what he's doing for us." Back to age twenty-something.

"Well, just send up your thanks to whomever. And you know, you're welcome here whether you buy anything for supper or not. In fact, I'd be delighted to see you, knowing you're not slaving over a hot stove!"

That made her giggle. She reached for another cookie.

57

Abit

I paced round that delivery room, but it was better than being stuck in the waiting room. The air was stuffy and overheated in there, and I would've been nervous and hot. And besides, I *wanted* to be with Fiona and soon Conor.

Fiona had to work awfully hard to bring that boy into the world. I think I held my breath the whole while, until that young'un let loose with a wail that rivaled the Southern Crescent. I stood by Fiona while they tidied him up, and we both sighed as the nurse laid our little boy in his mama's arms. I kissed his little towhead. We were both surprised he wasn't a redhead—or ginger nut, as Fiona called it—but I'd read where that could happen. It just made him all the more special.

But then being special, like me, was what scared me. But I was getting ahead of myself. I couldn't let thoughts like that ruin such a fine day.

Conor changed our lives, for sure. And for the better. I took to him like, well, the only expression that came to mind was flies to stink, but I knew that weren't quite right. Trouble was, I couldn't find any words big enough.

I managed to live most of the time like Della said— one day at a time. I enjoyed little changes in his eyes and how he moved round and wiggled his little arms and legs. We created new routines, and I especially enjoyed bath time, washing that precious little body.

But then his three-month checkup rolled round, and I was eat up again with worries. Fiona didn't seem the least bit concerned, as if she knew he wasn't like me. She admitted she'd never really taken care of babies before, not even as a nurse, but she said she just *knew* he was fine.

Well, I didn't. I barely slept the night before his appointment. I hated to think what the doctor might say.

58

Della

I heard Abit's car before I saw it. He and Fiona and the baby were heading my way while I was out front getting the mail. He slowed the Merc and pulled up next to the mailbox. Conor was so bundled up I could barely see him. His little knit cap had slipped down his forehead when Fiona cradled him close. But I'd seen this before with new parents, adding layers of protection against anything and everything.

Abit rolled down his window and called out, "Della, he's not Abit Junior!"

"He's not your baby?" I asked, puzzled that some changeling had come into their lives.

"No, silly," he said. "The doctor says he's perfect!"

He and Fiona were smiling broadly, and their happiness was contagious. I joined them with a smile of my own, relieved we could put those concerns behind us. But Abit wasn't finished.

"Conor's not like me, Della. He's *better* than me."

That time I couldn't agree. I knew that wasn't possible.

2004

59

Abit

I never gave the first thought to keeping that old house. I hadn't really lived there since I went to The Hicks when I was sixteen year old, and I wasn't about to live there again just because Daddy and Mama left it to me in their wills. As I walked through the almost-empty house, I was surprised to find it in such good shape, especially considering Daddy had died two years earlier—to the day—than Mama.

I'd been working on clearing out the house for some time. Amazing what two pack rats could collect over a lifetime. I could only stand to work on it a day here and there. Fiona'd offered to help, but I didn't want anyone else round.

I'd held a giveaway earlier in the month. I'd put up a notice in Della's store and a small ad in the *Mountain Weekly*. That Saturday, when I opened the doors, people came from all round to cart off old chairs and tables and such. I was happy to see the things go, happy they'd do someone else some good. I'd been working since then to clean out the rest so I could sell the house. But I was in no rush. It had to go to the right person, someone who'd be a good neighbor for Della.

I did find a few things I wanted to keep. Daddy'd stashed four of my best hubcaps in the back of his closet. That was so strange, so unlike him, I had to sit down and hold them for a while. They made my heart ache for him and how he just couldn't let himself show what he was feeling. Of course, I didn't really know why he saved the hubcaps, but it struck me that it musta been somethin' nice.

He'd made me get rid of the collection one summer between semesters at The Hicks, except for a few I'd mounted on my bedroom walls. I couldn't recall why, but likely he'd felt I was pretty much gone from home, and he wanted his barn cleaned out. We made a right penny on them, and I split the money with Daddy. Not sure why I felt I needed to do that. Rent, I guessed, on space for my collection all those years, as if I'd just been a tenant.

In Mama's dresser, I found my elementary school report cards from before Daddy yanked me out. I didn't even look at them. I ripped them into shreds and threw them in one of the bulging plastic bags I'd been dragging from room to room.

I also found a few old toys of mine I planned to share with Conor. He was a fine, imaginative lad. And musical. He could fiddle like a little champ, just like his mama. Thanks to him, the past seven years had been the best of my life. Where oncet I hadn't wanted children, I couldn't imagine life without Conor. I'm proud to say that neither could Mama or Daddy. They took to him like a house a fire. And not just because he wasn't like me. He had his own personality that couldn't help but win your heart.

Of course, everyone was relieved he didn't get my traits, no one more than me. At the same time, I was glad Fiona and I'd agreed not to have any more, if things went as they should. I didn't want to press our luck.

I'd left my room for last. I found a bunch of keepsakes and dusty books, including the two old diaries I planned to share with Della. I rarely wrote anything down any more—other than ideas for furniture or music. As I dug round, I uncovered a thing or two that musta belonged to Andrew, things he'd left behind when he'd stayed in my room so many weekends. Like the tooled leather belt my parents gave him one Christmas.

Oncet Andrew went off to Afghanistan, they needed something to fill their lives, and little Conor did that in a way I never could. It was as if they'd said *here's a clean slate so let's fill it like we never have before.* And by then in my life, that suited me just fine.

Some of my clothes were still in the closet. Flannel shirts with sleeves that wouldn't get past my elbows if I were to try them on. And pants that had been high-water when I wore them all those year ago. When I held them up, I got a good chuckle, somethin' I was needing real bad.

I walked through the house and ran my hand over counters and built-in bookshelves. There weren't any photos of me, but I'd convinced myself that was because they'd never owned a camera. I'd taken so many pictures of Conor I had to build a cabinet for them. Fiona said I should hold up some on the photos, but I didn't think so.

I thought I'd feel regret, revulsion even, when I pulled out all the things Mama and Daddy had collected over the years, but it just looked like somebody's old junk. Broken dishes—oncet part of Mama's best but used so rarely, I couldn't imagine when they'd had a chance to break. Or why she'd held on to all them pieces. And more figurines of happy children than could fit on the mantle or the few shelves we had in the house. Children smiling, holding balloons and puppies and kittens. She musta needed them. Pretending, because our lives were nothin' like that.

After Daddy died, Mama seemed different. Not so nervous, and she laughed more. Maybe because she spent more time with Conor; he couldn't help but make you feel good. Shiloh started visiting with her some, and when I'd stop by to check on her, I'd hear her chuckling over his jokes. (Of course, he told only the clean ones.) She even went on a church bus trip to Asheville and one to Blowing Rock. It seemed a shame she had only a coupla year to enjoy herself that way. But then maybe that kinda freedom proved too much for her.

I packed up for the evening, and I looked over at the store, which was closed at that hour. Della seemed to be working there less and less, Mary Lou keeping shop whole weeks at a time. I couldn't understand why Della had been holed up in her apartment so much; I'd been missing her. I knew she'd tended to Mama, and it was sad and all with her passing, but they were never really friends. Just neighbors doing a good turn for one another from time to time. Then my mind would go crazy worrying that maybe Della was sick or sick at heart. She'd been through a lot over the past few year.

Della did make it to Mama's funeral, which was well-attended. I knew Fiona and I had to be there, but I told her I didn't want Conor to come. She was all into Irish wakes and had a different take on death and funerals, but she agreed.

She did give me hell, though, when I bought a new suit for Mama's funeral. I didn't know about the Irish curse that fell upon anyone wearing new clothes to a funeral; Fiona said it would bring us no end of bad luck. But I couldn't go in my overalls, and the only suit I had was from our wedding, almost eight year ago, and I just didn't want to wear it. It was a happy suit.

The man at the men's shop in Asheville said the new suit I tried on didn't need alterations—that I was a natural. I wasn't sure what that meant, but he straightened the lapels and stood back and admired the fit. Not unlike the way I took a good look at my new furniture pieces.

I did wear an old tie—one of Daddy's. I found it in his closet, good as new; I'm pretty sure he'd never worn it. It was out of date and didn't look all that great with the suit, but it seemed right to wear it for Mama.

When I walked up to the front of the church—well, really, the VFW Hall—and started speaking, I struggled with what to say. I knew Mama loved me, and I loved her. But it was always different. Nothing like what I felt for Fiona or Conor. And I didn't want to make up flowerdy notions about her. I settled on the word *steadfast*. That coulda been her middle name. She'd bought me nice enough clothes, when she could, and she always kept a clean house and made good food, even if her menu was also steadfast. (I got a chuckle then; I think she always took the same two things to church potlucks.) I kept my comments short. I knew Mama would've approved of that.

Andrew sent a real nice note, all the way from Afghanistan. I don't know how he'd heard of her passing, but I appreciated his kindness. I read some of it to the people gathered in her honor. Della choked back a sob during my talk, but mostly she just cried quietly. Not as hard as Bettina Redgrave, who made it her life's work to cry at funerals.

Mama had requested that Fiona and I play "Will the Circle Be Unbroken" on the fiddle and mandolin. Fiona joined me up front, and she carried the melody for us. Glad she made us look good; I felt spent and not up to my usual playing.

After the funeral, I couldn't wait to get home to my boy. I *could* make *him* laugh. I was really good at something Fiona called silly buggers. Fun things together like running and tumbling and tickling. Mollie, a sweet dog who came to live with us when we lost Millie a year back, would join in, too. Fiona would just watch for a while and finally, when she couldn't hold back any longer, jump in and join us.

Times like that were the best. They felt more like family than any othern.

60

Della

Whole weeks had gone by when I didn't go to work. I just couldn't face that store. In fact, I could barely get out of bed. Mary Lou accepted the burden of handling everything herself without complaint, but I knew I was taking advantage. And yet the idea of dealing with those whiney customers sent me back under the covers. The price was too high, the can was dented, the bread didn't feel fresh enough (because it wasn't Bunny Bread with a thousand additives). One customer even complained that a new brand of ice cream was *too creamy*!

At that moment, I hated them all. They'd been part of the world that had made me jump through hoops because I wasn't born in Laurel Falls and made Abit live under a cloud of lies. All that hate—theirs and mine—made bile rise in my throat.

Often over the past weeks, when I looked out the window, I'd see Abit working hard on that house of horrors next door. I wondered who would become my neighbors. They'd need an exorcism to rid it of evil.

When Mildred got sick, a little more than a year after Vester died, I started going over and sitting with her. Just reading to her and chatting when she felt up to it.

After she told me her lie, I kept playing that pointless game of "if only." If only I hadn't gone over that day. If only she'd fallen asleep before she spoke to me that last time. But it had happened, and I didn't know how I could live with it.

I was reading *Gone with the Wind*, a book she loved. I wasn't so keen on it, but that wasn't the point. As I read a passage about Ashley Wilkes, she held up her hand for me to pause. With tears rolling down her cheeks, she said, "I wished I'd had a husband like that."

At first I thought she was hallucinating, but then I understood. She was comparing Vester to the man in the book. "He beat me, you know," she said, her voice so soft I struggled to hear. "Early on in our marriage, especially while I was in the family way with Vester Junior. One time, I fell down the steps, and I almost died. I should say *we* almost died. Vester and I never admitted how my fall happened, but the doctor knew. He warned Vester that if anythin' like that happened again, and I lost the baby, that would be, uh, oh, what did he call it? Infant side, or somethin' like that. I didn't want to think about it, so I never tried to look it up. Besides, I *knew* what it meant. The doctor did warn us that our baby could be damaged from my fall. Slow—or worse. Fortunately, he was just slow."

It took several long moments for what she had just told me to register. When I fully grasped it, I felt such rage, my fists clenched, wrinkling the pages of the book. I forced myself to relax, which sent the book tumbling to the floor. My hands now free, I imagined grabbing Mildred's pillow and smothering her. In all honesty, that was the least of the things I wanted to do to her.

She broke through my wicked thoughts. "Now, don't ever tell our boy about this."

My heart clenched at the words *our boy*, though I figured she'd meant hers and Vester's. But I couldn't let it rest. "Whose boy?"

"Ours, your'un and mine. Abit, Vester Junior," looking at me as though I were the one losing her grip on life. I could only nod, grateful I didn't have to speak. "Vester never touched me that way again, but I watched as he took it out on that poor boy."

I was amazed she was that insightful about Vester's behavior toward his son, but she was still awash in denial. Who was she kidding? She could have done so much more to help Abit. Later on, she did seem proud of him. Even Vester started to show his appreciation of Abit's woodworking—and Fiona and his grandson. But that was after three decades of ridicule and neglect.

But never against Conor. She and Vester loved him, and what wasn't to love about that little one? He was happy and playful and bright, as if his birth had vanquished all the sorrows and wants of generations before him.

The doctor told me Mildred had another month to live, but I knew she wouldn't last that long. (And not because of my thoughts of helping her along.) The next evening after Mildred made her confession, she seemed at peace and passed away.

That left me the one carrying an unbearable weight.

A darkness hung over me after her death, so pronounced that people asked about it. I made out that I was struggling with Mildred's passing—and troubles of my own. I would honor Mildred's wish; I'd never lay the burden of that truth on Abit. But I felt sick from so many secrets that colored our lives. Like the way Abit and Fiona, loving parents, were not planning on a larger family, all because of a lie.

Thoughts of how much pain had been inflicted by Vester's fists one day in 1969—and how he'd fostered even more pain over the next thirty years—made me recoil from the world. As I lay in my bed, day after day, I endured the darkest thoughts. I tried not to think them, but they came unbidden. I imagined digging up Vester and Mildred and stuffing them in my Jeep so I could drive them to the dump to lie among the detritus of life. No consecrated ground for them. Yank them out of those ridiculously expensive coffins they chose for themselves and throw them on the trash heap they deserved. And while I was at it, I'd round up those church members who'd made Abit's life so difficult and make them watch, tell them their high and mighty Mildred and her heathen husband had ruined that boy's life, until he went deep within and found the strength to make his life a wonder.

Eventually, I came to appreciate that my vile fantasies weren't all bad. As they played out, they burned through the painful story Mildred had thrust on me, and slowly I began to heal.

I moldered inside my apartment for a couple more days until I finally got sick of myself. I heard my own words *one day at a time* ring in my ears. I got up, showered, dressed, and made some toast and tea. I knew I had choices. Whether or not to be angry. Whether or not to ruin any given day.

I heard laughter outside and walked over to my bedroom window. Down in the meadow, Conor and Fiona, Abit and Mollie played with a joy they'd earned a hundred times over. Abit picked up Conor and did that raspberry thing that turned children into a bundle of giggles. I recalled how Jake and Abit had loved to romp around back there, and for just a moment, while I watched them play, memories of Jake melded with Abit's family now. Damn it was good to see that dog again. Then just as quickly, he was gone, but my heart felt fuller than it had in days.

As I watched Conor running around like a healthy seven year old, I felt relief knowing they wouldn't be moving into that house next door. The circle *had* been broken. Mollie began chasing Conor, and when he squealed with delight, I saw a look of love pass between his parents so strong I could feel it where I stood.

The words "indomitable human spirit" sprang to mind from somewhere bigger than me. At that moment, something washed over me that could only be called a blessing. I sensed how lucky I was to witness such strength and courage to live fully, whatever the odds. I knew all we really had was one another, and I wanted to be with them, the people I loved. I hurried to finish dressing.

When I opened my front door, I heard a familiar sound—Alex's noisy car approaching, which that day sounded as beautiful as a mockingbird's song. As I headed down the stairs, I quickened my pace, eager to join my family.

Discover how Della and Abit's saga started!

Excerpt from
Book One
in the Appalachian Mountain
Mysteries Trilogy: *A Life for a Life*

Prologue

September 2004

My life was saved by a murder. At the time, of course, I didn't understand that. I just knew I was having the best year of my life. Given all the terrible things that happened, I should be ashamed to say it, but that year was a blessing for me.

I'd just turned fifteen when Della Kincaid bought Daddy's store. At first nothing much changed. Daddy was still round a lot, getting odd jobs as a handyman and farming enough to sell what Mama couldn't put by. And we still lived in the house next door, though Mama banned me from going inside the store. She said she didn't want me to be a nuisance, but I think she was jealous of "that woman from Washington, D.C."

So I just sat out front like I always did when Daddy owned it, killing time, chatting with a few friendly customers or other bench-sitters like me. I never wanted to go inside while Daddy had the store, not because he might have asked me to help, but because he thought I *couldn't* help. Oh sure, I'd go in for a Coca-Cola or Dr. Pepper, but, for the most part, I just sat there, reared back with my chair resting against the outside wall, my legs dangling. Just like my life.

I've never forgotten how crazy it all played out. I *had* forgotten about the two diaries I'd kept that year. I discovered them while cleaning out our home after Mama died in April. (Daddy had passed two years earlier, to the day.) They weren't like a girl's diary (at least that's what I told myself, when I worried about such things). They were notes I'd imagined a reporter like Della or her ex-husband would make, capturing the times.

I'd already cleaned out most of the house, saving my room for last. I boxed up my hubcaps, picking out my favorites from the ones still hanging on my bedroom walls. (We'd long ago sold the collection in the barn.) I tackled the shelves with all my odd keepsakes: a deer jaw, two dusty geodes, other rocks I'd found that caught my eye, like the heart-shaped reddish one—too good not to keep. When I gathered a shelf full of books in my arms, I saw the battered shoebox where I'd stashed those diaries behind the books. I sat on my old bed, the plaid spread dusty and faded, and started to read. The pages had yellowed, but they stirred up fresh memories, all the same. That's when I called Della (I still looked for any excuse to talk with her), and we arranged a couple of afternoons to go over the diaries together.

We sat at her kitchen table and talked. And talked. After a time or two recollecting over the diaries, I told Della I wanted to write a book about that year. She agreed. We were both a little surprised that, even after all these years, we didn't have any trouble recalling that spring.

April 1985

1   Abit

Four cop cars blocked our driveway.

I thought I might've dreamed it, since I'd fallen asleep on the couch, watching TV. But after I rubbed my eyes, all four cars was still there. Seeing four black-and-whites in a town with only one could throw you.

All I could think was *what did I do wrong*? I ran through my day real quick-like, and I couldn't come up with anything that would get me more than a backhand from Daddy.

I watched a cop walking in front of the store next door, which we shared a driveway with. As long as I could remember, that store hadn't never had four cars out front at the same time, let alone four *cop* cars. I stepped outside, quietly closing our front door. The sun was getting low, and I hoped Mama wudn't about to call me in to supper.

I headed down our stone steps to see for myself. Our house sat on a hill above the store, which made it close enough that Daddy, when he still owned the store, could run down the steps (twenty of 'em, mossy and slick after a rain) if, say, a customer drove up while he was home having his midday dinner. But of an evening, those same steps seemed to keep people from pestering him to open up, as Daddy put it, "to sell some fool thing they could live without 'til the next morning."

I was just about halfway down when the cop looked my way. "Don't trouble yourself over this, Abit. Nothing to see here." That was Lonnie Parker, the county's deputy sheriff.

"What do you mean nothing to see here? I ain't seen four cop cars all in one place in my whole life."

"You don't need to worry about this."

"I'm not worried," I said. "I'm curious."

"You're curious all right." He turned and spat something dark onto the dirt drive, a mix of tobacco and hate.

That's how it always went. People talked to me like I was an idiot. Okay, I knew I wudn't as smart as others. Something happened when Mama had me (she was pretty old by then), and I had trouble making my words just right sometimes. But inside, I worked better than most people thought. I used to go to school, but I had trouble keeping up, and that made Daddy feel bad. I wudn't sure if he felt bad for me or him. Anyways, they took me out of school when I was twelve, which meant I spent my days watching TV and hanging out. And being bored. I could read, but it took me a while. The bookmobile swung by every few weeks, and I'd get a new book each time. And I watched the news and stuff like that to try to learn.

I was named after Daddy – Vester Bradshaw Jr. – but everyone called me Abit. I heard the name Abbott mentioned on the TV and asked Mama if that was the same as mine. She said it were different but pronounced about the same. She wouldn't call me that, but Daddy were fine with it. A few year ago, I overheard him explaining how I came by it.

"I didn't want him called the same as me," Daddy told a group of men killing time outside the store. He was a good storyteller, and he was enjoying the attention. "He's a retard. When he come home from the hospital, and people asked how he was doin', I'd tell 'em, 'he's a bit slow.' I wanted to just say it outright to cut out all the gossip. I told that story enough that someone started calling him Abit, and it stuck."

Some jerk then asked if my middle name were "Slow," and everybody laughed. That hurt me at the time, but with the choice between Abit and Vester, I reckoned my name wudn't so bad, after all. Daddy could have his stupid name.

Anyways, I wudn't going to have Lonnie Parker run me off my own property (or nearabouts my property), so I folded my arms and leaned against the rock wall.

I grabbed a long blade of grass and chewed. While I waited, I checked out the hubcaps on the cars—nothing exciting, just the routine sort of government caps. Too bad, 'cause a black-and-white would've looked really cool with Mercury chrome hubcaps. I had one in my collection in the barn back of the house, so I knew what I was talkin' about.

I heard some loud voices coming from upstairs, the apartment above the store, where Della lived with Jake, some kind of mixed hound that came to live with her when she lived in Washington, D.C. I couldn't imagine what Della'd done wrong. She was about the nicest person I'd ever met. I loved Mama, but Della was easier to be round. She just let me be.

Ever since Daddy sold the store, Mama wouldn't let me go inside it anymore. I knew she was jealous of Della. To be honest, I thought a lot of people were jealous a lot of the time and that was why they did so many stupid things. I saw it all the time. Sitting out front of the store most days, I'd hear them gossiping or even making stuff up about people. I bet they said things about me, too, when I wudn't there, off having my dinner or taking a nap.

But lately, something else was going on with Mama. Oncet I turned fifteen year old, she started snooping and worrying. I'd seen something about that on TV, so I knew it were true: People thought that any guy who was kinda slow was a sex maniac. They figured since we weren't one-hundred percent "normal," we walked round with boners all the time and couldn't control ourselves. I couldn't speak for others, but that just weren't true for me. I remembered the first one I got, and it sure surprised me. But I'd done my experimenting, and I knew it wouldn't lead to no harm. Mama had nothin' to worry about, but still, she kept a close eye on me.

Of course, it was true that Della was real nice looking—tall and thin, but not skinny. She had a way about her—smart, but not stuck up. And her hair was real pretty—kinda curly and reddish gold, cut just below her ears. But she coulda been my mother, for heaven's sake.

After a while, Gregg from the Forest Service and the sheriff, along with some other cops, started making their way down Della's steps to their cars.

"Abit, you get on home, son," Sheriff Brower said. "Don't go bothering Ms. Kincaid right now."

"Go to hell, Brower. I don't need your stupid advice." Okay, that was just what I wanted to say. What I really said was, "I don't plan on bothering Della." I used her first name to piss him off; young people were supposed to use grownups' last names, but she'd asked me to call her Della. Then I added, "And I don't bother her. She likes me."

But he was already churning dust in the driveway, speeding onto the road.

2   Della

I heard Jake whimpering as I sank into the couch. I'd closed him in the bedroom while the sheriff and his gang of four were here. Jake kept bringing toys over for them to throw, and I could see how irritated they were getting. I didn't want to give them reason to be even more unpleasant.

"Hi there, boy," I said as I opened the door. "Sorry about that, buddy." He sprang from the room and grabbed his stuffed rabbit. I scratched his ears and threw the toy, then reclaimed the couch. "Why didn't we stay in today, like I wanted?"

Earlier, I'd thought about skipping our usual hike. It was my only day off, and I wanted to read last Sunday's *Washington Post*. (I was always a week behind since I had to have the papers mailed to me.) But Jake sat by the door and whined softly, and I sensed how cooped up he'd been with all the early spring rains.

Besides, those walks did me more good than Jake. When I first moved to Laurel Falls, the natural world frightened me. Growing up in Washington, D.C. hadn't prepared me for that kind of wild. But gradually, I got more comfortable and started to recognize some of the birds and trees. And wildflowers. Something about their delicate beauty made the woods more welcoming.

Trilliums, pink lady's slippers, and fringed phacelia beckoned, encouraging me to venture deeper.

Of course, it didn't help that my neighbors and customers carried on about the perils of taking long hikes by myself. "You could be murdered," they cried. "At the very least you could be raped," warned Abit's mother, Mildred Bradshaw, normally a quiet, prim woman. "And what about perverts?" she'd add, exasperated that I wasn't listening to her.

Sometimes Mildred's chant "You're so alone out there" nagged at me in a reactive loop as Jake and I walked in the woods. But that was one of the reasons I'd moved here. I *wanted* to be alone. I longed to get away from deadlines and noise and people. And memories. Besides, I argued with myself, hadn't I lived safely in D.C. for years? I'd walked dark streets, sat face-to-face with felons, been robbed at gunpoint, but I still went out whenever I wanted, at least before midnight. You couldn't live there and worry too much about crime, be it violent, white-collar, or political; that city would grind to a halt if people thought that way.

As Jake and I wound our way, the bright green tree buds and wildflowers soothed my dark thoughts. I breathed in that intoxicating smell of spring: not one thing in particular, but a mix of fragrances floating on soft breezes, signaling winter's retreat. The birds were louder too, chittering and chattering in the warmer temperatures. I was lost in my reverie when Jake stopped so fast I almost tripped over him. He stood still, ears alert.

"What is it, boy?" He looked up at me, then resumed his exploration of rotten squirrels and decaying stumps.

I didn't just love that dog, I admired him. He was unafraid of his surroundings, plowing through tall fields of hay or dense forests without any idea where he was headed, not the least bit perturbed by bugs flying into his eyes or seeds up his nose. He'd just sneeze and keep going.

We walked a while longer and came to a favorite lunch spot. I nestled against a broad beech tree, its smooth bark gentler against my back than the alligator bark of red oak or locust. Jake fixated on a line of ants carrying off remnants from a picnic earlier that day, rooting under leaves and exploring new smells since his last visit. But mostly he slept. He found a sunspot and made a nest thick with leaves, turning round and round until everything was just right.

Jake came to live with me a year and a half ago when a neighbor committed suicide, a few months before I moved south. We both struggled at first, but when we settled here, the past for him seemed forgotten. Sure, he still ran in circles when I brushed against his old leash hanging in the coat closet, but otherwise he was officially a mountain dog. I was the one still working on leaving the past behind.

I'd bought the store on a whim after a week's stay in a log cabin in the Black Mountains. To prolong the trip, I took backroads home. As I drove through Laurel Falls, I spotted the boarded-up store sporting a For Sale sign. I stopped, jotted down the listed phone number, and called. Within a week, I owned it. The store was in shambles, both physically and financially, but something about its bones had appealed to me. And I could afford the extensive remodeling it needed because the asking price was so low.

Back in my D.C. condo, I realized how much I wanted a change in my life. I had no family to miss. I was an only child, and my parents had died in an alcoholic daze, their car wrapped around a tree, not long after I left for college. And all those editors and deadlines, big city hassles, and a failed marriage? I was eager to trade them in for a tiny town and a dilapidated store called Coburn's General Store. (Nobody knew who Coburn was—that was just what it had always been called, though most of the time it was simply Coburn's. Even if I'd renamed it, no one would've used that name.)

In addition to the store, the deal included an apartment upstairs that, during its ninety-year history, had likely housed more critters than humans, plus a vintage 1950 Chevy pickup truck with wraparound rear windows. And a bonus I didn't know about when I signed the papers: a living, breathing griffon to guard me and the store—Abit.

I'd lived there almost a year, and I treasured my days away from the store, especially once it was spring again. Some folks complained that I wasn't open Sundays (blue laws a distant memory, even though they were repealed only a few years earlier), but I couldn't work every day, and I couldn't afford to hire help, except now and again.

While Jake and I sat under that tree, the sun broke through the canopy and warmed my face and shoulders. I watched Jake's muzzle twitch (he was already lost in a dream), and chuckled when he sprang to life at the first crinkle of wax paper. I shooed him away as I unwrapped my lunch. On his way back to his nest, he stopped and stared down the dell, his back hairs spiking into a Mohawk.

"Get over it, boy. I don't need you scaring me as bad as Mildred. Settle down now," I gently scolded as I laid out a chunk of Gruyere I'd whittled the hard edges off, an almost-out-of-date salami, and a sourdough roll I'd rescued from the store. I'd been called a food snob, but these sad leftovers from a struggling store sure couldn't support that claim. Besides, out here the food didn't matter so much. It was all about the pileated woodpecker trumpeting its jungle call or the tiny golden-crowned kinglet flitting from branch to branch. And the waterfall in the distance, playing its soothing continuo, day and night. These walks kept me sane. The giant trees reminded me I was just a player in a much bigger game, a willing refugee from a crowded, over-planned life.

I crumpled the lunch wrappings, threw Jake a piece of roll, and found a sunnier spot. I hadn't closed my eyes for a minute when Jake gave another low growl. He was sitting upright, nose twitching, looking at me for advice. "Sorry, pal. You started it. I don't hear anything," I told him. He gave another face-saving low growl and put his head back down.

"You crazy old hound." I patted his warm, golden fur. Early on, I wondered what kind of mix he was—maybe some retriever and beagle, bringing his size down to medium. I'd asked the vet to hazard a guess. He wouldn't. Or couldn't. It didn't matter.

I poured myself a cup of hot coffee, white with steamed milk, appreciating the magic of a thermos, even if the contents always tasted vaguely of vegetable soup. That aroma took me back to the woods of my childhood, just two vacant lots really, a few blocks from my home in D.C.'s Cleveland Park. I played there for hours, stocked with sandwiches and a thermos of hot chocolate. I guessed that was where I first thought of becoming a reporter; I sat in the cold and wrote up everything that passed by—from birds and salamanders to postmen and high schoolers sneaking out for a smoke.

A deeper growl from Jake pulled me back. As I turned to share his view, I saw a man running toward us. "Dammit, Mildred," I swore, as though the intruder were her fault. The man looked angry, pushing branches out of his way as he charged toward us. Jake barked furiously as

I grabbed his collar and held tight. Even though the scene was unfolding just as my neighbor had warned, I wasn't afraid. Maybe it was the Madras sport shirt, so out of place on a man with a bushy beard and long ponytail. *For God's sake*, I thought, *how could anyone set out in the morning dressed like that and plan to do harm*? A hint of a tattoo— a Celtic cross?—peeked below his shirt sleeve, adding to his unlikely appearance.

As he neared, I could see his face wasn't so much angry as pained, drained of color.

"There's some … one," his voice cracked. He put his hands on his thighs and tried to catch his breath. As he did, his graying ponytail fell across his chest.

"What? Who?"

"A body. Somebody over there," he said, pointing toward the creek. "Not far, it's …" he stopped again to breathe.

"Where?"

"I don't know. Cross … creek." He started to run.

"Wait! Don't go!" I shouted, but all I could see was the back of his shirt as he ran. "Hey! At least call for help. There's an emergency call box down that road, at the car park. Call Gregg O'Donnell at the Forest Service. I'll go see if there's anything I can do."

He shouted, "There nothing you can do," and kept running.

Jake led the way as we crashed through the forest, branches whipping our faces. I felt the creek's icy chill, in defiance of the day's warmth, as I missed the smaller stepping stones and soaked my feet. Why didn't I ask the stranger more details or have him show me where to find the person? And what did "across the creek" mean in an eleven-thousand-acre wilderness area? When I stopped to get my bearings, I began to shiver, my feet numb. Jake stopped with me, sensing the seriousness of our romp in the woods; he even ignored a squirrel.

We were a pack of two, running together, the forest silent except for our heavy breathing and the rustle we made crossing the decaying carpet beneath our feet. Jake barked at something, startling me, but it was just the crack of a branch I'd broken to clear the way. We were both spooked.

I stopped to rest on a fallen tree as Jake ran ahead, then back and to the right. Confused, he stopped and looked at me. "I don't know which way either, boy." We were just responding to a deep, instinctual urge to help. "You go on, Jake. You'll find it before I will."

And he did.

3 Abit

Nobody paid me no attention. They either ignored me, like Daddy, or they thought I was a no count. Oncet I got over the hurt, or didn't care so much, I could see how that had its good points. They thought since they didn't notice me, I didn't see them. If they only knew.

That evening, all I could think about was Della and what them cops had been doing up in her apartment. Four cars and six men. I wudn't even hungry for supper. Mama looked at me funny; she knew I usually didn't have no trouble putting away four of her biscuits covered in gravy.

"Eat your supper, son. What's wrong with you?" she scolded, like I were eight year old. Well, what did she think? Like we'd ever had a day like that before. I asked to be excused, and Daddy nodded at her. I couldn't figure out why they weren't more curious about everything.

"Do you know what's going on?" I asked.

Daddy just told me to run along. Okay, fine. That was my idea in the first place.

Even though the store were closed, I headed to my chair. A couple of year ago, I'd found a butt-sprung caned chair thrown behind the store. I fixed it with woven strips of inner tube, which made it real comfortable, especially when I'd lean against the wall. I worried when Daddy sold the store that the new owner would gussy everything up and get rid of my chair. But Della told me I was welcome to lean on her wall any day, any time. Then she smiled at me and asked me to stop calling her Mrs. Kincaid; I was welcome to call her Della.

I liked sitting there 'cause I could visit with folks, and not everyone talked to me like Lonnie and the sheriff. Take Della's best friend, Cleva Hall, who came by at least oncet a week. She insisted on calling me Vester, which was kind of weird since I wudn't used to it. At first, I thought she was talking about Daddy. But then I reckoned she had trouble calling me Abit, which was pretty nice when I thought about it.

I'd been on my own most of my life. Mama and Daddy kinda ignored me, when they weren't worried I was getting up to no good. And I didn't fit in with other folks. Della didn't neither, but she seemed okay with that. She chatted with customers and acted polite, but I could tell she weren't worried about being accepted. Which was good, since folks hadn't accepted her. Sure, they bought her food and beer, but that was mostly 'cause the big store was a good ten or more mile away. They'd act okay to her face, but they didn't really like her 'cause "she wudn't from here." Truth be told, I liked her extra 'cause she wudn't from here.

I couldn't understand why she chose to live in our town. It weren't much, though I hadn't never been out of the county, so how would I have known whether it was good or not? I had to admit that the falls were pretty to look at, and even Daddy said we was lucky to live near them. And we did have a bank, a real estate and law office combined, a dry goods store, Adam's Rib and few other restaurants (though we never ate out as a family). And some kinda new art store. But there wudn't a library or gas station or grocery store—except for Della's store, which sat two mile outside of town on the road to the falls.

I felt kinda stupid sitting out front with the store closed and all, but I hoped Della would hear me tapping the chair against the wall and come down to talk with me. Mama didn't like me to be out after supper, though I told her I was getting too old for that. It was funny—Mama was a Bible-readin' Christian, but she always thought the worst things. Especially at night. She never told me this, but I figured she thought demons came out then. (Not that she weren't worried about demons during the day, too.) I hated to think of the things that went through her head. Maybe I was slow, but so be it if that meant I didn't have to wrestle with all that.

I looked up at Della's big window but couldn't see nothin'. I wanted to know if she was all right—and, sure, I wanted to find out what was going on, too. Then a light went on in Della's kitchen. "Oh, please, please come downstairs," I said out loud. But just as fast, the light went out.

4   Della

I switched off the kitchen light and limped back to the couch. No aspirin in the bedside table or in the bathroom or kitchen cabinets. Good thing I lived above a store.

Earlier in the woods, I'd twisted my ankle as I scrambled over a mass of tangled limbs trying to get to the open space where Jake waited, barking. Under the towering canopy of giant oaks, little grew, creating a hushed, cathedral-like space. Usually. Jake finally quit barking when he saw me, but he began a strange primal dance, crouching from side to side as he bared his teeth and emitted ugly guttural sounds. I closed my eyes, trying to will away what I knew lay ahead.

A young woman leaned against a fallen tree trunk blanketed in moss. Her head flopped to one side, long black hair covering half her face, though not enough to hide the vomit that pooled on her left shoulder and down her sleeve. She looked vaguely familiar; I'd probably seen her at the store.

I edged closer and reached out to feel her neck. Cold and silent. She looked up at me with the penetrating stare of the dead; I resisted the urge to close her eyes.

The woman, her skin smooth and clear, seemed no older than twenty or so, but her face was locked in a terrible grimace. Pain would do that, possibly the last sensation she'd felt. Just below her left hand lay an empty syringe. I thought about drug overdose or possible suicide. I'd seen both before.

I knew it wouldn't be long before the sun slipped behind the mountains and took the day's warmth with it. We needed help, soon. I held out little hope that Madras Man would call Gregg. And yet, for some reason, I didn't want to leave the young woman alone.

For the first time in what felt like hours, I thought about the store, which really wasn't that far away, as the crow flies. And Abit, who was usually around, even on a day the store was closed. I looked at Jake and recalled how he somehow knew the command, "Go home." I had no idea how he'd learned it, but he'd built an impressive reputation on it. Not long after we moved to Laurel Falls, Vester ordered Jake off his porch. (Leave it to Jake to find the sunniest spot to lie in.) He told him, "Go home, Jake." And he did. He stood up, combed his hair (that all-over body shaking dogs do), and trotted down to the store, scratching on the door for me to let him in. The men hanging out on the benches started laughing and calling him Rin Tin Tin, admiring his smarts.

I searched through my pack for something to write on, but it offered only keys, wallet, and remnants of lunch. I looked at the woman's backpack. *No, I couldn't*, I told myself. But as long shadows blanketed the mountains, I opened a side compartment and rifled through it. I found a small, blank notebook with an attached pen, tore out a sheet, and wrote a note describing the location, best I could. I wiped my prints off the pen and notebook, and put them back in the pack. The note went inside the bread bag I'd stashed in my pocket after lunch; I tied it to Jake's collar.

"Go home, Jake. Go home!" It was a longshot, but worth a try. His brown eyes looked sad, but then they always did. "Go home, Jake. Be a good boy."

The third time I said it, he turned and ran, though not down the path we'd taken. *God, I hope he knows where he's going*, I thought, as he raced up the creek bank. And I prayed Mildred hadn't called Abit inside.

I watched Jake climb the steep trail and head over the ridge. When the last of his golden fur disappeared below the horizon, I laid back against the red oak, avoiding the stare of the dead woman. It would be at least an hour before anyone could get there.

I tried to rest, but when my eyes closed, unwelcomed memories rushed to mind. I reopened them. That's when I saw the dead woman turn her head toward me. I screamed, but quickly felt foolish. It was just the wind blowing her long hair.

I knew not to touch anything. I'd been involved in several police investigations in D.C. and watched enough television shows to know the drill. But eventually, curiosity won out. I crawled over to her, pulled my sleeve over my hand to avoid fingerprints, and began carefully rummaging through the backpack again, trying to find out who she was and where she'd come from.

Her wallet contained twenty-six dollars and a few coins, but all the slots normally bulging with credit cards and driver's license were empty. I also found a syringe case, the kind diabetics carry with them. Otherwise, the pack held only an apple and a scarf. No keys or identifiers of any kind.

I was getting stiff, so I stood, stretched, and started pacing. From a different angle, I noticed a corner of white barely sticking out of the left pocket of her flannel shirt. I pulled down my sleeve again and removed the note. I clumsily opened the handwritten note with my makeshift gloved hand.

I'm tired of so much sorrow.
My life or death doesn't matter. L.

I struggled to refold the note and slip it back into the pocket. I knew I didn't have any connection to this death, unlike a tragedy I'd witnessed in D.C., but my nerves felt raw. I kept walking. I started to shiver from the cold, but wouldn't allow myself to borrow anything from her stash. I found another smooth beech tree surrounded by brush that sheltered me from the wind, scrunched down, and waited.

My thoughts drifted back to my home and office near Dupont Circle, where I wrote for a variety of magazines and newspapers. I had a nickname among colleagues—Ghoulfriend—because I somehow kept getting assignments for sad and even violent stories. I was good at it, maybe because I took the time to understand both the backstory and the current story. I covered unimaginable situations, except by those who'd suffered them. Men who passed as loving fathers during the workday but turned into monsters in the basements of their family homes. Women who grew up with abuse and perpetuated that pattern onto another generation. Men so troubled by wars that it seemed only natural to kill—including themselves, either intentionally or through the slow death of drugs and alcohol. I recalled the relief I always felt when I'd hear about their passing, and how I still grappled with that. It seemed wrong to be glad someone died, but when their suffering never stopped, it was hard *not* to be thankful they'd finally been released from so much pain.

I stood again and paced around the natural enclosure. I noticed some British soldiers, the green matchstick lichen with bright red "hats," standing at attention atop a huge fallen trunk, its center hollowed out by rain and time and animals seeking shelter. The birds were singing again—or was I just hearing them again? Two nuthatches flittered through a nearby stand of white pines. A cluster of spring beauty eased my mind, until I saw they were growing inside the skull of an opossum. I kept moving.

As I paced, I noticed that her youthful face was pretty in the way that most young people are. I couldn't imagine why her life had to end that way. I knew features were superficial, that the urge to kill yourself garnered energy from dark places deep within, but she didn't look tired or drained like the other victims I'd seen. No telltale lines that broadcast an unbearable hurt. But who really knew?

I shivered in my light jacket and waited. Finally, I heard Jake's bark over the grinding gears of a four-wheel drive.

My throbbing ankle brought me back to my apartment. When I stepped out onto the landing, I noticed the sun had dropped behind the mountains, carving the sky with angry slashes of purple. Swallows swooped through the air, as though they were drawing a curtain on the day.

I limped down the long wooden staircase that hugged the outside of the building, leading down to the driveway. Only the promise of aspirin inside the store kept me moving. As I turned toward the front door, I saw Abit craning his neck to see me. Jake had run ahead and jumped in Abit's lap, threatening to topple him from his chair. I couldn't help but smile at my makeshift family.

I recalled the first time I saw Abit, a lanky kid nervously pacing around the front of the store, afraid the new owner would throw out his chair and ban him from his perch near the door. He'd reminded me of a teenaged Opie Taylor, sporting a cowlick and overalls. Still did.

"Howdy, Mister. I suspect you'd like to come in." I'd started calling him that to avoid using his mean-spirited nickname, though that was hard to stick to since almost everyone called him Abit. Over the years, it seemed to have morphed into just another name, no more peculiar than Cletus or Enos; I hoped it had lost its sting for him. When he looked over his shoulder toward his house, I added, "I don't think your mother will mind today. Besides, it's after hours. You can't bother the customers, can you? Why don't you pick out something to drink, and we'll talk."

A Life for a Life
and the second book in the trilogy,
The Roads to Damascus,
are available at book retailers.

About the Author

Lynda McDaniel has written 18 books and more than 1,200 articles for major magazines. *Welcome the Little Children* is the third book in her Appalachian Mountain Mysteries trilogy, which started with *A Life for a Life* and *The Roads to Damascus*. Lynda is also a writing coach who enthusiastically helps others express their creativity and write with confidence. She lives in Santa Rosa, California, with her family.

Want to know more about the real people behind the characters? Join Lynda's mailing list. No spam, no pestering, just honest-to-goodness stories, updates, and a free copy of Lynda's first mystery short story (that she thought she'd lost!).

Sign up at www.LyndaMcDanielBooks.com.

Made in the USA
San Bernardino, CA
24 November 2018